W9-CFK-272

She was all his until Christmas...

Madeline must have heard their approach. She swung around to face them, and looked immediately wary to see Mitch with Neil, the officer who'd brought her to him. He tried to feel no emotion as they took each other's measure.

Her admirers hadn't exaggerated. She was everything he had heard—a tall, leggy beauty with amber eyes and a mane of dark red hair. What surprised him, though, was her youth. She couldn't be more than in her early twenties. Still, there was a self-possession about her that he had to respect, considering she must be terrified.

"Madeline." Neil introduced him. "This is Mitchell Hawke.

"Looks like I've been elected to take care of you," Mitch said.

"Thank you," she said simply.

If she was conscious of her looks and how they might be affecting a man she was meeting for the first time, she gave no indication of it. But Mitch was fully aware. And he didn't like his reaction. Not one bit.

Dear Harlequin Intrigue Reader,

Deck the halls with romance and suspense as we bring you four new stories that will wrap you up tighter than a present under your Christmas tree!

First we begin with the continuing series by Rita Herron, NIGHTHAWK ISLAND, where medical experiments on an island off the coast of Georgia lead to some dangerous results. Cole Hunter does not know who he is, and the only memories he has are of Megan Wells's dead husband. And why does he have these intimate *Memories of Megan*?

Next, Susan Kearney finishes her trilogy THE CROWN AFFAIR, which features the Zared royalty and the treachery they must confront in order to save their homeland. In book three, a prickly, pretty P.I. must pose as a prince's wife in order to help his majesty uncover a deadly plot. However, will she be able to elude his *Royal Pursuit* of her heart?

In Charlotte Douglas's *The Bride's Rescuer*, a recluse saves a woman who washes up on his lonely island, clothed only in a tattered wedding dress. Cameron Alexander hasn't seen a woman in over six years, and Celia Stevens is definitely a woman, with secrets of her own. But whose secrets are more deadly? And also join Jean Barrett for another tale with the Hawke Family Detective Agency in the Christmastime cross-country journey titled *Official Escort*.

Best wishes to all of our loyal readers for a "breathtaking" holiday season!

Sincerely,

Denise O'Sullivan
Associate Senior Editor
Harlequin Intrigue

OFFICIAL ESCORT
JEAN BARRETT

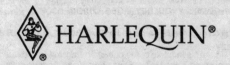

HARLEQUIN®

TORONTO • NEW YORK • LONDON
AMSTERDAM • PARIS • SYDNEY • HAMBURG
STOCKHOLM • ATHENS • TOKYO • MILAN • MADRID
PRAGUE • WARSAW • BUDAPEST • AUCKLAND

If you purchased this book without a cover you should be aware that this book is stolen property. It was reported as "unsold and destroyed" to the publisher, and neither the author nor the publisher has received any payment for this "stripped book."

ISBN 0-373-22692-6

OFFICIAL ESCORT

Copyright © 2002 by Jean Barrett

All rights reserved. Except for use in any review, the reproduction or utilization of this work in whole or in part in any form by any electronic, mechanical or other means, now known or hereafter invented, including xerography, photocopying and recording, or in any information storage or retrieval system, is forbidden without the written permission of the publisher, Harlequin Enterprises Limited, 225 Duncan Mill Road, Don Mills, Ontario, Canada M3B 3K9.

All characters in this book have no existence outside the imagination of the author and have no relation whatsoever to anyone bearing the same name or names. They are not even distantly inspired by any individual known or unknown to the author, and all incidents are pure invention.

This edition published by arrangement with Harlequin Books S.A.

® and TM are trademarks of the publisher. Trademarks indicated with ® are registered in the United States Patent and Trademark Office, the Canadian Trade Marks Office and in other countries.

Visit us at www.eHarlequin.com

Printed in U.S.A.

ABOUT THE AUTHOR

If setting has anything to do with it, Jean Barrett claims she has no reason not to be inspired. She and her husband live on Wisconsin's scenic Door Peninsula in an antique-filled country cottage overlooking Lake Michigan. A teacher for many years, she left the classroom to write full-time. She is the author of a number of romance novels.

Write to Jean at P.O. Box 623, Sister Bay, WI 54234. SASE appreciated.

Books by Jean Barrett

HARLEQUIN INTRIGUE
308—THE SHELTER OF HER ARMS
351—WHITE WEDDING
384—MAN OF THE MIDNIGHT SUN
475—FUGITIVE FATHER
528—MY LOVER'S SECRET
605—THE HUNT FOR HAWKE'S DAUGHTER
652—PRIVATE INVESTIGATIONS
692—OFFICIAL ESCORT

Don't miss any of our special offers. Write to us at the following address for information on our newest releases.

Harlequin Reader Service
U.S.: 3010 Walden Ave., P.O. Box 1325, Buffalo, NY 14269
Canadian: P.O. Box 609, Fort Erie, Ont. L2A 5X3

CLASSIFIEDS

HOUSE FOR SALE
3 bdrm, 2 1/2 bath Cape on 1/2 acre in nice family neighborhood. Washer/dryer, frpl, EI Kitchen. Close to schools and shopping.

HANDYMAN
Jack of all trades available to serve your every need!
Need pipes patched?
Walls painted?
VCR hooked up?
Hedges trimmed?
Floors sanded?
Will work cheap!
Call Joe

NEED TO LOSE WEIGHT?
New Ancient Diet Secret from the Orient guarantees that you will lose weight for your big event in just 3 days!
Look good for that
Wedding
Class Reunion
Hot Date
Make everyone sick with jealousy!
We use a combination of natural herbs and stimulants from ancient Asian texts!
Don't miss our introductory offer going on right now!

MEET YOUR PERFECT MATE!
Dating stinks!
Let an old-fashioned matchmaker find your perfect Mr. or Ms. Right!
All our applicants are thoroughly screened and tested. Our members are eligible, gainfully employed and waiting to meet you!

THE HAWKE DETECTIVE AGENCY
Do you yearn to find a lost loved one from your past?
Do you need protection from an enemy?
A mystery you desperately want solved?
All these, and much more, are possible at the family-owned Hawke Detective Agency. Its offices throughout the country are operated by the sons and daughters of the founders of the Hawke Detective Agency. You'll find a branch somewhere near you and a trained investigator eager to serve you. But before you walk through the door with the distinctive golden hawk on it, be aware that danger and romance are waiting on the other side....

PUPPIES FOR ADOPTION!
We have a large assortment of adorable puppies for adoption. All shots and spay and neutering available.
Pugs, Boxers, Poodles, Golden Retrievers, Labs, Beagles, Jack Russell Terriers, Yorkies, Poms and many more.
All waiting for a loving home!
Call now!

CAST OF CHARACTERS

Madeline Raeburn—On the run after witnessing a murder, she can trust no one, including her protector—a man who assaults her senses on every level.

Mitchell Hawke—Madeline Raeburn is the last woman on earth the hard-bitten P.I. wants to be responsible for. Though he will protect her with his life, he doesn't have to like it—or her. But he *does*.

Griff Matisse—He is determined to destroy the woman who betrayed him—Madeline Raeburn.

Gloria Rodriguez—Without Madeline Raeburn, the worried assistant district attorney has no case.

Neil Stanek—The cop needs Mitch to protect a vital witness.

Angel—He is a killer without mercy.

Morrie Swanson, Dave Ennis and Hank Rosinski—The three San Francisco officers were Neil's trusted friends. But could one of them be a cop gone bad?

To Chad
Here's the one you asked for. May it bring you the same
luck in your career as in your card playing—
except when I'm in the game, of course.

To Connie
Mach's gut immer.

And to Rebecca
May lucky horseshoes hang always
over your doorways.

Prologue

She knew the risk in coming here. It would be the first place he'd look for her. But she couldn't disappear without the collection that it had taken her years to accumulate. The precious objects could mean her survival in the months ahead.

But she must hurry, *hurry*. Take what she had come for and run before it was too late.

Madeline worked feverishly, thrusting the treasures one by one into the canvas satchel. She selected only those that were essential. The larger pieces weren't easily portable and, regrettably, would have to be left behind.

One of the items slipped through her fingers and clattered on the bench. She retrieved it with a shaking hand and stuffed it deep into the satchel.

This is no good. You're letting panic rule you. And, anyway, you're probably exaggerating the danger. It was dark out in the hall. Griff couldn't have had more than a fleeting glimpse of an unrecognizable shadow, before you turned and fled.

But Madeline wasn't able to shake the image of his victim sinking to his knees with a bullet through his head. Horrifying!

The velvet pouch was the last of the collection to go into the satchel. She placed her purse on top. It contained the funds she had cleared out of her checking and meager savings account this afternoon. Thank God she'd had the sense to do that before going to the club.

Nothing else mattered in the apartment. Not her furniture, not even her clothes. All of it was expendable. Time to leave.

You're going to make it.

She kept telling herself this as she picked up the heavy satchel and hurried toward the door. She made herself remember how lucky she had been that a cab had been cruising by when she'd burst out of the club. She had grabbed it and rushed straight to the apartment. That meant no wasted minutes. A comfortable head start on any pursuit. But she couldn't shake her alarm, her awful sense of urgency.

After dousing the lights, Madeline unlocked the door and eased it back on the chain, then peered out into the hallway. Nothing. No one in sight. Seconds later, without a backward glance at the apartment with all its poignant memories, she was on her way to the elevators.

The hallway continued to be silent and deserted, but when she reached the elevators, the indicator revealed that one of the two cars was rising from the ground floor. What if the occupant of that car wasn't another tenant, but someone who had been sent to find her? She couldn't take that chance.

Turning away from the elevators, she flew down the hallway and around the corner. It was nine floors to the lobby below, but she considered the enclosed stairway a safer route to the street. It wasn't. Madeline learned that when she shouldered her way past the metal fire door and, drawing a gasp, shrank back in fear.

He was waiting for her there on the landing, just as though he had expected her to choose this avenue of escape. He was the one they called Angel. An inappropriate name since, even in her days of innocence, she had always thought there was something lethal about him. It was there now in the smile on his bony face and in that low, breathy voice she found so chilling.

"I always said Griff knew what he was doing when he picked you. Said none of the other girls at the Phoenix could compare. Could be it's all that red hair. You think?"

She had been wrong. Madeline knew that now. Griff *had* realized it was her outside his office and had sent Angel after her. She had made a serious mistake in coming back to the apartment, one that was about to cost her her life.

"Yeah," Angel said, "I'm gonna be real sorry about that red hair." His cunning eyes went to the satchel she carried. "Put it on the floor."

"There isn't any weapon in it," she managed to croak, clutching the satchel protectively.

"Do it," he commanded.

She had no choice. He had no gun in evidence, but she knew he must be carrying one beneath that finely cut suit coat. Madeline lowered the bag to the floor.

"Now step back," he instructed her.

She retreated a few steps as he moved forward to take possession of the satchel. Her gaze cut to the stairs. Before she could even consider the possibility of plunging down them, he stopped her with a soft "I wouldn't—not if you want to live long enough for me to get you back to the Phoenix. Griff is real anxious about you, Madeline."

Trapped. There was nothing she could do. She watched him as he lifted the satchel, hanging it by its long straps on his shoulder in order to keep his hands free. He didn't seem interested in its contents. He was probably leaving them for Griff to examine.

"We'll go now," he said.

Angel motioned for her to precede him down the stairway, but at that moment the metal door on the floor below them burst open. A group of people trooped out onto the landing, chattering loudly.

Angel muttered an oath. "Guess we have to take the elevator," he said.

Madeline knew he couldn't risk taking her past all those people, who seemed in no hurry to leave the landing. She watched him glance one last time at the stairway, an expression of regret on his thin face that she didn't understand.

Conscious of him close behind her, she opened the fire door and returned along the hallway. They didn't have to call an elevator. The car that had risen earlier was waiting.

"Inside," Angel instructed her. He hesitated a second before following her into the elevator, where he stabbed the button for the ground floor and then stood so close beside her that she could smell his strong cologne.

Madeline was barely conscious of the door closing, the car descending. Her mind was on a desperate journey, searching for some means of escape. But there didn't seem to be any hope, not even when the car bounced to a sudden halt. She waited for the door to roll back to admit another passenger. But it stayed firmly shut.

There was a moment of total silence, and then Angel demanded sharply, "What's wrong? Why have we stopped?"

Her gaze lifted to the indicator above the door. They were stalled between the fourth and fifth floors. "We're stuck, that's all."

"What do you mean, *stuck?*"

"It's an old building. It happens." Apparently he had never been caught in an elevator before.

"How do we get out of this thing?"

"How do you suppose? You press the alarm button, and hope someone hears it and that the super is around to come to our rescue."

"And what if he isn't around?"

She glanced at him as he went to the panel and repeatedly punched the alarm button. His voice had become even more raspy, and he was breathing hard.

"Then, we wait," she said.

"How long?"

Madeline lifted her shoulders in a little shrug and eyed him warily as he leaned against the wall, cursing savagely under his breath. There was a frantic look now on his sharp-featured face. It told her why he had been reluctant to leave the stairs for the elevator. The deadly Angel suffered from claustrophobia. It was a situation that might be to her advantage, or prove even more dangerous for her. There was no way of knowing. She could only pray that, when help arrived, she could somehow make them aware of her plight.

They didn't speak as the long minutes passed. She watched him become increasingly restless. Every few seconds, his movements jerky and impatient, he would attack the alarm button with his thumb or smack the other buttons in a futile effort to move the elevator. They could hear the bell ringing somewhere in the distance, but no one came. There was a sheen of perspiration on his face now. Madeline feared he was so panicked that he was nearing a stage of hyperventilation.

What would she do if he lost all control? What *could* she do, when she was trapped in an elevator with a wild animal who wouldn't hesitate to kill her if she made the wrong move?

Madeline didn't know whether to be worried or relieved when he finally ruptured the silence with a growled, "I'm not taking this anymore! I'm getting out!"

She followed his lifted gaze, understanding his intention. There was a panel in the low ceiling above them, covering a service hatch to the roof of the elevator.

"Floor above us can't be more than a couple of feet higher than the top of the elevator," he said. "If I can get up there, maybe I can force the door, climb out. Get over here and make a step for me with your hands."

Madeline didn't want to touch him, but she didn't dare to refuse him. She joined him below the hatch where he had positioned himself. Leaning down, she braced herself as he placed his weight on the sling she created with her hands linked together. He shouldn't have been too heavy for her, not when she was nearly as tall as he was and his body was emaciated. But with the satchel still firmly in his keeping, he felt like a boulder.

Steadying himself, with his fingers biting painfully into her shoulder, he rose to his full height and shoved the loose panel up out of its frame. The hatch was now open to the elevator shaft. She wished he would hurry. Her hands wobbled under the strain, especially when he stretched himself to gain a hold on the frame. Having succeeded, he was ready to swing himself through the opening. That's when it happened. The elevator lurched without warning, dropping another several inches.

Madeline lost her footing, Angel his grip. With a yell, he plummeted to the floor of the car. The satchel swinging wildly from his shoulder cost him his balance. He went crashing into the steel wall.

When she'd recovered herself, she went over to check

on him. He was huddled tightly in a corner, unconscious, blood seeping from a wound where his head had struck the wall.

Madeline crouched beside him. The aroma of his cologne was overpowering, sickening. *Forget that. Find his gun.*

Her hands were on his coat, ready to search him, when there was a clang of metal from the floor above. She recognized it as the sound of a door scraping open. It was followed by the familiar voice of the small-statured Korean man who was the super for the building, calling down to her.

"Who is there, please?"

Madeline got eagerly to her feet. "It's me, Kim."

"You okay, Miss Raeburn?"

"I'm fine. Just get me out."

"Sure. I got a ladder. It's coming down."

By the time he managed to lower the ladder to her through the hatch, Madeline had the precious satchel back in her possession. With a last glance at the still-unconscious Angel, she swarmed up the ladder. The fifth floor, where Kim waited for her, was no more than three feet above the roof of the elevator. He reached down and helped her scramble to safety.

"You got anyone else down there, Miss Raeburn?"

"No, Kim, I was all alone on the elevator."

He started to mutter about how the tenants would complain again about the car having to be shut down until the engineer came to fix it. Madeline didn't stop to listen to him. She was already flying toward the stairs.

Nor did she permit her pace to slacken when she reached the street. She hurried down the hill, the clang of a cable car making her start nervously as she threaded her way through the evening crowds. From time to time she checked over her shoulder, fearing that Angel might be in pursuit again. Or, if not Angel, another enemy sent by Griff to find her. Nowhere in the city was safe for her.

The police? No, Madeline didn't trust the police to protect her. Hadn't she learned firsthand what happened to informers? Griff Matisse was too powerful, had too many friends in high places for her to risk staying here in San Francisco. Damn it, she was scared. All she wanted to do was to lose herself, go far away and hide.

You're doing the right thing. They're dead. You can't help them now. Stay and testify? Don't be a fool. He'd never let you survive long enough to mount a witness stand. You were planning to go away, anyway, weren't you? That's why you took all your money out of the bank, remember?

She wouldn't let herself feel guilty because she was running away. She *wouldn't*.

SCARS, THE RESIDUE of a severe adolescent acne, pitted his jaw. They were the only flaws on Griff Matisse's handsome face. He permitted nothing else to mar his appearance, which was as immaculate as his tasteful office in the Phoenix on Powell Street. Nor was Matisse willing to tolerate any mistakes from those who served him.

"I'm not happy," he coldly informed the man who stood on the other side of his desk. "I think I have every reason to be *un*happy, don't you?"

Angel, resisting the urge to finger the wound in his scalp, nodded slowly. For a moment the only sound in the office was the muted wail of a saxophone off in the elegant main room of the club.

"What are we going to do about making me happy again, Angel?"

"She's disappeared," Angel said in his hushed, raspy voice that was almost a whisper. "She could be anywhere."

"But she's somewhere, isn't she? And wherever that is, and whatever it takes, I want her found and eliminated. We have all the right connections. Use them."

Angel didn't need to be persuaded. He had his own score to settle with Madeline Raeburn.

Chapter One

Madeline didn't have a good feeling about this arrangement. Maybe the setting was responsible for that, at least partly. It wasn't very encouraging, she decided, gazing out the passenger window of the car as it bumped up the long, rutted farm lane.

It was a bleak situation, the fields brown, the trees leafless. Even the spiky evergreens that studded the hills on all sides were a dull shade of green. Snow would have softened the scene, made it more palatable. But even though it was late December and only a few days before Christmas, the ground was bare, though the gray sky was certainly cold enough to warrant snow.

The burly man beside her at the wheel, hair grizzled, face lined, must have sensed her anxiety. "We're doing the right thing," he reassured her gently.

He had been particularly kind to her since yesterday. Understandable, considering he had come within millimeters of losing her to an assassin's bullet.

Madeline nodded. "This man...you're sure he's safe?"

"I wouldn't be taking you to him if I wasn't."

But Madeline continued to be uneasy. There was no one

and nowhere she really trusted anymore, though this setting certainly seemed isolated enough to provide her with the protection that was so essential now. Funny that it should seem so remote when it was less than fifty miles from Milwaukee.

That feeling of loneliness was emphasized when they crawled around a bend and came in sight of the old farmhouse. The place had a look of neglect about it. It would have benefited from a fresh coat of paint. The outbuildings were in even sorrier condition, the roofs sagging, the walls weathered to a dismal gray. There was no sign of life.

"Animals," Madeline said. "Where are the animals? Farms are supposed to have cows and chickens and horses, at least a dog or a cat."

"This isn't a working farm," her companion replied. "The owners only use it in the summer on weekends and as a vacation retreat. But, of course, this winter it's being rented to—" He broke off to negotiate a particularly rough stretch of the driveway.

Madeline silently finished the explanation for him. *The man you're being taken to.* She was beginning to feel like a waif. Dumped for the holidays with whomever would take her. Not very cheerful holidays, either, she thought. She had just observed not only that the farm lacked animals, but that it was missing any evidence of the approaching Christmas. There was no welcoming wreath on the front door, no decorated tree mounted in the bay window. It was probably foolish of her to have expected them. Or, considering her perilous circumstances, to even yearn for them.

The car rolled to a stop at the edge of the front yard. The man at her side checked the lane behind them, making sure it was deserted. All the way out from Milwaukee, Madeline had watched him repeatedly glance in the rearview mirror to be certain they weren't followed. Neil Stanek was that sort of cop—conscientious, thorough. And considerate.

He demonstrated that now by turning to her with a concerned "You all right?"

He feels guilty, Madeline thought. Blames himself for what happened, even though it wasn't his fault.

"I'm fine," she assured him. She wasn't, of course, and they both knew that. But it helped to pretend otherwise.

"You'll be okay, then, if I leave you here in the car for a few minutes?" he asked, releasing his seat belt and opening the door on his side. "Just long enough for me to explain all the particulars to him."

Madeline was suddenly worried. "He is expecting me, isn't he?"

"Oh, sure, sure, no problem there. And, like I said, he's got all the right skills and instincts for this. You just sit tight. I'll leave the motor running so you'll have the heater. Keep the doors locked, and lay on that horn if you see or hear anything you don't like. Not that you will. No one now but us knows where you are, and we're going to keep it that way."

Madeline had no choice but to accept his word. Setting the lock, he slid out of the car and slammed the door. She watched his stocky figure trudge up the ragged path to the porch. The front door opened as he neared the house. A man stepped out and stood there in the dimness of the porch, waiting for Neil. She couldn't tell much about that figure at this distance, only that he was tall and lean. But there was another impression Madeline had. Maybe it was the way he stood there by the door, hands buried in his pockets in an attitude of detachment. As though he didn't mind the desolation of this place. As if it suited him because he, too, was using its seclusion to hide himself. Or was it merely her imagination, which lately had been working overtime?

MITCH WAS IN NO MOOD for visitors. These days he preferred his own company, rotten though it was. After all, that's why he had buried himself out here. He'd needed to get away from people—friends with their sympathy that had driven him crazy, his loving, well-meaning family offering a comfort he didn't want. Even strangers, who were apt to be curious, troubled him. That's why he'd resented the sound of a car arriving in the driveway, and why he had gone so unwillingly to the door.

Mitch had been relieved when his caller turned out to be Neil. He didn't mind Neil, didn't regard him as an intruder. The cop never asked questions to which, these days, Mitch had no answers. Never expected more of him than he was capable of being.

But Neil wasn't alone this time. Mitch could see someone else waiting in the car. That's why he hung back on the porch. All he could tell was that the figure was a woman, nothing else. Must be Neil's daughter, he figured.

"That Faye with you?" Mitch asked when the cop joined him on the porch, adding a reluctant, "She doesn't have to sit out there. Ask her to come in."

"It's not Faye," Neil said, shaking Mitch's hand.

Who else? Mitch wondered. Maybe that neighbor of Neil's, the widow who was trying to be more than just friends with him. What was her name? Claire Something-or-other. But Neil wasn't prepared to name his companion.

"How about we go inside," he suggested, "before one of us turns blue out here?"

Mitch led the way into the big farm kitchen with its sparse country furnishings. "Coffee?"

Neil shook his head and opened his coat. But he didn't

remove it, and Mitch noticed that he stood near the window where he could keep an eye on the car in the driveway. Mitch was beginning to have an uncomfortable feeling about this unexpected visit.

"Something up?"

Neil replied by removing a business card from his pocket and slapping it down on the sturdy table, his action like a challenge. Mitch had only to glance at the prominent logo of a golden hawk to recognize it. And why shouldn't he know it, since it was one of his own business cards?

The Hawke Detective Agency. That's what it read. Neil's silent message to him was very plain. This time his friend *did* expect something from him. Mitch was immediately resistant.

"Whatever it is," he said firmly, "you can forget about it. I'm out of the business. Anyway, I don't have a license to practice here in Wisconsin."

"You don't need a license for this. It's a simple matter of protection. Your specialty, remember?"

Mitch laughed. It was a brittle laugh without a trace of humor. "Yeah? Like I protected Julie, huh?"

"You weren't responsible for what happened to Julie. When are you going to stop beating yourself up over that?"

"I wasn't there for her, Neil. *I wasn't there.*"

"And that wasn't your fault, either. All right, I know you're hurting, but it's been five months. Hell, Mitch, when a man starts feeling sorry for himself, it's time to stop grieving."

"What would you know about it?"

The angry words were out of Mitch's mouth before he could stop them. Damn it, how could he have said something like that to Neil, of all people? Because, of course, Neil did know all about losing someone who mattered.

"Sorry," Mitch mumbled.

"Forget it. Look, I wouldn't ask, but there is no one else. No one I trust, anyway. I need you."

He would have been justified in saying that Mitch owed him, but Neil would never do that. It wasn't his way. Mitch would probably regret this, already did regret it, in fact, but how could he send Neil away without at least listening to him?

"Okay, who are we talking about? The woman out there in the car? Who is she?"

"A murder witness. A vital one. If we can keep her alive long enough for the accused to come to trial, we stand every chance of convicting the bastard for cold-bloodedly icing an undercover cop."

"Why come to me, when you've got the whole Milwaukee police force to guard her?"

"That's the problem." Neil turned his head to check on the occupant of the car before continuing. "We did have her in a safe house, only it turns out it wasn't so safe. She came close to swallowing a bullet last night. Guy got away. Probably a mob assassin. The bastard has some powerful connections. Anyway, they knew just where to find her."

"Are you saying there's an informer in the police ranks?"

"Looks like it. Now I'm afraid to trust her with any of our people."

"So you're in charge of her. Why you, Neil? This isn't exactly your area."

"Because I'm the one she came to when she finally decided to turn herself in."

"Turned herself— Wait a minute, just how long ago did this cop killing take place?"

"Couple of months. She's been on the run since then, too scared to do anything but hide."

It occurred to Mitch that there was something decidedly

wrong about this situation, a whole lot that didn't make sense. It also occurred to him that the uncomfortable feeling he'd been experiencing over his friend's visit was probably not just his imagination.

"Talk to me, Neil. Tell me exactly what this is all about. Like, for instance, why she happened to want you."

Neil's heavy shoulders lifted in a shrug. "I guess I'm the one she trusted. I guess because she thought I treated her fairly when I questioned her during another investigation last summer."

Mitch stared at him, his suspicion growing stronger by the moment. "You weren't with the Milwaukee department last summer. You were still on the San Francisco force."

"That's right."

It was more than just discomfort Mitch was feeling now. It was something raw and wrenching deep inside him. "You didn't phone me before you came out here," he said, his voice accusing. "Why is that, Neil? Because you knew I'd hang up on you after you told me what you wanted?"

Neil, looking decidedly awkward now, gazed at him silently.

"Who is she, Neil?" Mitch demanded. "Who is it you've got out there in that car?"

And that was when Neil dropped his bombshell, the one Mitch had been expecting.

"Madeline Raeburn," he said quietly.

Hearing the name was worse than anticipating it—a pain that tore at Mitch's gut. He fought for self-control, strove to keep his voice level. "Take your witness and get out of here. *Now,* before I forget you're supposed to be my friend."

"I'm not going anywhere. I'm staying right here, and you're going to listen to me."

"And what am I going to hear, Neil? You telling me

that I've got Madeline Raeburn all wrong? That she's a decent, caring woman who is in no way to blame for Julie ending up in San Francisco Bay?"

"I don't know what she is or isn't. All I know is that she's scared. She'd gotten as far away from San Francisco as her money could take her and was lying low somewhere in Indiana when she saw me on a newscast involving that Milwaukee Brewers case and learned I was in Milwaukee. That's when she found the guts to come to me and agree to testify against Griff Matisse."

Matisse. Another name that had Mitch's insides tightening in rage. "Matisse is your cop killer?"

Neil nodded. "Back in San Francisco."

"Then, what is Milwaukee doing protecting her? Why isn't one of those close friends of yours from the Frisco force taking charge of her? You always said they're the best."

"The DA's office in San Francisco *is* going to send an escort for her. They're just waiting until they can get a secure safe house set up for her out there—one that Matisse can't penetrate this time. You know how delayed everything gets around the holiday. Meanwhile, they think she's better off in this area."

"Even with a dirty cop on your force passing information to Matisse's connections here?" This just didn't make sense to Mitch. "You sure?"

"That's the decision."

Mitch shook his head, still puzzled. "It's a bad decision. And I'll tell you one that's even worse—you wanting to stash her out here with me."

"Just for a few days," Neil pleaded. "Just until after Christmas. By then, we'll either have plugged our leak here, or the safe house will be ready for her in California. Look, I'd keep her myself, but my house is no secret."

"And mine isn't vulnerable like that, huh? Besides, I should want to do it, now that I know Madeline Raeburn has found both a conscience and courage. Except," he added cynically, "I've got to wonder whether that's why she came to you or whether she finally realized she isn't safe anywhere and needed police protection to save her own neck."

"Maybe she sees it as *risking* her neck."

"Yeah? Then, if she's so good, why did she wait until now to talk? Why didn't she open up to you when Julie was murdered?"

Neil gazed at him, his face solemn. "When did you become so bitter, Mitch?"

Mitch squirmed under the sorrowful expression in his friend's eyes. He knew that Neil was right. He *had* become bitter since Julie's death. It was something he needed to lose, but he also knew that could never happen with Madeline Raeburn in his house.

"I'd like to help you out, Neil, but I can't do it. The answer is no."

His friend didn't say anything. He just went on gazing at him, while Mitch stood there, trying to look casual about his emphatic refusal. And then Neil delivered his final shot, the one he must have been saving for this exact moment.

"That's too bad, Mitch," he said quietly. "Because if Matisse was responsible for Julie's death last summer, and we don't keep Madeline Raeburn alive to testify against him, then he ends up not paying for any of it. You want to see him just walk away again?"

It was an argument for which Mitch had no defense, and his friend knew that. He stared at Neil in an explosive frustration that finally released itself when he snatched up the business card from the table, crushing it angrily in his fist.

Neil, understanding the surrender that anger signified,

nodded slowly. "You coming out to the car with me, or do you want to wait here while I bring her in?"

Mitch answered by striding across the room and snagging his leather jacket from a hook on the wall. "She know who I am?" he asked, shrugging into the coat.

"You mean that you're Julie's 'Mickey'? You don't think she would have agreed to come out here if she did, do you? And let's keep it that way, please. I don't want to risk her going on the run again. She's already nervous enough after last night."

Mitch nodded as he zipped up the jacket. He remembered how Neil, after questioning Madeline Raeburn last summer, had told him that Julie apparently had never referred to him at the Phoenix by anything other than her playful nickname for him. Their private joke. Mitch also remembered how Neil, with just short of physical force, had managed to keep him from going to Matisse and Madeline Raeburn. Mad with grief, he'd wanted to tear both of them apart. He realized as he joined Neil by the door that that memory was still painful.

"And, Mitch?"

"Yeah?"

"Anything happens—not that it will—you won't let me down, will you? You'll stick by her?"

Mitch promised, and they went out on the porch. The cop swore. "Damn it, I told her to stay in the car."

Madeline stood a few yards away from the car, her back to them as she gazed off into the wooded hills.

"Nice beginning," Mitch muttered. "A woman with her own mind."

"You just treat her right," Neil instructed him as they started toward the car. "She's been through a lot."

"Hell, Neil," Mitch said dryly, "before it's over we're gonna be best friends. Probably share the same toothbrush."

Madeline must have heard their approach. She swung to face them, looking immediately wary when she realized Neil was not alone. Mitch tried to feel no emotion as they stood there near the car, taking each other's measure. But holding his feelings in check wasn't possible, not with what felt like a fist slowly squeezing his insides as he looked at her.

Her admirers hadn't exaggerated. She was everything he had heard she was: a tall, leggy beauty with wide, amber eyes and a mane of dark red hair that was probably the result of Scottish ancestry. But he had expected no less. Griff Matisse wouldn't have owned her if she hadn't been stunning.

What did surprise Mitch was her youth. She couldn't have been older than her early twenties. Still, there was a self-possession about her, which he supposed he had to respect considering she must be terrified under all that seemingly quiet composure.

If she was conscious of her looks and how they might be affecting a man she was meeting for the first time—and in Mitch's experience women like her always were—she gave no indication. But, hell, she didn't have to be conscious of her looks. Mitch was fully aware of them for her. And he didn't like his reaction. Not one bit. Her mere existence was problem enough.

"Madeline," Neil introduced him, "this is Mitchell Hawke."

"Looks like I've been elected to take care of you," Mitch said. It was the best he had to offer her.

There was a bad moment while she went on silently regarding him. Did his name mean something to her, after all? Or had another recognition occurred, the physical one that was certainly possible?

Mitch relaxed, and Neil with him, when she finally nodded gravely and extended a gloved hand. Mitch accepted the slim hand. Her clasp was brief but firm; her voice was low and husky—the kind that did things to a man's imagination.

"Thank you for letting me be your guest," she said simply. And then her thickly lashed gaze flicked toward Neil. "It is all arranged, isn't it?" she asked, a note of concern in her voice.

"Everything's settled," Neil assured her. He opened the back door of the car and took out a single suitcase.

Madeline went to the front and removed a bulging canvas satchel. It looked heavy. Mitch tried to take it from her, but she clung to it possessively.

"I'll carry it," she informed him, holding it close.

Mitch, leading the way to the house, wondered what she was guarding in that satchel. It was one more complication in a situation that was already difficult. He knew this was not going to be an easy few days. How could it be, when, once Neil was gone, he would be alone with Madeline Raeburn and all that alluring red hair?

CLARK GABLE.

That's who Madeline had been trying to think of all afternoon. The actor from the golden age of movies. The name finally came to her all at once as she sat across the dinner table from Mitchell Hawke. He had the same prominent ears as Clark Gable.

Funny, she thought, how ears that were a bit too large for their wearer, and stuck out slightly, as well, could qualify as sexy. They certainly had for Clark Gable, and they did for this man. Maybe it was the way they were set on his head.

Or maybe it was that dark head itself with its other bold features—a pair of probing blue eyes, a strong nose and a wide, sensual mouth above a square jaw. All of this was carried on a solid body clad in a bulky, wheat-colored sweater and snug jeans.

Madeline had been making a concerted effort ever since her arrival not to notice just how well Mitch Hawke filled those jeans. This had become especially difficult during their preparations for dinner.

The kitchen was not small, but they had been forever bumping into each other. Brief as those contacts were, they had been charged with a kind of intimacy in which Madeline had been far too conscious of the heat radiating from his six-foot frame.

Neil Stanek trusted this man to protect her—Madeline kept reminding herself of that. Still, she couldn't seem to shake the conviction that Mitch Hawke was dangerous. Dangerous on some level she was unable to define but that had her fearing it was a mistake for her to be here with him in this house.

"Something wrong?"

He had looked up abruptly from his plate and caught her staring at him. Maybe his ears were a sensitive subject. Madeline felt herself flushing, the penalty of a fair, slightly freckled complexion.

"No. The meat loaf is very good."

She busied herself slicing it, but she was aware of him eyeing her across the table. Madeline was used to men looking at her. It was essentially what she had been paid for at the Phoenix. But there was a difference in the way Mitch Hawke looked at her. It wasn't admiration. It was something else, something that worried her. Something that was very wrong.

This, too, had been on her mind all afternoon. She had even asked him about it when she'd noticed all the somber looks he'd cast in her direction while helping her settle in to her room. But he had denied it in that brusque manner she found so troubling.

She could feel his gaze still lingering on her as she ate the meat loaf. That was why she asked him about his relationship with Neil Stanek, not because she needed to understand it but simply in an effort to ease the tension between them.

"You were friends with Neil back in San Francisco, weren't you?"

"That's right," he said, adding more dressing to his salad.

"I think he mentioned you were both in law enforcement there."

"Something like that."

"But you aren't here? In law enforcement like Neil, I mean."

"No."

He didn't elaborate, and she didn't press him for an explanation. She sensed that he wouldn't appreciate any probing in that direction.

Madeline helped herself to applesauce, trying to decide whether Mitch was just a private man by nature or whether he was hiding something. And if he did have secrets, ought she to be worried about that? After all, it was a little odd that a man of his robust age—somewhere in his early thirties, she guessed—should be living a solitary existence in this remote place.

On the other hand, Neil trusted him and she trusted Neil.

Which brought her back to the subject that she judged was a safe one.

"It's a long way from San Francisco to Milwaukee," she said. "What brought Neil here?"

He didn't answer her for a moment, and then he apparently decided there was no reason why she shouldn't know. "Neil lost his wife last spring after a long battle with cancer. It was pretty hard on him."

The loss of a loved one. Madeline certainly had no trouble relating to that kind of anguish. "I'm sorry," she murmured. "I didn't know."

"He can deal with it now, thanks to his daughter and her family. They live in Milwaukee. That's why Neil eventually moved here, to be close to them."

"And you helped him through that bad time, too, when you were both in San Francisco, didn't you. He said as much on the drive out here, although I didn't understand then what he was referring to."

Mitch didn't deny it.

And you ended up here yourself, Madeline thought, not daring to ask him why he also was so far from San Francisco, but wondering just the same. Had Neil somehow brought Mitch to Wisconsin, just as Neil's existence here had brought her? No, that wasn't right. It was guilt that had finally summoned her to a Milwaukee police station. The need to make a bad thing right. Because no matter how she had struggled to silence it, and wherever she had tried to hide from it in those long weeks on the road, the voice of her conscience had given her no peace.

Madeline was suddenly aware that Mitch was no longer eating. When she looked up from her own plate, it was to find those blue eyes fastened on her again. Intense, unreadable. But there was something now in that steady gaze that she did understand. Something that was both hot and potent, robbing her of her breath. Smoldering desire.

It had all the impact of a searing physical contact, and in a kind of panic she tore her gaze away from his and cast it about the kitchen in an effort to distract herself.

"What are you looking for?" he asked.

"There aren't any," she suddenly said.

"Any what?"

"Christmas decorations. Not a single one."

It was one thing not to have a wreath on the door or a tree in the window, but a house deserved some acknowledgment of the holiday season. Except, this house hadn't so much as a homely poinsettia in it, she thought sadly. Why? Because even a plant, in its need for water, demanded commitment? Was that why he kept no animals for company, either?

"No, there aren't," he said simply and without emotion. As if he were curtly telling her that he preferred his self-imposed exile to be without any attachment whatsoever, thank you.

Madeline was sorry about that. She had always tried to make Christmas special for Adam and her, filling their apartment with every ornament imaginable. Maybe it had been her way of expressing the importance of everything they'd been for each other.

And this year? This year, it seemed, she would be spending Christmas in a sterile farmhouse with a mystifying, disconnected stranger—one who was barely civil to her while managing at the same time to disturb her senses on every level.

Just what, Madeline wondered, had she let herself in for?

DAMN NEIL for saddling him with her.

Mitch, stirring restlessly in his bed, wasn't able to sleep.

He was too aware of the woman in the room just across the hall. Madeline Raeburn, with her tantalizing red hair and full mouth. He could still see her across the table from him, unconsciously playing with that distinctive enameled pendant resting above a pair of full breasts.

Dinner had been difficult, a really strained affair. She had been understandably curious about him. There had been all those questions, which, out of necessity, he had either avoided or answered vaguely. And all the while he had longed to blast her with the truth. *Yeah, there aren't any damn Christmas decorations. That's because I'm not here to celebrate. I'm here because I'm supposed to be healing. That's why Neil dragged me to this place. Because he thought I needed to get far away from San Francisco. Because I was so haunted by losing Julie that I was an emotional wreck, no longer able to function. A real hoot, huh?*

That's what he would have told Madeline Raeburn, and it would have satisfied him to watch the shocked expression on that bewitching face of hers. Then he would have followed it up by attacking her with a barrage of his own questions.

Why did you urge a vulnerable girl like Julie to get involved in a place like the Phoenix and with people like Griff Matisse and his kind?

What really happened that night, and why did you stand by and let it happen? And why did you keep your mouth shut afterward?

Why are you willing to talk now? Did your lover betray you, find someone else? That why?

Angry questions he hadn't dared to ask. And the worst of it, the absolute worst, was his realization that he could hang on to his torment and his memories, but he could no longer hang on to the woman they stood for. Julie's image was beginning to blur, beginning to slip away from him. And that worried him. It didn't seem right, somehow—felt like a betrayal of his grief for her.

Bad enough, but to have Madeline Raeburn in this house, to find himself actually aroused by her siren sexiness made him livid. Hell, he could feel himself thickening every time she came close to him. And, fair or not, he blamed her for that, too.

Barriers. That's what he had needed. He had to keep throwing up barriers against his desire for her. He had to tell himself over and over that she was here for protection, nothing else. Had to keep reminding himself of the kind of woman she was and that she'd been that bastard Griff Matisse's girl.

Even with these resolutions, sleep eluded him. It was long after midnight before Mitch finally drifted off. His restless night cost him in the morning. He slept late, and when he finally woke, it was to a clear sky with the sun already well above the hills.

He was aware of the silence in the house as he showered and dressed. He wondered if his guest was still in bed, but when he left his room to check on her, her door was open and her bed neatly made. There was no sign of her inside.

Mitch wasn't worried. He'd made certain last night that all the windows and outside doors were secure. He had also elicited a promise from her that she wouldn't try to go anywhere without him. He imagined she was in the kitchen, sitting over a mug of coffee.

"Hey, are you down there?" he shouted from the head of the stairs, feeling a little foolish.

He didn't feel foolish when there was no answer. Mitch began to experience the first stirrings of alarm. Ducking back into his room, he removed his Colt automatic from the locked drawer of the table beside his bed.

With his loaded pistol in hand, he raced down to the first floor and searched the rooms. They were all empty, and there was no evidence in the kitchen that she'd made any breakfast for herself.

Mitch felt a sick dread deep in his gut. It was followed immediately by guilt. Damn it, he had been careless in his preoccupation with his own roiling emotions, had failed to be alert. Neil had been counting on him, and if anything had happened to her—

The back door off the kitchen was still locked, but when he checked the front door, his worst fear was confirmed. It was unlocked. There was no longer any question. Madeline Raeburn was gone.

Chapter Two

Mitch paused only long enough to struggle into his jacket before tearing out of the house. Leaping off the porch, he swept a frantic gaze over the empty yard, then the outbuildings. No sign of her.

He was on his way to the barn, prepared to search both it and the crumbling granary, when he saw something. The sun reflecting off something hard and shiny, high on the wooded hill behind the farm. The quick flash through the trees told Mitch there was someone up there. Someone on the move, bearing an object bright enough to catch the glare of the sun. A metal object. Like a gun.

On the heels of that thought came a fear that was almost a certainty. *They* had somehow learned Madeline was here at the farm, had managed to invade the house and snatch her. He had heard no sound of a car in the driveway, but he remembered there was another lane down on the other side of the hill. Was she being taken to a car waiting there?

Mitch didn't hesitate. His long legs carried him swiftly across the frosted meadow behind the sheds and up the steep slope of the hill. The morning air was clear and crisp, and on any other occasion he might have found it invigorating. But now it was nothing but a hindrance, its sharp coldness burning his lungs as he struggled through the dry, brittle undergrowth.

He kept scanning the ridge above him, but he detected no further reflections or movements. And all the while he cursed himself for his lack of vigilance. He had to get her back. Whatever it took.

He must have covered half the distance to the top, his labored breath steaming now in little clouds, when he heard it. The sound of something approaching through the thicket above him. He dodged behind an oak tree, the enormous girth of its trunk hiding him as he waited, his gun ready.

Whatever, or whoever, it was came on through the dense growth, unaware of him concealed behind the oak. Seconds later, Mitch risked peering cautiously around the trunk. The sight that met his gaze was one of the oddest he'd ever seen.

There, emerging from the woods, marching blithely down the hill in his direction, was an upright evergreen tree. Nothing else. Just an evergreen that must have been a full six or seven feet in height.

Evergreens didn't walk by themselves. Someone had to be behind it, maybe using it as camouflage or a shield. He was certain of this when once again, this time through the thickness of the tree's boughs, he glimpsed metal winking in the sunlight. There was a figure supporting that evergreen.

Mitch announced his presence with a growled, "You've got a gun covering you, so drop it!"

The evergreen came to a startled halt and was perfectly still. There was a long, uncertain pause.

"Now!" Mitch barked. "And make sure that whatever else you're carrying back there gets lowered to the ground with it."

With a suddenness that took him by surprise, the object that had first captured his attention came sailing through the air from behind the evergreen. At the apex of its arc, it flashed again in the sun before descending to land with a *thump* in the weeds. Not a gun. Not even a weapon, unless you defined its polished steel blade as a weapon. In this case Mitch didn't, since he realized immediately that the ax had been used to chop down the evergreen.

A second later that same tree, which he identified now as a fir, was flung to one side, revealing the figure behind it. There was no further hesitation from her, no willingness to be challenged again by the assailant lurking behind the oak. In a headlong panic, not daring to look back, she charged down the hill.

What in the—

But Mitch had no time to question her reckless flight. Fearing she'd break her silly neck on the steep, rough slope, he took off after her. "Hey, hang on!" he shouted. "It's just me, you little—"

Too late. A root caught her by the ankle, throwing her to the ground, where she rolled over like a log before coming to rest in a little hollow. Slipping and sliding down the incline, Mitch reached her side. Pistol tucked now into his belt, he knelt in the dry grass and leaned over her, intending to help her to her feet.

By this time Madeline was so blind with terror that she failed to recognize him. Or, if she did, to comprehend that he hadn't become the enemy. When his hands started to close around her arms, she read his action as an attack and struck out at him. Mitch didn't know quite how her instant and ferocious struggle managed to rob him of his balance, but the next thing he knew he was lying full length on top of her.

It was a treacherous position, in more ways than one. Fighting for her release, she squirmed and heaved under his weight. Mitch took several blows, but they didn't matter. Not when he was aware of her tantalizing body under his, igniting a fire in him. He supposed he was a bastard for his arousal, for experiencing the excitement of her lush warmth.

To his credit, he did try to make her understand. "Madeline, it's all right. I'm not going to hurt you."

At some point she must have listened to his repeated pleas, must have realized who he was. Her body went still under his, and for a timeless moment their close gazes locked, their breaths mingling on the cold air as she searched his face. He could almost taste her. *Wanted* to taste her.

The moment altered when her anger surfaced. She pushed against him with an urgent, "Off! Get off of me!"

Dragging his head back, he levered himself into a sitting position. She sat up beside him and smacked him on the arm with her gloved fist. There were tears of rage in her eyes.

"What were you doing hiding behind that oak? You're supposed to protect me, not ambush me."

Mitch was angry himself, not just with her but with himself for being susceptible to that sweet body. "How was I supposed to know it was you under all that shrubbery? Why did you run like that?"

"Why wouldn't I run, when every time I turn around somebody points a gun at me?"

"I might have shot you, you little fool, and all for the sake of a— What *were* you doing with that fir, anyway?"

"Taking it back to the house, of course. And don't yell at me."

Mitch suddenly understood. "A Christmas tree! You were bringing in a damn Christmas tree! Probably planning this since yesterday. That's why you disobeyed Neil and left the car. You wanted to get a better look at the evergreens up here. Where did you find the ax? In one of the sheds, I suppose."

She wanted a Christmas tree. It was a sentiment that didn't jibe with the kind of woman he knew she was.

"What's wrong with that?" she said, getting defiantly to

her feet and brushing bits of leaves and grass off her coat and jeans. "And it wasn't planned. It was an impulse."

Mitch surged to his feet. "I'll tell you what's wrong with it. You made me a promise last night not to leave the house without me."

"No," she corrected him. "I made a promise not to leave the house without *telling* you."

"Which you didn't."

"Which I did. I left a note for you on the table."

"Which I didn't see, since I happened to be a little too busy going out of my mind with worry to notice it. Why didn't you just tell me in person what you wanted?"

"I meant to, but you were so sound asleep I...well, I didn't like to disturb you."

She couldn't have known that, Mitch thought, unless she had opened his bedroom door to check on him. And since he happened to be in the habit of sleeping in the nude, and sometimes in the night kicked off his covers, there was the possibility that she had—

He looked at her sharply. She lowered her gaze, flushing.

So she *had* gotten an eyeful of him. Interesting. Of course, he ought to be annoyed that she had caught him in the buff. Instead, the image of Madeline Raeburn standing there in his doorway gazing at him filled him with a sudden heat that made him think of a steamy night in July, not a frigid morning in December.

"Anyway," she mumbled, "I don't know why you're making such a fuss. We're in the boonies, and no one knows I'm out here but you and Neil, so how could I be in any danger?"

"That's what you thought about that safe house and— Where are you going?" She had started up the hill.

"To get the tree."

"You don't need the tree. Forget it."

"I *do* need the tree," she insisted stubbornly.

All this trouble, and she still wanted that blasted fir.

"Fine," he grumbled, "we'll get the tree, but I don't know what you think you're going to decorate it with. I don't have any lights or ornaments."

"You'll see."

If I manage to survive her, Neil, I'm not going to let you forget this. You're gonna owe me forever.

They trudged up the hill, rescued the evergreen and the ax, then dragged both of them back down the hill. Once they reached the farm, Mitch was prepared to turn his back on the whole project—which made him wonder how he ended up in the barn a few minutes later, searching through an accumulation of junk for a tree stand. Miraculously, he actually found one. Rusted and battered though it was, it managed—after a frustrating effort on his part, all of which involved mutters, groans and considerable exertion—to support the fir.

To his relief, Madeline assumed responsibility for the tree once it had been placed to her satisfaction in front of the parlor's bay window. She had turned up a supply of construction paper in one of the cupboards, which wasn't surprising since the wife of the couple from whom Mitch was renting the farm was a kindergarten teacher.

Madeline settled herself at the kitchen table with the paper and a pair of sharp scissors she had extracted from the depths of the canvas satchel she'd fetched from her bedroom. Mitch continued to wonder about that mysterious satchel. Once the scissors had been removed, she snapped the bag shut and kept it close to her side. Why was she so careful about it? What was so precious about the contents?

Mitch, fixing a late breakfast for them, tried to ask her about it with a casual, "I'm all out of cornflakes. You got any to spare in there?"

She responded with an unrelated query of her own. "Is there any glue in the house?"

"Try the drawer over there."

She was either so absorbed in her project that his curiosity hadn't registered, or else she didn't want him to know what the satchel contained. Probably the latter. He let it go. For now.

Madeline was interested in nothing but coffee. As he ate his own breakfast, he watched her work and was impressed by the ornaments she fashioned out of the simple stack of paper. A series of intricately designed snowflakes, whimsical angels, loops of paper chain. The pile grew. She was creative. He'd give her that.

Mitch would have been all right if he'd been able to keep his fascination focused strictly on her efforts and not on the woman who produced them. He couldn't. Gazing at her across the table as she frowned with concentration behind a pair of reading glasses, he watched her lips making quirky little movements that he assumed were silent directions to herself. He kept remembering their encounter on the hillside and how that same sultry mouth had been so close under his that it seemed to beg him to take it.

When he abruptly shoved himself back from the table, she looked up from her work. "Where are you going?"

"To split some wood for the fireplace."

He hadn't used the parlor's fireplace since coming to the farm, didn't even know if it worked. But he needed an excuse to leave the house, to get away from her and what she was doing to him.

He spent the rest of the morning and part of the afternoon in one of the sheds, attacking logs they didn't need, in an effort to rid himself of his mounting tension. When he returned to the house, she had the Christmas tree all decked out with her paper ornaments. Even without lights, the result was impressive.

He admired the tree, and she thanked him. Neither of them referred to the sparks they had been rubbing off of each other since her arrival yesterday. They got through the rest of the day politely pretending that the unbearable strain between them didn't exist.

Their truce lasted until the next morning, when Mitch, emerging from his room, passed her door and noticed that it was ajar. He figured she was in the shower. He heard the water running behind the closed door of her bathroom. An empty glass on the bedside table told him she must have been down to the kitchen to get herself some orange juice and hadn't bothered latching her bedroom door when she returned.

There was something else he could see through the gap. The canvas satchel was there beside the bed. It was an invitation he was unable to resist.

Spreading the door wide, Mitch entered the room and crossed to the bed. He hesitated before reaching for the satchel, knowing that what he was about to do amounted to snooping. But, hell, he was a PI, wasn't he? He was supposed to investigate, especially when it was a woman with a history like Madeline Raeburn's.

Burying his guilt, telling himself he was entitled to know just what he was dealing with under his own roof, Mitch opened the satchel and dumped its secrets on the bed.

MADELINE HOPED THE SHOWER would revive her. She had spent a sleepless night trying to quell the disturbing image of Mitchell Hawke. But even behind her closed bedroom door, those stormy blue eyes had haunted her.

All day long yesterday, whenever she had turned around or looked up from her work, she had caught him watching her. She could still feel his dark gaze on her, following her with a brooding hostility she didn't understand.

He had been right, of course. She'd had no business going out on that hill without him. But she'd badly needed to get out of the house for a while, away from its charged atmosphere, away from him.

There was another memory that Madeline couldn't seem to shake, one that was far more unsettling. She kept seeing him there on his rumpled bed when she'd so unwisely opened his door yesterday morning to check on him before slipping away.

It refused to leave her—the potent image of sleep-tousled hair, long legs and muscular chest, the covers barely draped over another area that didn't bear thinking about. There had been a kind of flush on all that hard, naked flesh, as if its owner had spent a long night of heated lovemaking. And then on the hill when he had—

You have to stop this. You're in no position to be intrigued by any man, much less some steel-eyed stranger who seems to resent you, maybe just because you've dared to intrude on his privacy.

Madeline's mind continued to question that privacy, wondering if it had a connection with the harsh lines of suffering around his bold mouth.

Enough. Forget about him.

Impatient with herself, she slammed a hand against the plunger that cut off the shower portion of the tub. She left the water running in the tub itself, however, to wash away the soap and scum.

Her cosmetics bag wasn't on the sink counter when she stepped out from behind the shower curtain. She then remembered having placed it on the chair just outside the bathroom door. Wrapping herself in her terry-cloth robe, she opened the door to retrieve the bag—

And caught Mitchell Hawke in the act of examining the contents of her satchel.

For a moment their gazes met, hers shocked, his wearing a challenge without apology. Then, outraged by his invasion, Madeline swiftly crossed the room and snatched the velvet pouch he was holding out of his hand.

She lashed out at him furiously. "If you have an explanation, I don't want to hear it, because nothing you say can—"

"Oh, I'm not going to try to make excuses for myself.

Why should I, when I'm supposed to be responsible for you?''

He made it sound as if he was her jailer. She could have smacked him for his smugness. ''And that entitles you to look through my belongings?''

''Maybe it does, when it turns up something illicit.''

Madeline frowned at him. ''What are you talking about?''

''Those.'' He nodded at the articles strewn across the bed. ''A hacksaw, blades, hammers, files. And then there's the matter of that little bag you're hugging. I saw the stones inside it. They must be worth a fortune. What would you say all of that adds up to, Madeline? Would you say it adds up to…oh, I don't know, maybe a case of safecracking?''

She stared at him, wondering if she ought to laugh or smack him, after all. ''I see. You think I'm involved in some form of jewel robbing.''

''Aren't you?''

''I don't know what branch of law enforcement you practiced back in San Francisco, but you couldn't have been very good at it.'' Opening the pouch, she emptied its shining contents on the bed. ''This,'' she said, picking up one of the stones, ''is carnelian. And that's a tigereye. The blue ones are lapis lazuli, the milky ones moonstones and opals. All of the others, including the garnets and amethysts, fall into the same category. There isn't a precious gem in the whole collection. Now, would you like to know about the tools?'' She scooped up the three hammers and held them out. ''This is a chasing hammer, this one here a raising hammer, and this is called a planishing hammer. I seriously doubt that any of them, or all the rest in the satchel, could get you inside a safe.''

Mitch said nothing for a moment. She watched his gaze travel from the bed to the table beside it. Next to the empty orange juice glass was the enameled pendant she had worn that first night. His eyes came back to her. She saw understanding in them, and something more. For the first time he actually looked contrite.

"You made the necklace thing yourself, huh?"

"And designed it, yes."

"Okay, so I made a mistake, and I apologize for it. But if all this is just about a hobby—"

"It isn't a hobby. I'm very serious about my jewelry making. I'm good, and one day I expect to make a living from it."

He had a look of surprise on his face, as if he thought such a pursuit uncharacteristic of the woman he believed she was. Obviously he didn't know her, any more than she really knew him.

"All right, not a hobby. Then, why were you so secretive about the satchel?"

"I wasn't being secretive, I was being protective. My tools are valuable, and I can't afford to risk them. It's bad enough I'll have to replace all the larger equipment I had to leave behind in San Francisco. Do you know what a good rolling mill costs?"

"No idea. Here, give me the pouch. I made the mess, I'll pick it all up and put it back."

His hand came out with the intention of closing around the pouch and taking it from her. Madeline, who was holding the pouch by the drawstring, wasn't ready to forgive him. She started to jerk the pouch back out of his reach. She wasn't certain whether what happened next was deliberate or merely an accident. She knew only that his hand was suddenly grasping not the velvet bag but her own hand.

Jolted by his touch, she tugged against his grip. She expected him to release her. He didn't. He went on clinging to her, his strong hand searing her flesh. Their eyes met, and she was instantly lost in his mesmerizing gaze, raw with desire. She stopped resisting, almost stopped breathing.

They stood like that for what felt like a long time. Then

slowly, insistently, he drew her toward him until she was resting against the hard wall of his chest. Madeline wanted to believe that when she lifted her head and parted her mouth, it was to voice her objection. But she would never be sure of that, either. Never know whether, instead, she issued a silent invitation he was immediately prepared to answer.

His mouth came crashing down on hers in a deep, blistering kiss—an explosion that involved his tongue plundering hers, the clean taste of him in her mouth, the virile aroma of him in her nostrils. For one uncontrollable, urgent moment, as he strained his hardness against her, his hand dipping inside her robe to stroke the softness of her bare skin, Madeline surrendered to his sensual assault.

Sanity was restored to her at the same time as his own awareness must have surfaced. When he suddenly released her, she felt she was being thrown away. If she experienced any sensation of loss, she denied it to herself. It would have been canceled, anyway, by the look in his eyes as she backed away from him to an area of safety. It was a wounded look, one of naked accusation. Then, without a word, he swung around and strode out of the room.

Shaken, Madeline went to stand by the window. She stared out at the leafless trees against the overcast sky and remembered his kiss. There had been a wild passion in it. There had also been a seething anger. It was the anger that decided her.

Recovering herself, she went back into the bathroom and turned off the water. She was still damp from her shower. She dried herself, fixed her hair and gathered together all of her belongings. When her satchel and suitcase were packed, the bed neatly made, she left the room and went to look for him.

She found him in the kitchen by the back door, hands thrust into his pockets as he gazed out at the barren landscape. Their situation had become impossible, one Madeline could no longer bear. He would have to understand and accept that.

"I can't stay here any longer. I won't stay here," she informed him, managing to keep her voice low and even, though she was trembling with emotion.

He turned away from the windowed door and looked at her. Then, without asking for an explanation or offering any argument, he nodded slowly. That's when she realized that he, too, could no longer endure this bewildering mixture of stress and sizzle that had been between them from the start.

"Neil will have to make other arrangements for me," she said. "I don't care what they are, just as long as he makes them immediately."

Again he made no objection. He must have known as well as she that they were a mistake together and that giving her back to Neil was the best thing for both of them.

"All right," he said.

He went to the phone on the wall and dialed. She listened to him speak briefly to someone at the Milwaukee precinct where Neil worked.

"He's off today," Mitch reported after he ended the call. "I'll try him at home."

Again she waited while he dialed and talked to someone who, by the tenor of the quick conversation, clearly was not Neil. He hung up and turned to her.

"It was the girl who cleans house for him," Mitch explained. "She'd finished her work and was just leaving. Neil isn't there. She said he went out to get a paper and coffee and would probably be back in a few minutes. We'll just have to wait."

Madeline shook her head, her frustration at an intolerable level. "I don't want to wait. I want you to drive me to his house."

Her tone was so insistent that one of his thick eyebrows quirked. "What are you saying? That if we wait I might change my mind, or that if I give Neil the chance, he'll change it for me?''

"There is that possibility," she admitted. "But if you deliver me to his door, he'll have to take me in. Please."

"Have it your way," he conceded. But she knew he was relieved by her decision.

Minutes later, with her suitcase and satchel tucked behind the front seat of his pickup, they headed in the direction of Milwaukee. They didn't talk on the drive. Glancing at him at the wheel, she wondered if he was experiencing either regret or uncertainty. If he was, he didn't express it by word or look.

Madeline thought about asking him again why he seemed to resent her, and just what had gone wrong between them. But at this stage, what was the point? Turning her attention from the man beside her, she diverted herself with the countryside through which they dipped and wound. Neil had told her on the drive out to the farm that the area was known as the Kettle Moraine. Even under a cold, dismal sky, it was a lovely region with wooded hills and gentle valleys.

When the first snowflakes of the season began to drift down from the darkening sky, Madeline remembered thinking two days ago how a blanket of white would soften the scene, enrich it. It seemed that her longing was being answered.

But as the snowfall thickened, the route began to seem less like a welcome Christmas card and more like a potential problem. She finally voiced her concern to Mitch. "This is getting heavy, isn't it?"

He shrugged. "It's Wisconsin. It snows."

There was no reason to be worried if he wasn't bothered himself. That's what she told herself, but by the time they reached the fringes of Milwaukee it was snowing in earnest. The wind had risen, driving a curtain of white against the truck as it crawled through the traffic. Snow was piling in the streets faster than the plows could remove it, making the going hazardous.

Madeline was relieved when Mitch pulled into the driveway of the small, suburban ranch house that Neil occupied. There was no sign of life along the quiet street. People were wisely staying indoors.

Mitch left the engine running and turned to her. "I want you to stay here in the cab while I go in and talk to him. Neil isn't going to be happy about this. I have some explaining to do, and I'm better off handling that without you on the scene."

Madeline was puzzled. What could he have to say to Neil that he didn't want her to hear? She started to object but decided that she wanted no more quarrels with him. All she needed was a fast resolution to the problem and a final parting from him.

"You'll be all right," he assured her, turning off the blower that had kept the windows clear. They immediately began to cloud over with moisture. "With the fogged windows and all that snowfall out there, no one will know you're even in here. Just stay in the cab and keep the doors locked. I'll try to be as quick as I can."

His coat strained against him as he opened the door and started to slide out of the truck, revealing an unmistakable bulge beneath the leather. He must have brought his gun with him. He couldn't have anticipated trouble, not here. He must simply be exercising caution, feeling a responsibility for her until he handed her back to Neil.

But before she could ask him about it, he was gone. Scrubbing the mist off a spot on the window, she could just make out through the swirling snow the dim shape of his tall figure disappearing around the back corner of the house.

Making sure the doors on both sides were secure, Madeline turned on the radio to hear a weather forecast. It was something they should have done on the drive in, but both of them had been too preoccupied to think of it.

She found a news station and learned what she already feared—that the snow was rapidly developing into a major winter storm. When the station started to announce early school closings and cancellations of public meetings, she switched off the radio.

She went on waiting, wondering what was taking him so long. It seemed forever before a sudden rap on the window of the driver's door startled her. Leaning over, she rubbed away the condensation and discovered Mitch's face pressed against the glass. She unlocked the door.

There was an urgency about the way he flung open the door and climbed behind the wheel, bringing a rush of snow and cold air into the cab with him.

"Is something wrong?"

He didn't answer her. Without bothering to buckle up, he turned the blower on full blast, threw the gear into Reverse, gunned the engine and backed out of the driveway. The wheels spun in the snow on the turn. Then, digging in, the pickup leaped forward and tore up the street.

Madeline stared at him. His face was granite hard and grim. "What is it?" she demanded. "What's happened?"

"Not now," he muttered, biting the words, each syllable uttered on a note of harshness.

They roared recklessly around a corner, the pickup skidding dangerously on the slick snow. Rocked against her seat belt, Madeline caught her breath and waited for an impact. But the pickup righted itself and went on speeding through the blinding whiteness.

"Slow down before you kill us," she pleaded.

He didn't seem to hear her. His hands tightened on the wheel. Her own hands clenched the seat. She felt sick. Something was wrong. Terribly wrong. Why were they fleeing?

"Tell me," she insisted.

And he told her, bluntly and without looking at her.

"Neil is dead."

Chapter Three

Mitch knew he couldn't go on risking their necks like this, that he had to pull over somewhere long enough to tell her the rest. He didn't trust himself to do that while they were rolling. He just wasn't steady enough.

There. A strip mall. The snowstorm had nearly emptied the parking lot. They should be safe for a few minutes.

Slowing, Mitch swung into the lot and tucked the pickup between a large van and a panel truck. It was a spot where their presence wouldn't be obvious but where he could still keep an eye on the street. He left the engine running and turned to her. She was frightened, of course, and looked it. He was sorry about that, but there had been no time to waste on explanations. They had needed to leave the scene as quickly as possible.

Hell, Mitch was badly shaken himself. Still so jolted by the whole thing that he had yet to take it in, to realize his terrible loss. Nerving himself, he waited for her questions.

"What do you mean, *dead?*" she whispered, voice husky with emotion, amber eyes wide with shock and disbelief.

There was no way to soften it, no time for niceties. He had to make her understand. "Dead," he said, managing not to choke on the words, "as in lying on his kitchen floor with a bullet in him."

Madeline stared at him, numb and silent. He was aware of the snow hissing against the windows, of the wipers slashing across the glass. Then he was conscious of something else. There was a disturbing expression in her eyes as she searched his face, and Mitch knew she was remembering he'd insisted on going into the house alone. She had no way of knowing it was because he hadn't wanted her to hear him tell Neil that he could no longer protect the woman he held responsible for Julie's death.

Her expression was followed by something even more unsettling. He saw her gaze drift in the direction of the place where he kept his pistol in the belt holster under his coat. The pistol that was no longer there. Then that same gaze flew back to his face in horror.

"Don't be a fool," he said gruffly. "I didn't kill him."

She shook her head, not in denial but as if to throw off the initial shock. "I—I'm sorry. It was just that for a second I thought—" She paused to clear her mind. "Then, why did we run like that?"

"It was necessary. Look," he explained, "I knew something was wrong when I got to the back door. I could see someone lying facedown on the floor of the kitchen. That's why I went into the house with my gun drawn. It was Neil on the floor. I was kneeling beside him, checking for life signs, when something heavy came down on the back of my skull. By the time I came to, the pistol was no longer in my hand, and Neil had a bullet hole in his head that hadn't been there before."

"What are you saying?" Madeline whispered. "Are you telling me—"

"Yeah, the bastard must have used my gun to kill him, because I don't think Neil was dead when I knelt beside him. I think he was just unconscious, knocked over the head like I was. I don't suppose you heard the shot?"

"Nothing. I had the radio on. What about the gun? What happened to it? Do you think the killer took it with him?"

"What I think is that it's still in that house, hidden some-place where I wouldn't easily find it but where the police are certain to after a thorough search."

"Did you look for it?"

"Yeah, and without luck. I would have looked a lot fur-ther if *she* hadn't waltzed into the kitchen with a casserole in her hands."

"Who?"

"Claire, his next-door neighbor. She was forever doing favors for Neil, trying to win his attention."

"And when she found you like that with his body—"

"That's right, she figured I killed Neil. I could see that much in her face. And she wouldn't listen. Too scared to stop for any explanation. The next thing I knew, the cas-serole was all over the floor and she was out of there. By the time I got outside, she was back at her own house barricaded inside—and you can be sure she was calling the cops."

"But if you had stayed there and waited for them to come, then explained—" She broke off in sudden under-standing. "But, of course, you couldn't, could you. The gun that killed Neil would be registered in your name."

"Not to mention my fingerprints on it. The murderer would have made sure of that. All the evidence is there, pointing straight to me. I had no choice but to run."

"And we can't trust the police, anyway, can we? Any one of them could be the man or woman in Griff's pay."

And if I'm arrested, sweetheart, that leaves you at the mercy of the enemy. I have to stay free, because right now I'm all you've got.

Mitch hated this. Hated suddenly having to behave like a guilty fugitive. All he had wanted was to be rid of this woman, give her back to Neil—but that could never happen now. Neil was gone, leaving Mitch with the maddening memory of the promise he had made. That he would protect Madeline, make sure she stayed healthy until it was reliably safe for him to do otherwise. It was a promise he continued to owe his friend. No choice, then. Madeline Raeburn was still his responsibility.

She was still gazing at him, looking more troubled by the moment. "Who could have killed Neil? This—this bad cop?"

"Don't know. But it must have been someone he knew, someone he even invited into the house. He was too good an officer to let a stranger take him by surprise."

"But why kill him?"

Mitch didn't answer her.

"Oh, yes," she said in a small, shaken voice, "I see. It was because of me, wasn't it. Because Neil refused to tell him where I was, and once he'd revealed himself to Neil, exposed his identity like that, he had no choice but to—"

"We don't know that for sure."

"But it's the most likely explanation."

Mitch could see that probability deeply distressed her, maybe just because it emphasized her own danger. He wasn't ready to credit her with any less self-interested motive than that.

"And all the time," she murmured, "what he was after was sitting out there in the driveway."

"Yeah, and if he hadn't slipped out the back and across the yard without looking around the corner of the house—which is how he must have made his exit—then…"

"I'd be dead."

In the silence that followed, those incredible eyes of hers, thick-lashed, beautifully shaped, remained fastened on him. Then she asked him slowly, softly, "What are we going to do?"

Before he could tell her, they both tensed in alarm at the sound of a siren far down the block. The siren could have been in response to any emergency, and even though the wail receded in the distance, it was a grim reminder to Mitch that they couldn't go on sitting here in this exposed lot.

"We need to go someplace where we can think this thing through and not be caught while we're doing it."

"Where?" she demanded, as he backed the pickup out of the parking space and headed for the street.

He had an idea. He'd once accompanied Neil and his grandson to the spot. "There is a place," he said. "It's not far from here. Providing I can find it."

The weather didn't help. Even if he'd been comfortably familiar with the area, the swirling snow hindered his vision while the streets grew more treacherous with every mile.

Madeline was quiet while he concentrated on the route. She waited until they were stopped at a traffic light. And then in that low voice that never failed to stir his senses, even when he knew it shouldn't, she said something completely unexpected.

"I'm sorry. Deeply sorry."

She didn't elaborate. She didn't have to. Mitch knew that she was offering her sympathy for the loss of his best friend. He wasn't sure how genuine her expression was until he turned his head and saw that those alluring amber eyes were misty with sorrow.

All right, so it surprised him that in this moment, when she had to be frantic about her plight, she could grieve for Neil. It still didn't make her an angel, even if she had the face of one.

"Yeah," he muttered hoarsely. It was all he could manage by way of acknowledgment. Any further effort would have cost him his self-control. He was already torn up inside—and he meant to keep it there.

Faye, he thought as the light changed and the traffic moved forward again. It was going to kill her to hear about her father. And there were Neil's friends on the force back in Frisco. The news would be hard on them.

But Mitch knew he had to stop worrying about Neil's

daughter and his friends. Had to put his own grief on hold. All he had time for now was to get them out of this mess.

A PLOW HAD BEEN THROUGH HERE recently, Mitch noticed, so the snow wasn't as bad as he'd feared. He was able to negotiate the winding lane without difficulty. The lot was understandably empty when they reached it. He parked the pickup facing the lagoon.

On any other occasion Mitch would have admired the setting. The dark waters of the lagoon, which for some reason was still unfrozen, were rimmed with evergreens. Their somber green boughs drooped with snow, making a scene that an artist might have effectively borrowed for a Christmas card.

But all he could appreciate was the seclusion of the place. Nothing stirred in the vicinity of the lagoon or on the equipment of the children's playground behind them. The park was as deserted as he'd anticipated, offering them a reasonably safe haven. For now, anyway.

Madeline had been silent for most of the drive. But her mind must have been very busy, because the instant he shut off the engine and turned to her, she gave voice to her decision.

"There's only one thing for me to do. I'm going to turn myself over to the Milwaukee police."

"And what do you think that's going to accomplish, except to make you a target?"

"I'll take my chances on their protecting me, even if one or more of them is in Griff's pay."

She was offering to free him of any responsibility for her, giving him the chance to focus all of his energy on clearing himself. So tempting. Only, he couldn't accept her offer, not when it meant he would be failing Neil. Because whatever else Mitch had either lost or intentionally abandoned after Julie's death, he was still a man of his word. That much he'd been unable to shed.

"Yeah, why not? It's your life if you want to risk it. Except a lot of people are counting on you to stay healthy long enough to put Griff Matisse away where he belongs. Neil was one of those people."

His tactic worked. She was immediately apologetic. "Yes, you're right. I wasn't thinking. Then, what do we do? Go back to your farm?"

Mitch knew that neither of them was happy about that prospect. In any case, returning to the farm was out of the question. Although Neil wouldn't have shared the existence of the place with any of his colleagues—not when he had chosen it as a sanctuary for Madeline—his daughter knew about the farm. So, perhaps, did his neighbor. And under the circumstances, neither would hesitate to reveal their knowledge.

"No good," he said. "It's the first place the cops will look."

"Then, where or who do we turn to?"

Under other circumstances, that would have been an easy question for Mitch to answer. A single phone call would have provided them with immediate assistance from his family. But Mitch's family wasn't available. Every member of the Hawke clan was out of the country on a holiday cruise. He was supposed to have joined them, but he couldn't bring himself to celebrate anything this year.

"There is no one. Neil was the only contact we could trust, and now that he's gone, Milwaukee is no longer safe for you."

She was quiet as she gazed out at the lagoon. Then she said, "There's something I've learned since leaving San Francisco. I'm not really safe anywhere as long as Griff Matisse is free and so powerful that he has connections everywhere. So I might as well return now to San Francisco. At least there the DA's office wants so badly to put him behind bars that they'll go to extra lengths to protect me until the trial. Maybe their safe house is ready for me by now.''

Mitch wasn't happy about that safe house. Neil had explained it as the reason for the delay in San Francisco's sending an escort to return Madeline to California. But Mitch had sensed all along that something wasn't right about this explanation. For the moment, though, he was prepared to put that argument aside.

He could see Madeline was determined, that it would be a wasted effort to challenge her decision. He had a better method for handling this situation.

''All right,'' he said, ''what do you want me to do?''

If she was surprised by his easy compliance, she didn't say so. ''Drive me to the airport and put me on a flight. That's all I ask.''

''Sounds simple enough. Then, once you're in the air, I can start clearing myself of Neil's death.''

''Exactly.''

Mitch made no objection. There would be time enough once they were under way to make her understand that her plan wasn't going to work. That he had no intention of simply dumping her in Matisse's backyard and forgetting about her. Oh, she would be flying to San Francisco, all right, providing this weather hadn't already canceled all flights, but it would be under his terms.

He started the engine. ''One thing, though,'' he said. ''You can't just land in San Francisco without security of some sort waiting there to meet you. We have to let the DA's office know you're coming.''

She thought about that and then nodded. She was being calm about the whole thing, but he knew she had to be scared. What she intended involved considerable risk.

''Look,'' he suggested, ''I noticed a public phone back there near the picnic shelter.'' They would have to use a public phone because, in his hurry to deliver Madeline to Neil, he'd left his cell phone at the farm. ''Let me make the call for you. I know the assistant DA, Gloria Rodriguez. She's a woman I trust, and right now you need someone like that in your corner. Besides, you'll need to know if that safe house is ready and, if it isn't, what alternative she has to guarantee that you're fully protected.''

She considered his offer and apparently saw the advantages of it. ''All right.''

Mitch drove them back through the park to the rustic picnic shelter at the side of the lane. When he pulled over and started to slide out of the pickup, she opened her door with the intention of accompanying him.

''What are you doing?''

''I said you could make the call for me. I didn't say I wouldn't be listening in on it.''

Damn it, he had counted on her staying in the truck. There were things he hadn't wanted her to hear until the arrangements were settled, after which it would be too late for her to object. But she wasn't giving him any choice. Okay, so she'd learn the program now, and whatever her reaction, he would deal with it.

There had been a lull in the snowfall, but now the stuff was coming down again at a furious rate. The phone was located in a glass-walled stall that was open at the front, offering little protection from the weather. Coat collars turned up, shoulders hunched, they were squeezed side by side against the instrument.

But it wasn't the wet snow in his hair and down his neck that made Mitch miserable as they waited for the assistant DA to come on the line. In that tight place he was aware of Madeline's closeness, her warmth breath steaming on the air and mingling with his, the provocative scent of her hair near his face, the creamy smoothness of her cheek almost touching his. These were the sensations that made him uncomfortable. Never mind that this was the wrong place, the wrong time, the wrong woman. He was still aroused.

And relieved when Gloria Rodriguez's sane, familiar voice finally reached his ear. "Mitchell Hawke, is that you? What on earth—"

He interrupted her by asking if she was alone in her office and if the line she was speaking on was secure. Once assured of that, he described the situation for the assistant DA as succinctly as possible, holding the phone so that Madeline could hear the conversation.

There was a pause after Mitch explained Madeline's wish to return immediately to San Francisco. Madeline's questioning gaze met his, and he knew she could sense it, too—the unmistakable anxiety in the silence on the other end. It was more than Gloria's shock over learning that Neil was dead. Something was wrong.

"Mitch," the woman finally said, her tone decidedly reluctant, "this isn't wise."

"It's necessary. Hell, Gloria, she isn't safe here in Wisconsin."

"The thing is..."

"What?"

"We may not be able to guarantee her safety in San Francisco, either."

And that's when she told them. How her office wasn't sure where the leak had originated. How it might be either in Milwaukee or in San Francisco. Because it was only after all the particulars, along with Madeline's deposition, had been sent to San Francisco by Neil that the attempt had been made on her life in the Milwaukee safe house. Which meant that the information on her could have been relayed from California to one of Matisse's connections in Milwaukee. They didn't know. They were trying to discover the source, but they just didn't know.

So that, Mitch thought grimly, had been the reason for the delay in returning Madeline to San Francisco. Preparing a safe house for her had either been an excuse or not the important issue, which was to try to plug that leak. He'd been right in not trusting Neil's explanation.

And why *hadn't* Neil trusted him with the truth? Because he hadn't known it himself? Or had he not wanted Mitch to know just how complicated the situation was?

"Gloria, Neil's killer is somewhere on the loose in this town. He's not going to rest until he finds Madeline Raeburn. And if this guy *is* hiding behind a badge, she doesn't stand a chance, not with the whole Milwaukee police department behind him. So you tell me, just who do we trust at this point?"

"I see what you mean. Under the circumstances, it would be better if she's here in San Francisco where my office can directly control the situation. Also, the DA has changed his mind and isn't comfortable about sanctioning Matisse's arrest until the witness is back in California."

California maybe, Mitch thought, but not San Francisco. Not with Griff Matisse sitting right there waiting for her. Mitch had his own ideas on the subject of a safe house, but he didn't think this was a smart time to share them with either the DA's office or Madeline. His plan could wait.

"Mitch," Gloria went on, "can you hole up with Ms. Raeburn somewhere long enough for me to send a reliable officer to escort her back? I want her fully protected on that flight."

"She will be," he said, his gaze on Madeline's face. "I'm escorting her myself."

Her eyes registered astonishment and then anger. She tried to snatch the phone out of his hand, but he'd anticipated her reaction and held it out of her reach.

Hearing their scuffle, Gloria sounded alarmed. "What's going on there? Is something wrong?"

Mitch managed to get his mouth against the phone. "Ms. Raeburn is just expressing her happiness over my being her personal bodyguard on the flight, that's all."

"Mitch," Gloria started to object, "I don't think—"

"Your people haven't done very well by her so far," he said, fending off Madeline, who was still frantically trying to grab the receiver. "That's why it's going to be me accompanying her. And, Gloria," he added sharply, "see what you can do about stopping the Milwaukee police department from mounting a wholesale manhunt for me, at least long enough for me to deliver your witness to you. I'll be in touch."

Before Madeline could prevent it, he slapped the receiver into its cradle. She was breathing hard, and there was fire in the amber eyes that glared at him.

"Just what do you think you're doing?"

"Exactly what Neil would have wanted me to do," he informed her with flint in his voice.

"But I don't need you to—"

"And there will be no arguments about it." He thrust his face down close to hers. "And no discussions, either. This is just how it's going to be. Okay, I know, you don't want me on that flight with you. You want me out of your life as much as I want you out of mine. Well, it's just not going to happen. Not until I hand you over to Gloria Rodriguez."

She stared at him in dismay.

"Yeah, that's right, sweetheart, it's just you and me now." He chuckled softly, his mouth mere inches from hers. "Ought to be an interesting trip, huh?"

MADELINE KNEW she had every reason to be nervous as she waited for him in the pickup. This was a chancy errand, though imperative. She had only a modest sum in her purse, while he had no more than a few bills on him and a couple of credit cards that couldn't be used because they would leave an immediate trail.

They had to have funds in the form of cash to get to California, a need that had resulted in this stop at one of the branches of his bank. He was in there now, emptying his account. But if the police had managed to learn of his bank and to alert its tellers—

Yes, she should be nothing but worried, only she wasn't. She was too busy smoldering over the memory of his mocking grin back there in that tight little phone booth in the park. She could still feel his hard body pressed against her, still hear him taunting her in that slow, deep drawl that promised her his maddening company all the way to California.

He had tricked her with that phone call to San Francisco, and now she was stuck with him. What choice did she have, when he had the essential funds? At least, she hoped they were in his possession when he strode out of the bank a moment later and joined her in the cab.

"No problem," he reported, patting the pocket of his coat as he slid behind the wheel. "Nobody questions the withdrawal of large sums around the holidays."

Madeline nodded without comment. An expression of relief would have been premature in any case, because the money wasn't their only problem. He had earlier pointed out the risk of driving around the city in a pickup that the police might already be looking for. In that respect, though, the weather was their ally. The snow had escalated into a serious blizzard that made the identification of any vehicle difficult. Anyway, they needed the pickup, because securing a taxi in these conditions would be next to impossible.

However, the heavy snow hindered them in their crawl through Milwaukee's storm-snarled traffic as they worked their way south in the direction of Mitchell Field. It was another reason for Madeline to be nothing but anxious. Except, there was no room for anxiety. She was still seething.

She didn't like the man beside her. Mitchell Hawke was high-handed, devious, arrogant. And she needed him. She needed his strength and resourcefulness because, whatever his flaws, she realized she could trust him to see them through this crisis. It was this, her dependence on a man who assaulted her senses on every level and at every turn, that Madeline found so infuriating.

"This mess is getting worse," he said.

She knew he wasn't talking about just the weather, although that was bad enough, with high winds piling up drifts in the open areas and the visibility poor. It was the result of these conditions, and increasingly strangled traffic on the expressway they now traveled, that made him taut with impatience.

"How much farther is it to the airport?" she asked him, noticing another stalled car at the side of the road. She had already counted several.

"Several miles, but at this rate…"

He didn't finish. He didn't have to. She knew what he was thinking. If they were delayed too long, there was every possibility that all flights out of Milwaukee would be canceled. Which was why he had the radio on and tuned to the local news. So far, however, there had been no announcement that commercial air traffic was grounded.

But what happens, she wondered, *if we can't get out of the city, if we're trapped here with the police hunting for us?*

Madeline decided it was time to stop being apprehensive about her companion and to start worrying in earnest about their situation, especially since the traffic had now ground to a halt.

Mitch slapped the wheel in frustration. "Must be an accident up ahead."

"Yes." Would they be able to get through?

They sat there for several endless minutes. He used the washer to clean the worst of the slop off the windshield. The snow was still whirling against the glass. There was silence between them as they waited.

In the end, he lowered the volume on the radio and spoke to her abruptly. "This is as good an opportunity as any."

She turned her head, gazing at him in bemusement. "For what?"

"For you to tell me just what you witnessed that put you on the run. I'm in it now, so I'd better know exactly what we're up against."

"Then, Neil didn't—"

"No, not the particulars."

Both his tone and the expression on his face told her that, until now, he hadn't wanted to hear any of the details, that he'd refused to involve himself beyond what was absolutely necessary. Why? Because her story might have aroused emotions he chose to keep dormant? She didn't know. He was still very much a mystery to her.

Madeline was quiet for a moment, gathering her thoughts. Then, keeping it as simple and impersonal as possible, she told him what he'd asked to hear. "I'd been working as a hostess at Griff Matisse's club, the Phoenix. Since you lived in San Francisco yourself, you probably know the place. It's a very successful nightspot."

He nodded without comment.

"Anyway," she continued, "I'd decided to quit."

This seemed to surprise him, and he glanced at her sharply. "Any particular reason?"

Madeline had no intention of discussing Adam with him. She was much too vulnerable where Adam was concerned, and she meant to keep him private.

"I'd begun to get orders on my jewelry, and I thought it was time to concentrate on that." It wasn't the truth, of course, but it would do.

"Go on."

"So I went to the club to tell Griff of my decision. It was early, probably an hour or so before opening. Griff wasn't expecting me, but he was usually in his office around that time. The place was quiet, no one around when I went upstairs to find him— Look, we're moving."

The traffic had begun to creep forward again.

"And?" Mitch urged her.

"Griff was in his office, but he wasn't alone. The door was open, and I could hear them talking as I came down the hall. They didn't know I was there. Either the lights hadn't been turned on in the hall, or else one of them was burned out. It was very dim, and I was busy feeling my way. That's when I heard it."

"It?"

"Griff being angry in that slow, wounded way of his, whenever somebody crossed him. He was saying something like, 'I liked and trusted you, was getting ready to bring you in on things. That would have been a real mistake, wouldn't it? Good thing I was tipped in time, huh, because now, Woody, I've got to see that you don't hurt me.'"

Along with the other solid lines of vehicles in the three lanes, the pickup continued to move forward at a stop-and-go pace.

"Woody was one of the barmen," Madeline explained. "I thought he must have been caught helping himself to the receipts. That happened once before with another barman, who was fired on the spot. That's all I thought it was. I didn't understand what it was really about, that Woody was an undercover cop. I didn't know until it was too late, until I got to the door and heard him say, 'You can't kill a cop and get away with it.' Griff laughed and said, 'Sure I can.' And then—" she paused, struggling to get the rest out through the sudden thickness in her throat "—Griff shot him. Just like that, he shot him. It was all so—so horribly casual."

"And you ran," Mitch said.

"And I'm still running."

"Maybe you didn't need to. Considering the way Matisse felt about you, maybe he would have forgiven you for what you saw."

Madeline stared at him, shocked by his careless speculation. He wasn't looking at her. He had his eyes on the road. "How would you know what Griff Matisse felt about me, or didn't feel?"

His broad shoulders lifted in a faint shrug. "Thought I heard he was fond of you. Must have been Neil who mentioned it."

"He was fond of all his employees at the Phoenix. He called us his 'family.' But I had no illusions about that, not toward the end. And after I caught him cold-bloodedly murdering Woody like that—" Madeline shuddered over the memory "—well, I knew he couldn't afford to let me live."

"So what was the undercover cop—this Woody—investigating?"

"I don't know."

"No clue?"

"Why should I?" What was he implying?

"I just figure since you were—what did you call it?—one of the family, you might have— Damn!"

They had reached the scene of the accident where the traffic was being slowly channeled into a single lane. An eighteen-wheeler lay on its side, blocking the right lane. The middle lane was occupied by a pair of police cruisers, their lights flashing threateningly.

"Careful," Mitch muttered through his teeth.

She knew his warning referred to the two officers who were out in the middle of the expressway directing the flow of traffic. And eyeing each vehicle as it was waved on through. Were they checking for a pickup? Mitchell Hawke's pickup?

There was a bad moment when it came their turn to pass along the left lane into which Mitch had already eased the pickup. They were suddenly halted by the uplifted arm of the officer directly in front of them. Was it her imagination, or was he gazing at them suspiciously? Madeline felt herself sliding down in her seat in an instinctive effort to become invisible. The tension in the cab was unbearable.

"You can relax," Mitch murmured. "It's not us. Not yet, anyway. There's the reason for the holdup."

An ambulance squeezed past them. When it had cleared the lane, the traffic was allowed to proceed again. Madeline didn't know she'd been holding her breath until the flashing lights were behind them. She sagged against her belt, gulping air.

"Yeah, we got lucky," Mitch said. "*This* time."

He turned up the volume again on the radio, and that's when they heard what they had been fearing since leaving the park. All the air traffic at Mitchell Field had been grounded until the weather lifted, which could be hours from now. *Dangerous* hours.

"What are we going to do?" she asked.

"Get out of the city."

"But driving much farther in this weather—"

"Is out of the question. The pickup is history, anyway. We've pushed our luck with it, because if the cops aren't looking for it already, they will be soon enough. We'll have to leave it behind."

"And use what?"

He didn't answer her. He concentrated on edging over to a lane that carried them off one of the exits into Milwaukee's downtown area.

"Where are we going?"

"The Amtrak station. Radio hasn't said anything about the trains not running, and if we can manage it, one of them is going to be taking us out of here."

I hope you know what you're doing, Mitchell Hawke, Madeline was still silently hoping twenty minutes later, when, after abandoning the pickup in an obscure corner of a parking garage and bearing her things between them, they trudged through the slop and falling snow to the Amtrak station three blocks away.

The looming brick structure faced with faux arches was a welcome sight, although, like so many of the train stations in the country whose traffic had seriously declined, the interior had a shabby look.

There was no shortage of traffic this afternoon, however. The vast waiting room was crowded with travelers anxious to reach holiday destinations by whatever means was available to them. Long lines waited at the ticket windows.

Pausing inside the entrance, they consulted the huge board displaying arrivals and departures. There was a train leaving for Chicago in forty minutes. Mitch drew her off to the side next to a newsstand.

"I'm going to try to get us on that train. If the weather down in Chicago is any better than here, then we ought to be able to catch a flight out of O'Hare." He handed Madeline her suitcase. "While I do that, I want you to go into the women's rest room over there and lock yourself in one of the stalls."

She stared at him. "That's a plan. Not a very good one, of course, considering the police must be looking everywhere for you. You're the one that ought to stay out of sight while I buy the tickets."

"I don't want you at risk in that mob."

"What risk? The police aren't looking for me. They think I'm still safe wherever Neil put me."

"In case you've forgotten," he said, shoving his face down into hers, the expression on it suddenly harsh with anger, "there's a killer out there somewhere, stalking you. And if that's not enough, you might remember that a man lost his life today. And maybe he lost it because he was protecting you."

Madeline couldn't have been more stung if he'd struck her. Was he blaming her for Neil Stanek's death? Did he resent her that much?

"I didn't deserve that," she whispered. "I'm as sick as you are about Neil."

The heat of accusation that had flared briefly in his eyes

subsided. "Look, there's no way I'm going to be recognized. Not yet, anyway, because it's too soon for—"

He broke off abruptly, the expression on his face freezing as his gaze locked on to something behind her. Madeline twisted around. There was a TV monitor mounted above the racks of magazines and paperbacks. It was tuned to a local newscast. Someone had turned down the sound and forgotten to turn it up again.

But sound wasn't necessary. The image on the screen delivered its blow to them in absolute silence. It was the face of Mitchell Hawke.

Chapter Four

"Seems I was wrong," Mitch said grimly, turning away from the sight of his own face staring out at him from the screen. "Looks like I'm already Milwaukee's main attraction."

Madeline glanced around nervously, expecting to find a sea of faces gazing at her companion in shocked recognition. But no one was paying any attention to them or the TV monitor. "How could they broadcast your photograph this soon? Where could they have gotten it?"

Mitch thought about it. "I recognized the photo, at least the part they used. The cops must have lifted it from Neil's house. He kept it on the wall in his living room. The whole picture was of me, Neil and three of his friends on the force back in Frisco. It was our weekly poker group smiling for the camera. That neighbor of Neil's must have led the cops right to it."

"What do we do now?"

"Cops don't like it when one of their own is slain. They don't rest until the perp is in cuffs, and with my face so famous now in this town..." He paused, drew a deep breath and released it slowly. "Guess there's a new program. You buy the tickets while I keep out of sight."

"Where will you be?"

She watched him, seeing his reluctance over the necessity of his decision as he cast his gaze around the terminal.

"That should do," he said, nodding toward a deserted alcove where lockers lined the walls.

Madeline left her things with him, took the money he gave her and joined one of the lines waiting at the windows. She was still quivering with emotion, and not all of it was due to the shock of seeing Mitch's face up on that screen. In fact, most of it was due to his unreasonable performance when she'd first suggested she buy the tickets.

Remembering this, she could see in her mind those distinctive ears of his. She had noticed before how they flamed red when he was angry. It was one more thing about Mitchell Hawke, along with those stormy blue eyes and sinful mouth, that unnerved her, kept her constantly on edge.

Everything had happened so quickly that Madeline had had no time to examine any of it. Now, waiting here in this frustratingly slow line, she realized all over again that she was dependent on a man she didn't completely trust. And although instinct told her he would go to any lengths to safeguard her, she sensed there was something wrong about him. Something that made her reluctant to confide in him, had her fearing that, even if she shared the truth with him, he wouldn't believe her. That, in fact, he wanted, for some dark reason of his own, to believe nothing but the worst about her.

She thought again about that wicked mouth and how it had felt devouring her own. Hot and demanding, the mouth of a devil. She had wanted to get away from him, still wanted to, but need was dictating another scenario. One that had bound her to a man who might ultimately prove more dangerous to her than the people who wanted her dead.

He should never have let her go out there on her own! Anything could happen!

Mitch prowled restlessly from one end of the deep alcove

to the other, resisting the urge to poke his head around the corner and check the main hall of the terminal. He tried to remember that the lines were long, that it would take time for her to reach a window. Tried to tell himself that she would be all right. But he couldn't stop worrying about her.

What was keeping her? Where was she?

Mitch was tense with impatience by the time Madeline finally trotted around the corner and into the alcove, tickets in hand. He was about to express his relief, when he noticed the sober expression on her face. Something was wrong.

"What is it?" he demanded. "What happened?"

"The police. One of them came in from his cruiser out front and showed up at the window just as I reached it. He spoke to the attendant and handed him copies of a circular to be passed out to all the windows. I didn't hear what they said. I didn't have to. I could see your face on those circulars."

Mitch muttered an oath and started to move around her in the direction of the main hall.

"It's all right." Madeline stopped him. "He's gone now. He got a call on his two-way and left. I caught a glimpse of the cruiser pulling away."

"It's not all right," Mitch said. "This is all moving too fast. What about you? The cop pay any attention to you?"

"He never even glanced at me."

Then the guy didn't have eyes in his head, Mitch thought, or else he was immune to the kind of face that can twist a man's gut. Either way, it meant they were safe again. For now, at least.

"The attendant told me the Chicago train is delayed by twenty minutes," Madeline said. "And since we have to wait…well, there's a canteen out there serving fast food."

"You can eat?"

"I'm sorry, but I'm hungry."

Actually, it surprised him that she had waited until now

to mention food. He had noticed that first evening at the farm that she didn't suffer from a poor appetite. He had to admit he was hollow himself. He hadn't had breakfast or lunch, and it might be hours before they had another opportunity to snatch a meal.

"All right," he said, "we'll risk it. But we're not sitting down at one of those tables. You get whatever they have that's quick, and meet me out on the platform."

By the time she joined him with sandwiches and sodas, he had found a secluded bench for them. It was a poor place for a picnic. The platform was cold and drafty, which was exactly why Mitch had decided on it. Only a scattering of people was willing to wait out here, and none of them were interested in the couple on the bench.

He and Madeline ate without talking. He appreciated her silence. It was the first interlude he had experienced since walking into Neil's house, and it gave him a chance to think, to cast his mind back over what had happened in that kitchen.

Events had moved so swiftly, he wasn't clear about any of them. He tried to remember if he had heard someone behind him when he'd knelt there beside Neil's body. Seen something before whatever heavy object was wielded had come crashing down on his skull. Even smelled a revealing scent. Anything at all that might provide a clue to the identity of his attacker and Neil's killer.

Nothing. He hadn't heard a sound, hadn't glimpsed so much as a fleeting shadow, and there had been no odors. The attack had occurred with the same deadly surprise that Neil must have suffered from his assailant.

"Your head," Madeline said.

He turned to her in bemusement. "What?"

"You've been sitting there rubbing the back of your head. Does it hurt?"

He'd been so preoccupied he hadn't realized he was massaging his scalp. He lowered his hand. "It's nothing."

"Are you sure? Because from the way you described it before, you took a nasty blow, and if you've got an injury that needs attention—"

"I'm fine," he insisted. "A little swelling that's maybe tender, but no headache."

"Well, if you're sure…"

She went back to eating her sandwich, leaving Mitch with his thoughts again. Neil's assailant. His mind kept coming back to that and what he had told Madeline earlier—that Neil's visitor must have been someone Neil had known. Someone he had admitted into his house without suspicion, because there had been no sign of any forced entry, no evidence of anything like burglary.

A friend, then, or at least an acquaintance he trusted. Maybe a fellow officer. But Neil would have been careful about any member of the Milwaukee force if he was convinced that one of them was an informer. Assuming, that is, he hadn't yet learned what Gloria Rodriguez had shared with Mitch in that phone call. That the leak could have originated in San Francisco. In which case…

No, it was too fantastic.

But Mitch couldn't stop thinking about San Francisco and Neil's closest friends on the force there. Three other officers. Three men whose company Mitch had shared almost weekly in their poker sessions: Morrie Swanson, Dave Ennis, Hank Rosinski. He knew them, but not well—not like Neil who had worked with them, visited them in their homes. Was it possible, just possible, that one of them had arrived from Frisco to persuade Neil to—

"Didn't you hear?" Madeline interrupted him again. "They're announcing our train."

"Right." He got to his feet, disposed of the containers from their meal and took her suitcase. They headed toward the train.

Mitch put the subject of Neil's killer out of his mind, knowing he had to concentrate now on getting them safely

on board the Chicago-bound train. He would return to that
subject another time, he promised himself, and maybe by
then it would make more sense.

To his relief, no one challenged them as they moved
down the platform, joining the lines filing into the train. He
overheard someone claim that it was the last passenger train
leaving Milwaukee that afternoon. He could believe it. The
train was crammed with travelers.

Their own car had a crowd of boisterous football fans
on their way to a Packers–Bears game in Chicago. But
Madeline let neither their noise nor the tight space in which
she and Mitch had to fit themselves bother her. The two of
them were scarcely settled side by side on their portion of
the seat when she drifted into an exhausted sleep.

Mitch didn't blame her. The worst of the tension was
behind them, at least for the present, giving her a chance
to rest. Mitch himself remained alert as the train rolled
southward. Even if he had allowed himself the luxury of
relaxing his guard, he doubted he would have been able to
doze off. Not with Madeline Raeburn's lush body pressed
against him, reminding him of everything he wasn't supposed to feel about this woman, and couldn't help feeling.

That kiss. He kept remembering what they had shared
back at the farm this morning, the way his senses had rioted
on him, the longing he'd experienced to plunge his hands
even deeper inside her robe, to savor with his fingertips and
then his mouth her warm, naked flesh.

The kiss had been a result of his own weakness, a serious
mistake almost as bad as the one he made now by looking
down at her where she nestled against his side. Her head
rested on his shoulder, a position she wouldn't have permitted had she been conscious of it.

Unable to resist the temptation, Mitch slowly explored
her with his gaze, marveling at the thickness of her sable
lashes, noticing a tiny crescent-shaped scar at the corner of
one eye. The way she looked at this moment, hair tumbled,

full mouth slightly parted as though in invitation, had images chasing through his head. Wanton images that made him ache in areas that could prove to be a real problem.

Worse, far worse, was the tenderness that suddenly swelled deep inside his gut. All right, he had agreed to protect her. But to have that determined protectiveness accompanied by any degree of softness...

Damn it, what was he doing? How could he forget that he had lost Julie because of this woman? No matter what she had told him on the way to the airport, Madeline was no innocent. She couldn't be—not if she'd been Griff Matisse's girl. And most of San Francisco knew that she was. Nor, if she'd worked for Matisse, could she have been unaware of his criminal activities. And Mitch was convinced it had to be one of those activities that was responsible for Julie's savage death last summer.

He had to remember all of this. Had to keep reminding himself that Madeline was withholding something. Maybe a lot of somethings. That she wasn't who she pretended to be. Hadn't she already demonstrated this? She was forever surprising him, failing to match his expectations of her, keeping him on edge with her elusiveness.

But as much as he wanted to resent her, *did* resent her, there was something he couldn't deny. For the first time since Julie, he felt alive again, needed. And that, more than all the rest, worried the hell out of him.

Mitch had kept himself aware of the other passengers, but none had seemed to be interested in him or Madeline. That is until the Illinois border when a heavyset man began sneaking glances in Madeline's direction.

Mitch's warning system immediately signaled him of a potential danger. It was unlikely that any of Matisse's men had managed to find them and was on this train. But it wasn't impossible. Fully vigilant now, Mitch kept his eye on the stranger and regretted that he no longer had his gun.

There was, of course, a more probable explanation for

their neighbor's interest. Madeline was an alluring woman who commanded masculine attention.

That other men admired and desired her, had fantasies about her similar to his own, was understandable. What wasn't acceptable was how much this frustrated, even infuriated Mitch. And when he thought about her with Griff Matisse—

Enough! If he was going to get her safely to California, he had to control his urges. Otherwise, the situation could be fatal, because there was nothing that made a man as vulnerable as lust did. Particularly lust for a woman you had sworn to hate.

A moment later Madeline stirred, opened her eyes and sat up. "Sorry," she murmured when she realized she had been pillowing her head on Mitch's shoulder.

Before he could respond, the man across the aisle, who had continued to eye her, leaned toward her with an amiable smile on his florid face. Mitch stiffened, prepared to challenge him.

"Excuse me," he said, "but could I ask you about the bracelet you're wearing?"

Madeline must have been used to this. Even though she was still drowsy, she obligingly stretched out her arm. Unique silver disks dangled from the bracelet that clasped her wrist, flashing in the light.

"I've been admiring that thing since Milwaukee," the man explained. "Would you mind my asking where you got it? I know my wife would love to find one just like it in her Christmas stocking."

"Thank you, but I didn't buy it over the counter. Actually—"

Mitch pressed a hand against her side, warning her not to reveal that the bracelet was her own creation. Information like that had a way of getting back to the wrong people.

"Uh, it was made for me back east."

She probably hated having to lie like that. Mitch had

learned how proud she was of her jewelry designs. But, hell, if he hadn't stopped her, she might have gone on to take an order from the guy.

"Yes, I was afraid it might be one-of-a-kind. Well, thanks, anyway." Losing interest in them, he went back to the newspaper in his lap. Madeline leaned back and closed her eyes again.

Her bracelet, Mitch thought. That's all the guy had cared about. Harmless. Still, it was a lesson to him. People were curious in prolonged situations like this. They took notice, asked questions. Public transportation wasn't safe for them. No more trains, no planes or buses. Besides, by this evening there probably wouldn't be a terminal anywhere that wasn't under a careful watch for Neil's killer.

While Madeline slept, Mitch considered the options. By the time they reached the northern suburbs of Chicago, he had a plan shaped and ready to execute. It was an arrangement that had several advantages, one of which was his intention not to escort Madeline to San Francisco until Gloria Rodriguez could assure them that information was no longer being passed to Matisse.

A secure hiding place. That's what he needed for them. And he'd already decided back in the phone booth in the park just what it would be. There was a secluded little cabin in the California mountains. It wouldn't be easy taking Madeline there, not when he had once shared that cabin on a vacation with Julie. He'd avoided the place since her death.

No choice. The cabin was ideal for his purposes. He would deal with the memories when the time came. Somehow he would overcome them.

MADELINE WAS PERPLEXED when they left the train in Evanston.

"What are we doing?" she demanded, as Mitch hustled her onto the platform. "This isn't Chicago."

"Next door to it," he said, hailing a taxi.

She was further bewildered by the address he gave the driver. It wasn't O'Hare Airport, which she had assumed would be their destination. "Where are we going? What is this all about?"

He waited until the cab was under way, headed south toward the edge of the city, before he told her. "We're not flying to California. We're driving there."

Madeline stared at him. Here it is, she thought. More evidence of this man's overbearing, take-charge and be-damned-if-you-don't-like-it attitude. "Excuse me? Did you say something about a road trip? A *two-thousand-mile* road trip in the middle of winter?"

"Yeah, by interstate. Interstates aren't a problem. They're always kept open for the truck traffic. Even the far northern interstates are clear most of the time, and I figure we'll be taking a more central route. In case you haven't noticed, we're already out of the worst stuff."

It was true that the storm was behind them. There was only a light snow falling on Chicago's streets. That didn't mean conditions couldn't change and become severe. "All right, suppose we get lucky and don't run into another bliz-zard. It's still two thousand miles to San Francisco."

"We can make California in a couple of days if we take shifts at the wheel and drive straight through without any stopovers. You drive, don't you?"

"Oh, I'm a dandy driver. Now, suppose you convince me of just why I would want to see America by highway instead of spread out below me from the comfort of a 747. And just when were you planning on telling me of this little change in plan?"

"I'm telling you now, and I think it's necessary." He proceeded to give her his reasons for avoiding all forms of public transportation, stressing how it was to their advan-tage to keep on the move until San Francisco could plug that leak.

Madeline had to agree that if descriptions of both of them had been issued by now, they could be recognized and apprehended in any terminal, very possibly by the wrong people. She could even appreciate his argument that, by delaying their arrival in San Francisco, the DA's office had time to secure the situation. But to hide out on the long highway, which was essentially what they would be doing...well, that was the problem.

It was one thing to endure a few hours on a plane with this man, but to be trapped with him on a cross-country trip of several days' duration conjured up an intimacy that panicked Madeline. How had all of this gotten to be so complex, so charged with volatile emotions? All she had wanted was to testify against Matisse, leave the anguish behind her and find somewhere safe and quiet to make her jewelry. What she had *not* wanted was a Mitchell Hawke, putting her life in jeopardy.

"You know I'm right, don't you?" he urged.

"What I know is that we don't have a car for this proposed little jaunt of yours, although I'm assuming the mysterious address you mumbled to the cabbie means we're on our way to get one. I'm also assuming that since we abandoned a perfectly good pickup back in Milwaukee, we can't use a rental car, because that, too, could be traced."

"Exactly. Don't look so worried. This is all going to work out just fine."

What choice did she have? As she had realized back in Milwaukee, she had to trust him. There was no one else. Surviving him was another matter entirely.

It had been hours since they left the farm, and the afternoon light was already fading when the taxi delivered them to their destination. Madeline wasn't happy with the neighborhood. It was definitely not the best part of town.

"Where are we?" she asked, eyeing the brick building they approached. It had the seedy look of a run-down warehouse, one whose windows had been painted over to discourage any casual interest in its contents.

"Somewhere that, for the right price and no questions asked, we can get a safe car."

Madeline didn't like the sound of that any more than she cared for the appearance of the individual who answered Mitch's ring. With his wealth of tattoos, a bushy beard and a black leather vest over a sizable paunch, he looked like someone who dealt in motorcycles, not cars.

Mitch was greeted like an old friend. "Well, now, ain't this a sweet surprise! The Hawk hisself. Been a while, man."

Madeline shouldn't have been surprised that Mitch was familiar to this character, not when he'd known the address of this place and its purpose. Just how this was possible was a question that could wait. Right now she was too busy being grateful that their portly host, having decided he could trust his callers, was admitting them into his establishment. It was a gloomy barn of a place, but after the bitter wind out in the street, she welcomed its warmth.

"This is Hog," Mitch indicated.

Appropriate, Madeline thought, acknowledging the introduction with a nod. Hog nodded back, offering her a careless, "Howdy." She had decided by now that she was not in the company of a legitimate used-car dealer and that, in fact, this place was probably a chop shop.

Mitch lost no time in getting down to business. "We're shopping for a car, Hog. A dependable one, and something that's not so hot we'll get burned by the first cop who spots it."

If Hog was curious about Mitch's purpose or his companion, he knew better than to ask questions. "You need speed?"

"Not a requirement, but endurance is."

"Got just the merchandise for you. Follow me."

He led them toward the far end of the building, switching

on lights along the way. Madeline found herself avoiding mounds of clutter, most of them car parts. Among this assortment of junk were cars in various stages of being dismantled.

"There she is," Hog said when they reached the last bay.

She was a vintage station wagon whose forlorn appearance was not in the least encouraging. When they approached the vehicle, Madeline could see evidence of rust on the body. Peering through a lowered rear window, she noticed duct tape covering a tear on the seat and could sniff the faint odor of something suspiciously like the inside of a barn, one that had housed too many animals.

Madeline waited for Mitch to tell Hog that he had to be kidding, but she was astonished when she turned her head and saw the expression on his face. If ever she had witnessed love at first sight, this was it. How could he? How could this tough man, who'd had no trouble abandoning a perfectly good pickup, go all soft over this excuse for an automobile? There was no understanding it.

At least he had the sense to play it cagey with Hog. "I don't know, Hog. She's pretty old."

Hog defended his offering with a brisk, "Don't let her looks fool you, man. She's got new tires and an engine that purrs."

"And a door that doesn't open," Madeline observed sourly when she tried the front passenger door, which yielded no more than a fraction of an inch.

"Yeah, sometimes it sticks, but that's all. This baby will get you anywhere you want to go."

"Let's hear it," Mitch said.

Hog obliged him by attaching an exhaust hose to the tailpipe and starting the engine. Mitch spent several minutes walking around the car, sitting behind the wheel and poking under the hood. Madeline had no idea if he knew what he was doing, but in the end he seemed satisfied.

"How much?"

Hog named a price, Mitch called him a bandit, and for the next five minutes they haggled. Madeline, looking again through the window of the wagon, interrupted the negotiations.

"Uh, why is there a grille dividing the front seats from the back?"

Hog shrugged. "Dunno. Maybe the last owners had pets they wanted to keep out of the front. If it bothers you, I can have one of the boys try to remove it first thing in the morning."

"We're not hanging around that long," Mitch said. "The screen stays."

Lovely, Madeline thought. A stolen car that had been used to transport animals. Or maybe something not that innocent. She decided it was best not to think about it.

"Come on into the office," Hog said after the two men had settled on a price, "and we'll make up owner's registration and insurance cards for you. You got a preference for a state? I've got plates for all of them except Hawaii and Alaska."

"We'd better make it California," Mitch replied. "It ought to correspond with my driver's license. And, uh, Hog, what are my chances of getting a gun from you? I seem to have lost mine."

Hog hesitated, then nodded. "I can manage that, too."

"You're a prince. Is that discount store still around the corner?"

"Yep."

"Well, look, Hog, we're gonna pop around there while you handle the paperwork and attach the plates."

"I'll have her ready when you get back. Gun, too."

Mitch had them halfway to the exit before Madeline was able to express her concern. "Phony identification? That is what he's going to create for us, isn't he? The gun I don't want to even think about. And why do we need a discount store?"

"What else do you expect for a car that's changing hands this way? Stop worrying about it. Hog may look disreputable, but he's an artist when it comes to counterfeiting documents. Anyway, it's just a precaution. And I need clothes, a razor and whatever for the road. Remember, I wasn't the one who came away from the farm with a suitcase." He glanced at his watch. "I wonder if I ought to phone Gloria Rodriguez again and let her know about our change in plans. I guess, though, even with the time difference it's too late to catch her in her office. What do you think?"

"You don't want to know," Madeline said, convinced that this whole undertaking was fast approaching a stage of insanity.

"Come to think of it, maybe it's better Gloria doesn't hear from us right away. What she doesn't know can't slip through the cracks and reach Matisse. Yeah, I think we'll wait on that and call her from the road."

He isn't even listening to me, Madeline thought. *How am I going to stand two thousand miles of him?*

MITCH KNEW THE QUESTIONS would come. He just hoped he was prepared to answer them.

She waited until they were on the road. Night had fallen, but there was no darkness on the Chicago freeway they traveled. The dazzling lights of the traffic and the city cast a perpetual glow into the sky.

"You know this town," Madeline said, a note of accusation in her voice. "You knew all about Hog and his shady operation. You remembered the discount store. I think I'm entitled to an explanation."

"Yeah, all right." How much should he tell her? How much was safe for her to know? Maybe it was time he risked the truth about himself, at least some of it. "I grew up in Chicago."

"No wonder it's familiar to you."

He could feel her gaze on him, curious and puzzled.

"But, uh, someone like Hog—"

"No, we didn't steal bikes together when we were kids. Hog and his kind are the outcome of my family's business. Private investigators encounter all sorts of unscrupulous characters in their work. And when you're hunting for information, it's smart to keep those connections friendly ones."

Her surprise was evident. "Your people are private investigators?"

"That's right. The Hawke Detective Agency. Ma and Pop started it. They still run the home office here in Chicago."

"Meaning there are branches?"

"All over the country. My brother, Devlin, operates out of Denver, Roark out of San Antonio. My sisters, Christy and Eden, are in New Orleans and Charleston."

"All of them PIs?"

"All of them."

She sounded amazed, impressed even. And why that should please him he couldn't imagine, particularly since he knew his admission could very well lead to trouble. Probably would.

"And you?"

Her question was inevitable. He could lie about it. He didn't. "San Francisco."

"Not an ex-cop, then," she said slowly. "You're a PI with an office in San Francisco. Only, you're not in San Francisco doing whatever PIs do."

"That's right. Let's just say I burned out and needed a break."

That was all the explanation he was going to give her. Would she be satisfied with it? He was afraid she wouldn't.

She was silent. *She's working it out,* he thought. Remembering what Julie must have told her. Mitch braced himself for the explosion.

"There's something I don't understand," she said.

There was no anger in her voice. None whatsoever. He was relieved. And puzzled. She and Julie had been friends, even though they'd known each other for only a few weeks. Julie must have mentioned him. So why wasn't Madeline making the obvious connection between him and Julie's "Mickey"?

There was a probable explanation, of course, and after a second it occurred to him. Being who she was, Julie wouldn't have considered it cool to reveal that her boyfriend was involved in any form of law enforcement.

Madeline was waiting for his response. "What is it you don't understand?"

"If your whole family is in the business of helping people in trouble, and your mother and father operate an agency right here in Chicago…"

"Why aren't we turning to them?"

"Well, yes."

"I'd give anything to do just that, only we can't. The entire family is somewhere in the Caribbean on a holiday cruise."

"But you didn't join them?"

"No, I didn't join them."

Mitch thought about the irony in that. The cruise had been originally planned by his sisters to benefit him. Meant to ease his sorrow over Julie. It had been a good intention, but in the end he hadn't been capable of the effort. All he had wanted was to grieve for Julie in the seclusion of the farm, not celebrate a holiday in the Caribbean. The family had reluctantly gone without him.

They were nearing the junction for the Illinois interstate that would take them out of the city and across the state into the west. The traffic was heavy here. Mitch concentrated on the highway, not wanting to miss the lane they needed.

Madeline was quiet again. He began to worry that he was wrong in thinking himself still safe, that this time she would figure it out. And if that happened, the result might be what Neil had feared. Madeline could bolt. He'd been a fool to share with her anything about himself. But again she surprised Mitch.

"Your family means a great deal to you, don't they."

Damn it, what was she trying to do?

"I could hear it in your voice," she said softly. "The pride and the love you have for them."

She was trying to understand him, that's what she was doing. He didn't *want* her understanding him. He didn't want her caring like that. Because even though he would protect her with his life, even though she tantalized him at every turn, in the end Madeline Raeburn was still a woman whose motives and character he didn't trust.

Chapter Five

The explosion that split the blackness was so loud, so alarmingly close that it jerked Mitch out of a deep sleep. His reaction was instinctive and instantaneous.

As his hand flashed toward the gun in his holster, Madeline stopped him, her own hand plucking at his sleeve. "It's all right," she said quietly. "It's just thunder."

His hand relaxed and dropped back to his side. In the dim light from the dashboard she watched him shake his head, clearing the fog from his brain. It wasn't until he sat up that he seemed to become aware that the station wagon was parked along the side of the highway and that a torrent of rain was beating at the windows.

"What happened to the snow?" he asked.

"That was hours ago. Now we've got this," she said, indicating the lightning that slashed across the sky, followed by another crash of thunder.

"Talk about extremes," he grumbled, peering into the darkness outside. "Where are we, anyway?"

"Somewhere on the western side of Iowa."

"I can't see a thing."

"Which is exactly why I pulled over. The rain got so heavy, the wipers couldn't keep up with it anymore."

"Better this than another blizzard, I suppose. What time is it?" He leaned forward to consult the clock on the dashboard. "After three. Long past time for my shift at the wheel. You should have called me."

"I had a chance to sleep on the train, you didn't. And until the storm got so bad, I was doing just fine."

"Car okay?"

"Humming along."

"See, I knew we could count on her."

"I'm even getting used to the smell."

"What smell?"

"Never mind."

Fully alert now, Mitch unbuckled his belt. "Let's switch places. Rain's easing up, and I'm ready to move on."

"Are we in the same part of Iowa? Because I have to tell you that on my half of the state it's still coming in buckets out there."

"Okay, I don't mind getting drenched. I'll run around and you slide over."

Madeline watched him struggle to open the famous passenger door. It had worked back at the Illinois border when they had traded shifts at the wheel. Now it was being stubborn again, refusing to yield.

"You were saying about the car?" she commented dryly.

His response was a muttered obscenity.

"Of course," she pointed out, "if we didn't have this grille thing behind us, one of us could climb over into the back while the other scoots across. But since we don't have that option, I guess we both get soaked."

She started to open the door on her side. Mitch stopped her. "All right, we can still do this without either of us getting wet. If you lift yourself up while you come across, I can manage to pass under you."

Madeline wasn't sure she cared for his proposal. There was no way such an exchange could be achieved without some form of contact, and contact of any kind with this man was a definite risk.

Her hesitation was too lengthy. He understood it and

challenged her. "Come on, this isn't a seduction. It's just a practical solution."

Although still reluctant, she agreed. "All right. Ready?"

"Go."

Using first the wheel and then the top of the dashboard as support to raise herself, Madeline attempted to ease over to the passenger side of the car.

"Can't you go a little higher? I'm not having much luck here squeezing under you."

"My head is already bumping the ceiling."

This whole thing was a mistake. She could feel the heat of his solid body under her backside. The near contact made her woozy.

"Are you moving at all?" she asked. "It seems like you're just sitting there."

"I'm trying to inch over. Just need a little more maneuvering room."

"And I'm trying to give it to you, but I'm stalled here."

"Swing your leg over to my side," he directed her, "and then you'll have better leverage."

"How do you suggest I do that when your own legs are in the way?"

"Here, let me help." His big hands captured her hips in an effort to guide her across.

"Don't!" she warned him.

Too late. Panicked by his searing touch, she lost her grasp on the dashboard, and her balance. Before she could recover herself, she was on top of him with their limbs tangled and her derriere nestled against his groin. It would have been a comic situation ripe for laughter, had the intimacy not been so wildly provocative, so charged with sensuality.

The heat of his hardness was strained against her bottom. She tried to wriggle away from him, but her squirming only made it worse. He was clearly aroused. A low groan issued from his warm mouth somewhere close to her ear. She had the feeling that in another moment he would be nibbling her lobe. Madeline had never been in such a vulnerable position. She didn't know whether to blame the situation on him, the weather or the car. Because if she didn't know better, she'd swear his beloved wagon had deliberately helped him to mount this erotic assault.

"Sweetheart," he whispered, his voice deep and raw, "if you don't stop stirring that fanny of yours, something is going to happen here that I promise you will mean trouble for both of us."

"I'm trying to get off you, which I could do if you would remove your hands from my thighs."

"Just trying to steady you so you don't land on the floor."

"I believe that like I believe this little exercise was smarter than getting drenched."

"Kind of like a clown car, huh? All right, we move together, you to the right and me to the left. On the count of three."

He counted, they somehow sorted themselves out, and he transferred himself to the driver's side and she to the passenger seat.

"I'll be damned," he said as he settled himself behind the wheel. "It's stopped raining. When did that happen?"

Madeline didn't trust herself to respond to his innocent observation, not when it might have involved her hand connecting with his jaw. Instead, she secured her seat belt, thrust the rolled-up coat he'd been using for a pillow behind her head, and, as he pulled out onto the highway, prepared to go to sleep.

But she was too restless to sleep. She blamed the coat for that. It was *his* coat, and his warmth and the faint male aroma of him still clung to it. In her shaken state, it reminded her of another sort of warmth. She had heard it in his voice back in Chicago when he talked about his family. It had stayed with her, mostly because it was something she had never expected from this hard-bitten man at her side.

With each passing mile he became more of an enigma. Just who, she wondered, was the real Mitchell Hawke? And why did she care?

GRIFF MATISSE HAD A CRAVING for things that were rare and beautiful, and with his wealth he could afford to possess them. It satisfied him to surround himself with only the best, both in his apartment and here in his sumptuous office at the Phoenix. The club was successful, of course, but its profits were modest compared to what all of his behind-the-scenes operations earned him. Most of them were considerable, and all of them were illegal.

The office boasted several of his prized collections. There was a display case containing pre-Colombian art and a wall on which were arranged Far Eastern daggers with richly embossed hilts. But the collection that pleased Griff the most was a live one.

He was stationed now in front of the aquarium, watching the exotic tropical fish it contained dart toward the food flakes he had just shaken into the tank. He could see his own image reflected in the glass as he leaned close to the tank. A smile curved his mouth above his pitted jaw. It amused him to watch the swift movements and fantastic colors of the fish.

His smile vanished when another shadowy reflection appeared in the glass. He didn't have to turn around to know that Angel had entered the office and now stood behind him, waiting to be acknowledged.

Griff was no longer pleased. He knew that Angel was here to report on another beautiful creature he had collected. This one had turned on him. Madeline Raeburn's betrayal was unforgivable.

Coming erect, an impatient frown on his handsome face,

he swung around to confront the gaunt figure of his chief mercenary. "Where is she, Angel?"

"She's no longer in Milwaukee, Griff," Angel informed him in his low, breathy voice. "Our contact says she's on her way back to San Francisco."

"When does she arrive?"

Angel shook his head. "Don't know. She ain't flying in. Phoned the DA's office from the road to say she's coming by car."

"*Where* on the road?"

"Didn't say. She's being real cagey." Angel paused, an expression of reluctance on his bony face. "Griff, she ain't alone. There's someone with her."

"Who?"

"A PI, name of Mitchell Hawke. He has an office here in Frisco. Or did before he shut it down. Word is that Neil Stanek turned her over to Hawke for safekeeping."

"So she has a protector now, does she?"

The whole business infuriated Griff. He had more than just a need to silence a witness who was dangerous to him. Her continued elusiveness was a personal challenge, making him more determined than ever to destroy her. Nor would he let this Mitchell Hawke stand in his way.

"I want her found, Angel."

"Griff, we're working on it," Angel promised him, "but it's not gonna be easy to locate them. Not when they're on the move. Not when we don't know what they're driving or what route they're using. You know?"

"What I know," Griff said, his face hardening, "is that I want her eliminated before the DA has her back in San Francisco and his case solid enough to put me in handcuffs. And if this PI gets in the way, we'll take him out with her."

MITCH HAD NO ARGUMENT with the hard blue sky. It meant the weather was favoring them for a change. But the bright, clear sunlight did nothing to improve the monotony of the flat Nebraska terrain. Wheat fields, their stubble blanketed under a cover of snow, stretched to the horizon on both sides of the clear, ruler-straight four-lane highway. Nothing relieved them except for the occasional grain elevator.

The music that Mitch favored helped to prevent total tedium. He'd found a classic rock station on the radio, and at the moment Bruce Springsteen was keeping him company. Madeline, in the passenger seat beside him, had her own remedy for boredom.

Sketch pad on her lap, reading glasses in place and pencil in hand, she busied herself creating a new design for a piece of jewelry. This had to be the third or fourth drawing she'd executed since breakfast.

What intrigued Mitch was how she could extract inspiration from the most ordinary things. A dry leaf clinging to a shrub outside a gas station, the feather of a hawk fluttering on the sidewalk in front of a rest stop, the pattern in a patch of frost on the back window of the station wagon. All of them were material for her original designs.

"I like to take my ideas from nature," Madeline had explained when he'd asked her about it. "They make the most effective pieces for me."

Mitch was interested, but he was far more fascinated by the things she did with that enticing mouth of hers as she worked. He remembered noticing back at the farm, as she'd fashioned paper ornaments for the Christmas tree, how her mouth had been as busy as her hands. It was the same here in the car. She had a whole catalog of maneuvers involving lips, tongue and teeth.

Stealing a glance at her from his side of the car, he caught her pursing her mouth in concentration. When he looked again, her lips moved soundlessly in some silent direction to herself. Another glimpse revealed her lips drawn back over clenched teeth, as if she was dissatisfied with her effort.

But it was what she did with her tongue that had Mitch squirming behind the wheel. Sometimes the wet tip of it would protrude from the corner of her mouth. Or it would slowly lick back and forth across the fullness of her bottom lip—a sensual business that had all manner of hot possibilities chasing through his head.

Hell, was she even conscious of her quirky habits with that mouth? Probably not. All the same, it was damn seductive. He was relieved when she closed the sketch pad, removed her glasses and complained, "I'm hungry."

That was another thing. She had the appetite of a linebacker. It amazed Mitch the quantities of food she managed to put away at each of their stops for meals, apparently without any negative effects on that trim figure of hers. Her metabolism was probably the envy of every woman she'd known. That and her mane of red hair.

"It's time for lunch," she pointed out after checking the clock on the dash.

"All right, we'll see what the next exit offers."

"Please," she pleaded, "no more take-out. Couldn't we just this once sit down to something that isn't fast food?"

Since Illinois, Mitch hadn't trusted anything but drive-up windows. Those, a quick call to Gloria Rodriguez, gas fill-ups and necessary breaks at interstate rest rooms—where this morning they had managed to clean up and change clothes—had been their only stops. He thought about her request.

"I guess if we're careful we can risk it," he said.

The exit provided a sprawling truck stop just off the highway. Attached to it was a large restaurant. The place was lively with lunchtime traffic, but Mitch was able to snag a booth for them. Its tall back and position in a rear corner of the dining room provided moderate privacy.

As they waited for their orders to be filled, an obnoxious woman several tables away began complaining in a loud voice to the waitress serving her. "This is the wrong dressing. I distinctly told you blue cheese. Why can't you people ever get it right?''

"I'm sorry, ma'am. I'll get you a new salad."

"And my coffee needs refilling."

Madeline's gaze sympathetically followed the young waitress as she hurried away with the rejected salad. "Why do people have to be so rude?" she murmured. "Waiting on tables is hard enough without customers turning on you like that."

Mitch, recognizing the opportunity for further confidences from a woman who'd been reluctant from the start to share her history, leaned toward her across the table that divided them. "That sounds like someone with firsthand knowledge."

Madeline hesitated. And then, in that throaty voice that never failed to remind him of her allure, she revealed another facet of herself. "Waiting on tables is how I supported myself all those weeks on the run."

"Not jewelry making, huh?"

"I planned to, until I realized that Griff might be able to trace me through the pieces I sold. Waiting on tables was safer. Places were too glad for the help to ask a lot of questions. Besides, I was an experienced server. That's what I did at the Phoenix before I was promoted to a hostess."

"Not much opportunity in it, though, is there."

Before she could respond, their orders arrived. Mitch waited until the waitress retreated and they began to eat before he resumed the conversation.

"I would have figured with your looks there would have been other options for you."

Madeline swallowed a mouthful of omelette and shook her head. "Don't say it."

"What?"

"Modeling. Everyone used to tell me that, with my height, I would be a natural. I wasn't. Too self-conscious for the camera. Anyway, looks aren't worth much without a good education or marketable skills, and I didn't have either.''

''But you have a talent,'' he said, referring to her creative jewelry, ''and an ambition.''

She spread grape jelly on a piece of toast. ''You think I was wasting them at the Phoenix.''

She was perceptive, Mitch thought, because that's exactly what he'd been thinking. He learned just how perceptive after she bit into the toast.

''And that a woman with any real character wouldn't have been working at a place like the Phoenix.''

He'd been thinking that, too. All along. Was that why he was urging her now to confide in him? Because he'd been weakening in his resolve to believe the worst about her and needed fresh ammunition to feed his conviction?

''It wasn't like that,'' she said. ''It was respectable work.''

''Was it?''

''Just because a club hires attractive young women and dresses them in abbreviated uniforms doesn't make it unsavory. The Phoenix had strict rules of conduct for both the servers and the customers. We were never allowed to mix.''

''How about the man who operates that club? Or are you telling me you didn't hear any of the rumors before you hired on there?''

''Envy of a successful businessman. That's what I convinced myself those rumors were. It wasn't until later that I realized how naive I'd been and that the Phoenix was probably a front for organized crime.''

And by then, Mitch thought angrily, you were involved with Griff Matisse. Too *intimately* involved to walk away. That was the talk, anyway, in San Francisco, that they spent a lot of time together, that she was Matisse's girl. And

Madeline hadn't told Mitch anything so far to make him believe differently.

He had lost interest in his sandwich. He watched her go on with her omelette and toast, thinking she had nothing more to tell him. But she wasn't finished with the conversation. Stirring sweetener into her coffee, she gazed at him solemnly.

"The talent and ambition you said I have… I wasn't wasting them at the Phoenix, you know. They were the reason I was there."

"Yes?"

"The club paid their help the best salaries in the city. It was money I needed, and the hours were right."

"For what?"

"The college courses I was taking during the day. Education is expensive, and I was trying to earn a degree in business management. Or, at least, enough credits so that one day I could set myself up as a successful jewelry designer."

Mitch knew about those college classes. It was in one of them that Julie had met Madeline Raeburn and been recruited by her for the Phoenix. He remembered how he and Julie had argued over that, how he had asked her not to take a job at the club. But Julie was stubborn and the money too attractive for her to resist.

Madeline continued to gaze at him. "I don't know why I told you all that, because it doesn't change anything."

"Like what?"

"The opinion you have of me. It isn't very good, is it."

Why did she care? he wondered. What difference did it make to her whether he approved of her or not? All right, so her motive for working at the Phoenix was an honest one, her pursuit of higher education commendable. But if she was so damn decent, why had she stayed on with Matisse after Julie was murdered?

Maybe Madeline hadn't told him the whole story. Maybe

she was withholding part of it. Something vital. Mitch decided to risk asking her—

"Oh, this is intolerable! First you mess up my order, and now you spill coffee on me!"

"Ma'am, I'm sorry, but you bumped me when I—"

"I want the manager! I demand to see the manager!"

The voice of the obnoxious woman at the nearby table was so shattering this time that it immediately captured the notice of the entire dining room. There were turned heads, curious stares in their direction. Mitch realized he had lost his chance.

"This isn't good, is it," Madeline murmured.

She was right. They couldn't afford to be close to any unpleasant scene that might, before it was all over, draw attention to them.

"Damn it," he growled. "I knew I shouldn't have let you talk me into coming in here. If you're finished, let's go."

Slapping a tip on the table and snatching up the check that had been left when their orders were delivered, Mitch rose from the booth. The manager hurried by them on his way to soothe their ridiculous neighbor, who continued to abuse the waitress. Madeline and Mitch slipped away from the area as unobtrusively as possible.

There was a delay at the front desk before Mitch was able to pay the check. Madeline used the opportunity to visit the rest room off the minimart portion of the facility.

When Mitch finally came away from the dining room, he found her waiting near the front door. There was a Christmas tree just inside the entrance. She was gazing at its tinsel-laden branches with a melancholic expression on her face.

"It's Christmas Eve day tomorrow, and I was just thinking of the tree we abandoned back at the farm," she said. "With no one there to put fresh water in the stand, it won't last."

"It's a tree, Madeline. It's not going to get lonely without us. And you should have joined me at the desk when you came away from the rest room, not waited out here. No more stopping in restaurants. It's too risky."

She stared at him, saying nothing, but the wounded look in her eyes had him regretting his anger with her, both here and back in the dining room. What was the matter with him? Why had he gone and barked at her just because she'd been admiring the tree? Admiring it with the same wistful look she had worn in the car when she had switched his rock station over to one playing Christmas music. Once again, he failed to understand her. All this sentiment over a holiday just wasn't in keeping with the woman he knew her to be. Or was it the woman he *wanted* her to be? He was more confused than ever about that.

She provided no answers for him when they were back on the road. Mitch knew it would be useless to try to press her into continuing with the conversation that had been interrupted over lunch. It was his own fault. He had gone and blamed her for the truck stop, when he should have been blaming himself for exercising poor judgment.

His rash anger with her had cost him what had promised to be her first real trust in him. There would be no more confidences today. She had reverted to her mode of wariness with him, and was silent again. But Mitch was less worried about her withdrawal than his own growing frustration with himself.

Damn it, what was wrong with him, anyway? Why did he persist in hurting her? Maybe it was because, despite all his best efforts, he was beginning to like her, and he didn't trust that affection any more than the desire that accompanied it. He still wanted her, and wished he didn't.

SNEAKING A GUILTY GLANCE at her companion, as though fearing he would wake up and challenge her, Madeline polished off the last of the cheese-filled crackers she had bought from a machine at their last rest stop. It was the morning after their lunch in the restaurant, and she certainly didn't need the crackers, not when they'd eaten breakfast less than an hour ago.

Madeline knew that she was going to end up paying for those crackers, along with all the other food she'd been devouring since leaving Chicago the day before yesterday. The waistline of her slacks already felt tight. What was the matter with her, anyway?

Nerves, of course. That's what it was. And the reason for those nerves, she decided, casting another glance in the direction of the passenger seat from her position behind the wheel, was the man at her side. He was resting after his own shift at the wheel, arms folded across the breadth of his chest, clad in a gray sweatshirt, long, muscular legs encased in jeans sprawled out in front of him. The way those jeans were stretched over the bulge at his groin didn't bear thinking about.

Why did she have to be so aware of every part of him, including those prominent ears? Why, even when he was asleep, did he disturb her senses, leaving her as taut as a wire about to snap? And why, as had been the case yesterday at that truck stop, did she care about his opinion of her?

The truck stop had been a mistake, of course. She had been on the verge of telling him the rest of her story, everything that had happened, including the part about Julie. For the first time, he had seemed genuinely sympathetic. But then that interruption had occurred, followed by his unreasonable anger.

A painful lesson, that scene. One she didn't care to repeat. So, no more confessions. They weren't necessary when he already knew what was essential. Anyway, what did it matter whether the irascible Mitchell Hawke understood or approved of her, when she would part from him once they reached their destination, probably never see him again? And that would be a relief.

Would it?

Of course it would, and at the pace they were traveling, they would be in California in another day or so, providing the weather held. There had been no form of precipitation since Iowa. The interstate remained clear and dry, the sky a brittle blue.

They were currently rolling across the far southwestern side of Wyoming. There was no dramatic mountain scenery in this particular part of the state, but the hilly terrain was more interesting than Nebraska's. Sheep grazed on the tough grasses that lifted their stems above a thin cover of snow.

They were making excellent time, all right. And at none of their stops had either of them been recognized or challenged. What's more, to her grudging acknowledgment, the aging station wagon continued to perform like a thoroughbred. They were lucky.

But not for much longer, unless we do something about the gas, Madeline thought, eyeing the gauge. The tank was getting low. The wagon did not have the best record for fuel consumption.

Mitch roused himself when she exited the four-lane a few minutes later. "What's happening?"

"We need to fill up."

"I don't see a quick-stop."

"No, but there is a town close by. The county seat, I think. We'll have to go there to find a station."

They reached the town and a gas station on one of the corners of its main street. While Madeline used the rest room, Mitch filled the tank, paid the bill and claimed the driver's seat for his own turn at the wheel.

"Man, it's cold out there," he complained as they rolled away from the pumps.

Braking at the exit to the street, he checked both directions. To their right, a vehicle approached the four-way stop. Mitch had the right-of-way, but apparently the other driver was cheerfully unaware of that simple rule.

Madeline's alarmed, "Watch out!" came too late. The other car plowed through the intersection without pause, its stout nose smacking into the right front end of their wagon. Both vehicles rocked to a halt.

"Of all the idiotic—" Mitch interrupted his thundering anger, turning to Madeline with a concerned, "You okay?"

"I'm fine."

"Which is more than the jerk who hit us is going to be when I get my hands on him!"

Flinging open his door, his ears a vivid red, he stormed out of the car to confront the other driver. Madeline slid across the seat and followed him. The "jerk," emerging from her own vehicle, turned out to be a woman of diminutive height and advanced years.

"Do you realize what you did, young man? You went and pulled out right in front of me."

"I went and— Lady, you ran a stop sign!"

"What stop sign?"

Madeline approached her. "Are you all right?"

"Of course I'm all right. I have a very safe car."

What she had, Madeline noticed, was an ancient sedan, one of those vehicles built like a tank, too large and too heavy for its tiny owner. It looked like it hadn't suffered any dents, nor even a scratch, in the impact. Their own wagon had a crumpled fender, but none of the folded metal obstructed the wheel. As for their engine, which Mitch had left running, it seemed unaffected. And since no one was hurt and the damage was not serious...

Madeline plucked at Mitch's sleeve. "Don't you think," she murmured, "it would be a good idea to simply apologize and be on our way?"

Her message was clear. If they remained here arguing

about it, the situation could be potentially dangerous to them. But before Mitch could agree, trouble bore down on them in the shape of a car with the sheriff's emblem on its door.

Chapter Six

"Vera, this is the second time this month you've run that stop sign."

The elderly woman, dwarfed by her accuser and wearing a pair of furry earmuffs that, like her car, were much too large for her, glared at the sheriff. "I've driven down this street for more than fifty years, and suddenly the town decides to put up stop signs where there weren't any before. How can you expect me to remember overnight that they're there? After fifty years it takes time to get used to something like that."

The sheriff was bluff and burly. He was also incredibly patient. "Now, Vera, those aren't new stop signs. They've been there for almost two years."

The woman sniffed in disapproval. "Well, they shouldn't be. They're just a nuisance."

Madeline glanced at Mitch. She could see he was still fuming over the battering of his beloved wagon, though he had the good sense to keep silent. She knew he realized, as well as she did, that this scene was already a threat to them.

"The point is, Vera," the sheriff reminded her, "you went and hit these folks' car. Banged it up pretty good here in the fender. What's the rest look like?"

Without waiting for an invitation, he ambled around the

station wagon, inspecting it on all sides. Madeline watched him pause at the back of the vehicle. *He's checking out the license plate,* she thought nervously.

"California, huh?" he observed. "You're a long way from home."

"We're on our way back there," Mitch explained swiftly. "Hoping to be with our family by Christmas morning."

The sheriff nodded and peered into the window, checking out the interior of the wagon. *We're strangers in his town,* Madeline tried to tell herself calmly, *and driving a rather disreputable-looking vehicle. It's only natural he'd be a little suspicious of us.*

"I notice you've got a shield in here dividing the front from the back. Don't see barriers like that except in law enforcement vehicles. A little unusual, isn't it?"

Madeline offered her own quick explanation. "Beagles," she said. "My husband and I breed beagles."

"We just delivered a pair to a buyer in Nebraska," Mitch added. "Christmas present for his wife."

"They're a rather rambunctious dog," Madeline said. "We like to keep them contained in the back. It makes for safer driving."

The sheriff chuckled. "Guess that explains the duct tape on your seats."

There was another long pause while he gazed first at them and then along the length of the station wagon. Did he buy their story? Madeline wondered tensely. Would he let them go without further questioning?

"Doesn't seem to be any other damage," the sheriff said.

"I'm willing to forget about the fender," Mitch said. "It isn't serious. And, like I said, we're anxious to get home for Christmas. So if we could just be on our way…"

There was a hearty smile now on the sheriff's round face. "Well, we won't delay you. We'll let you get back on the road. Just as soon,'' he added offhandedly, ''as I fill out the accident report.''

''Is that necessary?''

''It's the law, son. Won't take long. I'll just need to see your driver's license, owner's registration and insurance card, then get a few details about what happened. You, too, Vera,'' he said severely to the elderly woman, who was looking more disgruntled by the moment.

Madeline shivered. It was probably more from fear than the bitter wind sweeping down the street. Either way it was a mistake. The sheriff didn't miss her reaction.

''It's danged cold out here,'' he agreed. ''No sense standing in the street when we can handle this in my office just around the corner.''

Madeline and Mitch exchanged worried glances. The situation had just gone from bad to worse. What would happen when the sheriff examined the phony vehicle identification Hog had provided back in Chicago? Could it stand the test?

''Vera,'' the sheriff directed the old lady, ''you lead the way. These folks will follow, and I'll bring up the rear. And you watch those stop signs.''

Grumbling her displeasure, Vera climbed behind the wheel of her car.

''Sorry about this, folks,'' the sheriff said to Madeline and Mitch. ''Judge McCrea should have revoked her license long ago, but he won't. Not that I'm saying their having been sweethearts back in high school has anything to do with that, you understand. Anyhow, I keep telling him that car's too big, and she's too small. She can barely see over the wheel. Don't get too close to her.''

''This is trouble, isn't it?'' Madeline murmured to Mitch a moment later as they headed down the street behind Vera's sedan.

''Not unless he learns our wagon is a stolen vehicle, and if Hog is as good as I think he is, he won't.''

She was aware of the sheriff's car following ominously behind them. "I don't suppose there's any way to avoid this."

"Short of a high-speed chase out of town, I don't think we have a choice. Just stay cool, and we'll be all right. Anyway, the car is performing okay."

He *would* worry about that, Madeline thought dryly.

The sheriff's department appeared on their left. Leaving their cars, the four of them trooped into the building. The facility had all the timeworn, rural ambience of an era when wood prevailed over plastic. Its equipment, however, was modern enough. Behind an oak counter that stretched across the reception area, an office assistant worked at a computer. In a corner a deputy manned a radio.

Vera was still objecting as they lined up in front of the scarred counter, facing the sheriff, who had stationed himself on the other side of the barrier where he shuffled through a pile of forms.

"I hope you realize I'm late for my hair appointment and that Dolly Harris just hates it when you're not on time. It throws off her whole schedule."

The sheriff ignored her, found the form he'd been looking for, and slapped it on the counter. Producing a pen from his pocket, he leaned toward them, his manner both official and efficient.

"Now, folks, if you'll just lay those documents out here in front of me…"

He wasn't interested in Vera, who dug through her purse, searching for the articles he'd requested earlier. Madeline noticed that the sheriff's attention was fixed on Mitch as he removed his driver's license, vehicle registration and insurance card from his wallet and placed them on the counter.

He *was* suspicious of them, she thought. She went rigid with panic while, one by one, he picked up each piece of identification and examined it with care. Mitch maintained an impassive expression on his face. But Madeline, fearing that her own concern was evident and would betray them if the sheriff should look up and glance at her, drifted to the farther end of the counter.

Once out of immediate range of the sheriff's gaze, she leaned against the counter in what she hoped was a casual pose. In truth, she needed the counter for support. From this position, she risked another look in the sheriff's direction. He was still peering at the documents.

He's going to realize the owner's registration and insurance card aren't genuine, she thought. He probably had a list somewhere, and he'd check them against that and discover the station wagon was a stolen vehicle. And even if that didn't happen, there was Mitch's very real driver's license and the possibility the sheriff would connect it with a man wanted for murder in Milwaukee.

Madeline was so sick with dread by now that the sheriff's cheerful, "Everything seems to be in order here," didn't register with her. It wasn't until Mitch sent her a look of reassurance that she was finally able to relax. The worst was behind them.

"We'll just get a description of the accident down here on the report," the sheriff said, "and then you folks can leave."

While Vera and Mitch related their versions of the fender bender, Madeline enjoyed the luxury of going limp with relief. There was a fax machine just below her on a lower level of the counter. Its phone rang, and then it began to chatter with an incoming communication. None of the occupants of the office paid it any immediate attention. The sheriff was involved with his report, the assistant was still at her computer and the deputy had left the radio to use a rest room off the rear of the office.

Madeline also ignored the machine. Until, that is, it spat the fax into the receiving tray. Then something familiar leaped into her peripheral vision. Turning her head, she gazed down in puzzlement. Her bewilderment became alarm.

The image of Mitch was located dead center on the communication. Madeline assumed it was taken from the photo that had been circulating in Milwaukee. And now that likeness had reached a small town in Wyoming, for the fax was a bulletin to law enforcement agencies across the country. It contained all the pertinent information, before ending with a plea for the apprehension of Mitchell Hawke.

Madeline was so dismayed for a moment that she was unable to act. Then it was too late. The assistant shoved away from her desk, got to her feet and started toward the counter to check the fax. The breath caught in Madeline's throat.

At that merciful second, the radio crackled to life. In the absence of the deputy, the assistant turned her back on the counter and went to take the call. Madeline breathed again, but she knew that, unless she found a way to remove the fax, she and Mitch would never leave this office.

He must have sensed her panic. When she looked his way, he turned his head and met her frantic gaze, a baffled frown on his face. She signaled her urgency with an imperceptible nod in the direction of the fax machine. He understood.

The sheriff's head was still lowered over his report, and Vera was busy tucking her documents back into her purse. But any sudden activity from Madeline would immediately capture their attention. A distraction was necessary, and Mitch provided it.

Using his body in an effort to shield Madeline, he turned sideways and leaned over the counter. "Sheriff," he said loudly, "it seems pretty clear at this point just whose fault the accident was. Like I said at the scene, I'm not asking the lady to pay for the fender. Heck, the car is so old it doesn't matter. But it seems to me she does deserve to get a ticket for reckless driving."

As expected, Vera erupted in a storm of fresh indignation. The noisy scene that resulted was the opportunity Madeline needed. With lightning speed, she reached over the counter and snatched the bulletin from the tray. There was an earlier fax under it. She could only hope that when the assistant finally got around to checking the machine, the first fax would be regarded as the latest communication.

By the time everything was sorted out, with Vera pacified by the sheriff, the deputy back at his radio and the assistant diverted again by a phone call at her desk, Madeline had the fax whisked out of sight under her coat. Minutes later she and Mitch were free to go.

They didn't talk on their way out of the building. Nor was there any conversation between them as they hurried to the car. Madeline was still anxious, fearing that at any second there would be a shout behind them. That they would hear a stern order from the sheriff or his deputy calling them back to the office.

She was thankful that there was no pursuit, and when they were in the car she opened her coat and withdrew the rumpled fax, showing it to him. Mitch glanced at the bulletin.

"Looks like the police hunt for me has gone nationwide."

He started up the car. They didn't speak again as they headed out of town. Not until they were several miles away, and nearing the ramp to the interstate, did Mitch feel it was safe to pull over to the side of the road. He turned to her, a note of relief in his voice.

"I don't know about you, but I could use a minute to just breathe again."

"I'll think about breathing normally after I stop shaking."

"*Were* you shaking?"

"Couldn't you tell? I thought the fax would start rattling under my coat and everybody would hear it and know."

"Hell, you didn't look nervous. You were cool through the whole thing. Beagles, huh? Now, that was an inspiration."

"And you picked up on it without blinking an eye."

"So maybe we make a team. What do you think?"

"That I wouldn't care to repeat that little performance."

"Hey, that was great, and you pulled it off by—"

"I couldn't have, without you noticing I needed—"

"But it was you in the first place, who—"

"Yes, but poor Vera."

"Don't feel sorry for old Vera. She's got Judge What-chamacallit on her side, remember? All we've got is—"

"Each other?"

"Yeah," he said softly, "each other."

Realizing what she had just said and what he had echoed, her excitement subsided. The rapid and giddy exchange of fragmented compliments, with which they had been congratulating each other as a means of easing their tension, had been wonderful, but it was at risk of turning serious. And though Mitch's praise warmed Madeline, she suddenly feared the result of its glow.

To forestall that danger, she gave him the fax so he could look at it again. "There was another fax under it. Something that must have come in a little while before."

"Anything connected with us?"

She shook her head. "I only had a glimpse, but I think it was something to do with a charity drive. I just pray that assistant doesn't remember there were two arrivals on the machine and start wondering what happened to the second one."

"Maybe we'd better get rid of the evidence, then. Unless," he added, a gleam in his eye as he held up the fax, "you'd like to keep this thing as a souvenir."

Madeline shuddered. "I don't need any reminders, thank you."

"In that case…"

She watched him slowly, systematically tear the sheet into strips, then into small bits. When he was finished, he had what amounted to a handful of confetti. That wicked gleam was still in his eyes as he weighed his effort. Then, with an impulsive heave, he tossed the pieces into the air.

"Happy holidays, Madeline Raeburn."

The stuff came down in a blizzard, showering her head and shoulders. She must have presented an interesting sight, with paper snowflakes in her hair and clinging to the collar of her coat. So entertaining that, head thrown back, Mitch began to laugh.

Had it been anyone else, there would have been nothing extraordinary in that reaction. But beyond an occasional mocking grin, he had never exhibited anything resembling hilarity. Madeline hadn't considered him capable of honest, unrestrained mirth.

His laughter—rich, robust, and displaying teeth that must be the pride of his dentist—shocked her. And at the same time filled her with wonder, because it so utterly transformed him. He had been dangerously appealing before this. Now, suddenly, he was incredibly sexy, destroying all her defenses.

Madeline was completely vulnerable when, still chuckling, he leaned toward her, his blue eyes glowing with mischief.

"It looks," he said, his voice deep and lazy, "like we'd better clean you up."

Madeline had neither the will nor the desire to resist, when his big hand reached out and began to pluck the bits of paper out of her hair. His long fingers worked with a leisurely care, frequently grazing her scalp—a series of tingling contacts that felt like caresses.

"What have we got here?" he murmured, bringing his face in so close to hers that she could feel his warm breath on her, detect his arousing masculine aroma. "There's just a little…"

With his forefinger, he flicked away the tiny scrap that had been pasted to her bottom lip. She could feel that lip quivering from his touch. Totally susceptible, hardly daring to breathe, she waited for him to withdraw. But his strong face remained mere centimeters from hers, sober now, all trace of teasing vanished from his expression. His gaze searched her mouth.

"Anything else?" she whispered.

"Let's make sure."

It wasn't his finger this time that cleaned her lip. The tip of his tongue lightly traced the contours of her mouth, laving it with long, erotic strokes.

"Better?" he asked.

"Much."

"And just in case I missed something…"

Fitting his lips over hers, his tongue penetrated her mouth, performing a slow, sensual sweep from side to side. Unlike that episode back in her bedroom at the farm, there was nothing fierce or brutal in this kiss. In all aspects, from the clean flavor of him to the manner in which his tongue now stroked hers, it was infinitely loving, demonstrating that he was capable of a genuine tenderness.

Like laughter, gentleness was not a quality she had encountered before in Mitchell Hawke. She found herself both dismayed by it and prizing it. And although his kiss was deep and prolonged, when it finally ended, Madeline felt cheated, wanting more.

His mouth parted from hers and he drew back slightly. His gaze held hers in a long, captivating silence. She could see pinpoints of light in his compelling blue eyes, signifying—what? Something that was intensely emotional, but that's all she could tell.

His voice was husky when he finally spoke. "Maddie?"

"Yes?"

"There's a lot more than just that mouth of yours I'd like to bathe with my tongue," he said boldly.

She could feel her face flame in a response that was more pleasure than embarrassment.

"And," he continued, "if we had a half hour to spare, you and I would be stretched out behind the grille back there with me doing my damnedest to convince you that's just what you need. Only, we don't have that half hour to risk. We have to move on before the office assistant starts complaining to the sheriff that there's a fax missing, and asking, could that nice couple who raises beagles possibly have had anything to do with it?"

Madeline managed to mask her disappointment. "Yes, you're right, we have to clear out of here."

"After," he said, moving briskly toward the door on his side, "I take a good look at the damage to the fender. Can't take any chances with this baby."

Madeline couldn't believe it. They had just shared a riveting kiss that had her lips swollen from his marauding mouth and her senses still raw and aching, and all he could think about was inspecting his precious station wagon.

"You already looked at it back in town," she said angrily. "And, anyway, as long as it still runs, what difference does it make how many dents and scrapes it has? It's a heap!"

If she had struck him, he couldn't have looked more hurt. He actually patted the wheel of the car, as though apologizing to it for her callous judgment. "Don't say that. She's a classic."

Piece of junk. That's what Madeline thought of his classic, but this time she held her tongue. "Will you please do what you have to do so we can get out of here?"

"Back in a minute."

He popped out of the car, releasing the handful of confetti he had collected from her hair and shoulders. The bits were blown away on the wind. The heater had sufficiently warmed the interior, so while she waited for him to examine the fender, she struggled out of her coat, muttering to herself in aggravation. That kiss and its aftermath had wounded her more than she was prepared to admit.

"Needs a body shop," he reported when he slid back behind the wheel, "but everything should be okay. I didn't see any leaks, and the engine is still purring."

Madeline waited until they were back on the interstate, headed toward the Utah border, before she asked him the question that had been nagging at her since Chicago. "Will you do me the favor of explaining to me exactly what the love affair with you and this excuse for an automobile is all about?"

"There you go again, insulting her."

"*She* is just a car," she reminded him, "and I'd really like to be enlightened here."

At first she thought he wasn't going to tell her. He was silent for a moment before he made up his mind to share his secret.

"Not just a car," he said solemnly. "*The* car. Or one pretty much like it."

"Don't tell me. This wagon reminds you of the first car you ever owned, when you were sixteen."

"She wouldn't have been cool enough for me when I was sixteen—and it was *seventeen*. Sorry, old girl."

Madeline tried to control her exasperation, as once again he patted the wheel in apology. "So what's the connection, then?"

"Something that goes back before that. My parents had a station wagon like this. Of course, it was a much earlier model, but it had the same metallic-green paint job and dark green upholstery. That was in the days before vans, when big families were loyal to their wagons. I was just a kid, probably nine or so."

"And you have fond memories," she guessed.

"Well, yeah," he said, a little embarrassed to admit his nostalgia. "They were some good times, with the whole clan piling into the wagon on weekends to drive out to my uncle's place, or Pop taking us fishing for the day on Fox Lake. Things like that." He grinned sheepishly. "Pretty corny, huh?"

Madeline only wished that she had the same corny memories. Her childhood had been vastly different, something she preferred to forget. "You're forgiven," she said, "and from now on, I'll try to be more tolerant of your girlfriend."

He loved his family, was sentimental about an old car that he associated with them. He was capable of a wonderful, rumbling laughter that made her mellow inside just thinking about it. And he had a lethal kiss.

This was not the Mitchell Hawke of that Wisconsin farm. This was another man, one with broader dimensions and deeper emotions. What was she going to do about him? What was she going to do about their tricky relationship?

She was on the run. And because of her, he was a fugitive now, one whom she had just helped to evade the law. It was an impossible situation, growing more complicated with each passing mile. Madeline feared the outcome. Feared her growing feelings for him even more.

THE TRAFFIC WAS LIGHT, consisting mostly of the usual trucks perpetually crossing the country with their heavy loads. Mitch didn't have to concentrate on his driving, so he had plenty of time to punish himself.

What the hell had he been thinking when he kissed her like that? Hadn't that reckless intimacy back at the farm been lesson enough? She was a risk to the promise he had made to himself not to betray the memory of Julie, to see those responsible for Julie's death suffer for it.

Now he was the one who was suffering. He was still painfully hard just thinking about that sizzling kiss, about the way her mouth had felt under his, all hot and wet and eager. Damn, what was he doing to himself?

Frowning, Mitch glanced in Madeline's direction. The

sketch pad was in her lap again, but this time her pencil was still. She wasn't creating a new jewelry design. Her gaze was lost in the view from her window. But it was so dreamy and faraway that he didn't think she could be admiring the scenery.

When she was like this, looking so innocent and almost angelically vulnerable, he forgot the woman she was supposed to be. He'd been doing that a lot lately. Tormenting himself with what he'd once cynically convinced himself was only a beautiful delusion.

But what if he'd been wrong about Madeline? What if, all along, he'd been blaming her unjustly in his need to hate her? Or, at least, exaggerating her role in Julie's death? His indecision about her had him so worried that he began to examine all that he'd learned about her in connection with Julie.

There had, of course, been her arrangement for Julie to work at the Phoenix. Well, that wasn't so damning—although, at the time, he had objected to Madeline Raeburn's influence on Julie, even accused her in his mind of luring Julie to the club.

She had been with Julie at the Phoenix the night she'd died. They'd been together in the bar after hours. Or so claimed a cleaning woman, who remembered overhearing Madeline tell Julie she was wanted upstairs. The cleaning woman had moved on to another region before Julie's departure, which meant Madeline Raeburn had been the last known person to see her alive.

Maybe Madeline hadn't been in any way responsible for Julie's death, but then, why had she been so reluctant a witness when Neil and his partner questioned her the next day? Denying that she had ever tried to send Julie upstairs, insisting she had no possible explanation for Julie Cleary's body, which had been sunk in San Francisco Bay and would have stayed there if a fisherman that morning hadn't caught his line on it. *My cop's instinct tells me she's hid-*

ing something,'' Neil had admitted to Mitch. *"And you can bet it's related to Matisse.''* That's what Mitch couldn't forget or forgive.

So just how guilty was the woman beside him? It was time he found out. Time he stopped pretending and told her all about Julie and him. Demanded her version of that night.

You'll lose her if you do.

Should he listen to that warning inside his head? The same warning that Neil had expressed when he'd left Madeline in Mitch's care. A prediction that amounted to: *Tell her the truth and she's bound to feel betrayed. She won't trust you at all after that. She'll want to get far away from you.*

All right, it was a risk, but he could no longer stand this deception. His mind was made up.

"You're going to hate me," she said.

Jolted by Madeline's sudden pronouncement on the heels of his decision, he cast a startled look at her. "What are you talking about?"

"I need a rest room."

So she wasn't a mind reader. "Madeline, you had a rest stop back at the service station just before the accident. That couldn't have been more than an hour ago, maybe less."

"Well, if you don't want an accident, then I suggest we get off at this next exit coming up. I'm sorry, but it's urgent. The result of tension around our close call with the sheriff, I guess."

Given the look of desperation on her face, Mitch had no choice but to accommodate her. There was a quick-stop just off the exit. He parked close to the side of the building that faced away from the interstate. Before he had the engine off, Madeline was out of the wagon and scooting into the women's facility.

Mitch sat there behind the wheel, thinking this would be

an opportunity to call California. It was time he checked in with Gloria again.

California, where both friends and enemies waited for them. Could one of those enemies be any of the three men with whom he and Neil had regularly played poker? Morrie Swanson, Dave Ennis, Hank Rosinski. Had one of them betrayed Neil?

Incredible though the possibility still seemed, it had haunted Mitch ever since Milwaukee. He had come back to it again and again on the long drive from Chicago, pondering it from all angles, searching his mind for an explanation. Nothing. Unless…

Something had been nagging at Mitch. He didn't know what it was, but he had an idea it might be a casual remark he'd once heard in connection with one of the three men. Trivial at the time but maybe of value now, if only he could recollect it. Whatever it was, it was buried deep in his memory, refusing to surface. On the other hand, he could be imagining things.

Madeline was still in the rest room when Mitch left the wagon and went looking for a phone. There was none mounted on the wall on this side of the building. Maybe out front.

The interstate was less than a hundred yards away. From the front of the quick-stop, it was in clear view. Mitch couldn't help spotting what was on it as he rounded the corner. Red light flashing, blue emblem prominent on the white door, it sped up the highway in urgent pursuit of—

Mitch ducked back around the corner just as Madeline emerged from the rest room. His facial expression must have registered the alarm going off inside his head.

"What is it?" she asked. "What's wrong?"

"The sheriff's cruiser. I just spotted it tearing up the highway in the direction we're headed."

"The same cruiser that—"

"Oh, yeah. Had to be."

"Maybe it isn't about us. Maybe he was chasing a speeder."

"Not likely, on the interstate. That's usually the duty of the state troopers."

He could see that Madeline shared his worry now.

"They must have gotten around to missing that fax, after all, realized I was responsible for lifting it," she said.

"Or else another bulletin about me came in."

"You saw him going by. Could he have seen you?"

"If he had, he'd be here by now."

"Mitch, we still don't know if it was us he was after."

"We know enough to get out of here."

"Where?"

"Not back on the interstate, that's for sure." He hurried her to the wagon, climbing in after her with a quick, "Break out that map, will you?"

Seconds later, after consulting the map, he made his choice. "Here, the old highway. Look, it parallels the interstate a little to the south, and we can access it from that underpass out there. Let's go. And, sweetheart, whenever you need a rest room again, remind me not to complain. If we hadn't stopped, we'd be on our way back to that sheriff's office, in cuffs."

Another rest room, however, was not an option. There was no sign of one on the back highway they traveled. And scarcely any traffic, either, which satisfied Mitch. Not that he was prepared to relax, even when the road carried them out of the sheriff's county and over the border into Utah.

No more distractions, he promised himself. There would be time enough later for confessions, for exploring any further his obsession with the woman he was protecting. Right now, he had to concentrate on his driving, which had become more of a challenge. They were in the majestic snow-clad mountains, and although the road was clear, it dipped and wound, presenting dangerous curves.

Madeline, too, was silent, possibly because she had made

the same promise to herself for the same reason. He could sense her tension. Neither of them was happy about this lonely road.

Mitch was wondering when, and if, it might be safe to return to the interstate, when Madeline ended her silence with a sharp "Treachery."

"Huh?"

"Your girlfriend, whose reliability you've been bragging about since Chicago. She's acting up."

"The car is fine."

"Mitch, the engine is laboring."

"It's because of climbing up and down these mountains, that's all."

"It's more than that."

She was right. The engine didn't sound good.

"Do you suppose it was because of the accident?" she asked. "Something that's just now showing up?"

Hell, he wasn't a trained mechanic. All he could do was guess. "Maybe."

"What can we do?"

"Pray."

But they would have to do more than that, Mitch realized. The engine was not only straining now but cutting in and out, the power surging one moment, and the next, threatening to expire. He nursed the gas pedal. A useless effort. The wagon limped like a sick animal, and within another half mile it died altogether.

Mitch managed to coast onto the shoulder of the highway before they came to a stop. With Madeline anxiously watching him, he spent a few minutes trying to coax the engine to life again. The wagon was having none of it.

"Do you think," she suggested, "if you look under the hood that maybe you might—"

He turned his head, eyeing her in blank-faced silence. She got the message.

"No, I guess not."

Mitch searched the road ahead of them through the windshield and then twisted around, looking back the way they had come. There was not a car in sight. Nor had they encountered another vehicle in some time. Not a sign of a house, either, or any building for that matter.

He smacked the wheel in frustration. "Stuck in the middle of nowhere."

By this time Madeline had the map open again on her knees and her reading glasses in place. "It looks like the nearest sign of any civilization is this dot here. A place called Silver Dollar. I don't think it can be very big."

"Big enough, I hope, to have a garage with a mechanic on duty. How far? Can you tell?"

She shook her head. "I don't know. Maybe five miles or so. What are we going to do?"

More than ever, Mitch regretted the absence of his cell phone. "You interested in seeing the country on foot?"

"Do I have a choice?"

"Doesn't look like it."

He certainly had no intention of leaving her behind in the car. She made no objection, though he could see she wasn't happy about abandoning her satchel of precious tools, which they locked in the wagon with the rest of their things. Seconds later, they were hiking down the deserted highway in the direction of Silver Dollar.

It was past noon on Christmas Eve day. What chance would they have, Mitch wondered, of finding a service center still open, even if one existed in this remote place? Taking everything into account, he would have to say that the situation was not encouraging. No, definitely not.

"Mitch."

"Yeah?"

"We're being stalked."

"What are you talking about?"

"Up there. Can't you hear it?"

There was a steep embankment off the left side of the

road. A long, unbroken hedgerow grew along the crest of it, so thick that it offered no glimpse of what occupied the other side.

"No."

"There's something up there," she insisted nervously, "and it's following us."

Mitch listened. He could detect nothing, except strands of barbed wire peeking here and there through the heavy growth. "It's probably just cattle." He hoped. "Relax. Enjoy the mountains."

"We're in the wilderness, and I'm not enjoying any of it."

They went on. Less than a mile farther along, she stopped again. "Whatever it is, it's still with us, and I don't like it. What if it's dangerous? Like a bear."

Mitch could hear it now, too, something rustling in the undergrowth behind the fence. Beast or man? He decided it was time to investigate. There was a gap a few yards along in the hedgerow.

"Wait here," he cautioned Madeline.

Hand ready to produce his gun, he started up the snow-layered embankment. He was halfway to the top when he caught the sound of a car approaching from around the bend behind them. Madeline heard it, too, because when he looked back, she was out in the center of the highway prepared to flag it down.

"Don't!" he called out to her, afraid for them to trust any strange vehicle.

"Yes!" she called back stubbornly. "I'm cold, tired of picking road pebbles out of my boots, and in no mood to tangle with whatever is behind that hedge!"

By the time Mitch had scrambled down the embankment and was on his way to rejoin her, the vehicle had swung into sight around the bend and had eased to a halt in front of Madeline's frantically waving figure. It revealed itself as a battered pickup. A window rolled down, and a head with a round, friendly face poked out.

"You folks in trouble?"

"I'm afraid we are," Madeline answered. "For one thing, there's something behind that hedgerow up there that doesn't seem too happy about us being here."

Her concern was met with a chuckle. "That would be Pete Nelson's pair of llamas. He's grazing sheep in those pastures, and llamas are very protective of sheep."

"And for another thing," Mitch said, catching up with Madeline and not liking it one bit that she had approached the open window of the truck, even though its driver was probably a harmless local, "our car is broken down."

"Yeah, I noticed it parked at the side of the road back there. You on your way to Silver Dollar?"

"Yes, hoping to find a garage there," Madeline replied.

"Well, there is one, but I don't know what luck you'll have getting repairs today. Be happy to give you a lift, though."

Mitch hesitated. He wanted to limit their contact with people as much as possible, especially after the episode with the sheriff in Wyoming. But in their current predicament, he didn't have much choice.

"We'd appreciate that."

He was being paranoid, he knew, worrying needlessly. There wasn't much chance, if any, that he would be recognized. Neil's murder might have been major news back in Milwaukee, but it was unlikely that any report had reached this remote region. His face wouldn't have appeared anywhere but in bulletins to law enforcement agencies.

On the other hand, people were naturally curious, and their rescuer was no exception. He demonstrated that after they'd managed to fit themselves into the cab beside his corpulent body squeezed behind the wheel.

"You folks headed back to California?" he asked as they

headed up the highway. "Noticed the California plate on your wagon."

"We're on our way back from Iowa," Mitch said.

"And planning to stop over for Christmas with friends in Salt Lake City," Madeline added quickly. "We wanted to see a bit of the backcountry along the way."

Their driver bobbed his head in understanding, his fat chins quivering. "Wondered why you weren't driving through on the interstate. I hope you can make it. Silver Dollar ain't much of a spot to spend Christmas."

"Oh?" He'd given Mitch the opportunity to arm himself with information about the place they were going, while avoiding any further questions about them. "Why is that? What's there?"

"Precious little. About all we got these days is the service station, Vi's grocery store and a motel. No traffic to speak of at this time of the year, but it gets visitors in summer for the ghost town up on the mountainside."

"Sounds like Silver Dollar used to be much more."

"That was long ago before the silver mine played out and just about everybody left. Got a railroad museum, though, around the back side of the mountain. It ain't open in winter, of course."

"Any kind of sheriff or police station there?" Mitch asked him casually. "I was thinking I ought to report our abandoned car."

"Don't mind about that. The closest peace officer is way over in Fraser, and he don't get this way too often. No action. Here we go."

The pickup rounded the shoulder of a mountain and descended a long slope into Silver Dollar. As their driver had indicated, it was a depressed community. Its few active buildings were stretched out beside the highway in a deep hollow tucked between the mountains. Mitch didn't have much hope for the place, not where he and Madeline were concerned.

THE ATTENDANT at the service station was young, pencil-thin, and had a chin trimmed with a goatee. He was not encouraging.

"I'd like to help you, but I don't see what I can do. Mike is our mechanic, and he's spending the holiday with family over in Fraser. He won't be back on duty here until the morning after Christmas."

"And there is no one else?" Mitch asked him.

"My brother and I operate the place. He's good with small engines, but he won't touch a car. Especially not one that sounds like it could have a serious problem."

"Any chance I can get my hands on a rental?" Mitch asked him.

The attendant looked at him in disbelief. "Mister, this is Silver Dollar. There aren't any cars here for rent."

"What about paying someone to drive us to Salt Lake City?"

"Man, have a heart. It's Christmas Eve day. You're not going to find anyone willing to drive you anywhere."

Mitch and Madeline exchanged looks of silent acceptance. It seemed that they had no alternative. They would be spending Christmas in Silver Dollar. But where?

"Is the motel open?" Madeline asked the young man, indicating the long, low structure situated on a knoll up behind the grocery store.

"Year-round."

"We had to leave our things in our car. I don't suppose…"

In that respect he was willing to accommodate them. "My brother's out on a call trying to repair a snowmobile. When he gets back, we'll haul your wagon down here."

Mitch left the keys with him, and they climbed the hill to the motel. It wasn't much of a motel. Painted an ugly shade of lime green, it had all the character of those road-side tourist cabins from decades ago.

Madeline was noticeably silent beside him. "You worried?" he asked her.

"It isn't that. It's the thought of spending Christmas in an impersonal motel room. Though I don't know why that should be any worse than spending it out on the road or, even if we had reached San Francisco, in a safe house somewhere."

The holiday saddened her. Mitch didn't blame her. It suddenly saddened him, too. He thought about offering her words of sympathy, but what could he say?

The front office was empty when they entered the motel. Mitch rang a bell on the counter. The door at the back of the office opened, affording them a glimpse of an apartment. A woman appeared and moved to the desk to serve them. She was stout, had a head of dirty-blond hair in need of disciplining, and a warm, friendly manner.

Maybe too friendly, Mitch thought. In under two minutes she'd introduced herself as their hostess, Betty Schultz, and learned from them that their car had broken down and that they were forced to lay over in Silver Dollar. She was distressed that they would miss Christmas with their family— but wasn't it lucky that the motel was available for them, which it wouldn't have been at this time of the year if she and her husband didn't live right on the premises.

Betty had yet to get around to the subject of rooms, when the front door opened abruptly behind them, admitting a blast of icy air and a threatening voice shouting, "Mickey, you are one hard man to catch up with!"

Mitch went rigid with alarm, and before he could stop himself, his hand moved instinctively in the direction of the gun under his coat.

Chapter Seven

"Hell, Mickey, didn't you hear me calling you all the way up the hill?"

Mitch, who had swiveled around at the first sign of trouble, checked himself just in time. He gazed with relief at the two men who entered the office. The older one carried a toolbox and had a pair of earmuffs clamped to his bald head.

"Didn't hear you with these on," he said, removing the muffs.

"You're getting deaf, Mickey," the younger man accused, moving into the office behind him. "I just came by to tell you about the snowmobile that conked out on you when you were doing the rounds over at the museum. I got it fixed. Left it at the side of the depot and left the key where you asked. You can stop by the station and settle up with my brother when you're ready."

He departed. The other man, with a curt nod in their direction, rounded the counter and disappeared into the apartment behind the office.

Mitch, having understood by now that it was another "Mickey" who'd been accosted and that it had nothing to do with him, suddenly realized his hand still hovered in the area of the holster carrying his pistol. He hastily covered his mistake by tugging at his coat, as if straightening a stubborn fold.

But as he turned back to the desk, he found Madeline staring at him. She couldn't have missed his startled response to the challenge, the way he had moved protectively in front of her at the same time his hand had gone for his gun.

"Something wrong?" he asked, making an effort to be as casual as he could.

She shook her head, but there was a puzzled expression on her face. *Mickey.* Did she realize it was the name itself that had alerted Mitch? Was she remembering that *Mickey* was Julie's pet name for her boyfriend? And if she knew that, would she be able to put it all together?

"My husband," Betty said, cheerfully explaining the dour-faced man with the toolbox, "Mickey, is winter caretaker for the railroad museum. Sure helped Silver Dollar's economy when they added that attraction a few seasons back."

"About our rooms," Mitch reminded her.

"Connecting rooms, right?" She seemed puzzled about that.

"I snore," Mitch said.

Betty chuckled. "I guess I can relate to that. Mickey is like a buzz saw."

They registered, were handed their keys, and then were given directions to their rooms, which were located toward the end of a gloomy hallway that divided the motel lengthwise.

Madeline was disturbingly silent as they made their way along the corridor. Mitch had the uncomfortable impression that she was sneaking glances at his damn ears. That they were flaming under her scrutiny and about to betray him.

"About what happened at the desk," he said. Feeling the situation was increasingly awkward, he made an effort to explain. "The guy sounded genuinely angry when he burst into the lobby like that. I was just being cautious."

"I know."

Why didn't her calm reply satisfy him? Why did he still read puzzlement in her manner, sense that she was striving to understand?

Their rooms were at the back of the motel. Although a bit on the shabby side, they were scrupulously clean. What mattered to Mitch, however, was security. He immediately checked out the locks on the doors and found them dependable. Satisfied, he turned to Madeline. She was still watching him.

He would tell her about Julie and him, just as he'd intended to do before their trouble on the road. She deserved to know. But he wanted a tranquil moment for his difficult confession.

"We missed lunch," he said. "Why don't we visit that grocery store? We'll need to load up on provisions, anyway, before it closes."

She shook her head. "Not yet. I haven't seen a tub since we left the farm. All I want is a bath."

Her famous appetite hadn't failed since the start of this long haul. Not a good sign, Mitch thought. "You sure?"

"Yes."

"All right," he agreed. "You take your bath, and I'll try to reach the DA's office in Frisco. Gloria Rodriguez will need to know we've been delayed. Hopefully, she'll still be at her desk."

"Fine."

"I'll check back with you after your bath." He would tell her then. "And, uh, leave the connecting door ajar. Just in case."

He left her and went reluctantly into his own room, still worried by her reticence. He picked up the phone on the bedside table. Making sure that he blocked caller ID, even though Gloria had assured him the first time he'd phoned her from the road that her line was a safe one, he placed his call.

Gloria was frantic when she answered. "Mitchell Hawke, I am going to have your head! I should have been out of this office hours ago and home with my kids, not hanging around here worrying about you and wondering where you are and if I stood a prayer of hearing from you! But I don't suppose it ever occurred to you that I have a family and a personal life, and that this happens to be the day before Christmas!"

Her voice was so strident that Mitch held the receiver away from his ear. He didn't try to interrupt her. He let her vent.

When Gloria finally paused to draw a breath, he asked her calmly, "You wound down yet?"

"Don't get smart with me, mister. Not when I've been risking my career by letting you—"

This time Mitch did interrupt. "Are you alone, or is half your office listening in?"

"I may be a fool, but I'm not that big of a fool. Of course I'm alone. My assistant is gone, and the door is closed. And since this line is secure, as I told you before, there's no one to overhear us." The assistant district attorney ended her tirade by demanding furiously "And why *haven't* I heard from you?"

"You're hearing from me now. And why are you making such a case of it? Hell, didn't I phone our first morning on the road to let you know the change in plans?"

"That was a lifetime ago. And you should have been checking in with me regularly. I thought that was the understanding when you told me you were coming by car. Though why I ever agreed—"

"Gloria, don't fuss. There was nothing to report. Until now, anyway."

"What's wrong?" she asked sharply.

"Nothing I'm not handling." He went on to tell her

about the problem with the car and their necessary stopover until it could be repaired.

She was silent for a few seconds. He could picture her sitting there at her desk, a small, attractive woman shaking her dark head.

"Mitch, I don't like this. I don't like the two of you being out there on your own. I still say it's a mistake. Why don't you let me send someone reliable to accompany our witness back here by plane?"

"*I'm* reliable," Mitch stubbornly insisted, "and until you can tell me that you've identified the informer in the ranks, the highway is a lot safer for Madeline than San Francisco. Can you tell me that, Gloria?"

"We're working on it."

"Which means no result yet." He didn't add that, as long as that danger existed, he meant to avoid San Francisco altogether. Time enough when they reached California for both Gloria and Madeline to learn about his plan involving the cabin in the mountains.

"You haven't told me where you are."

"Uh-uh. Secure line or not, I'm not risking it. You don't need to know where we are."

"Damn it, Mitch, I'm sticking my neck out for you, and I *do* need to know where you are. In case you've forgotten, I'm ultimately responsible for Madeline Raeburn. What if something happens to you, and one or both of you don't turn up? I need to at least have a starting place to look for you."

He had to admit that Gloria had a strong argument. If something did happen to him, and in their situation anything was possible, then Madeline would be alone, maybe unable to seek help. There probably should be someone who knew where she was and had the resources to get to her without delay. Someone she could rely on without hesitation. But as persuasive as Gloria's argument was, and as much as he trusted her, he couldn't bring himself to chance it.

"Sorry," he said, "but I'm still not telling you where we are."

He could hear Gloria issuing a long sigh. "Then you leave me no choice, because there's a bottom line here, Mitch. My boss," she explained, referring to the DA, "has had it with you. My last instruction from him was that, if you don't tell me where you are, he's making it a top priority to find you. That means requesting every lawman in the west to use their full resources to track you down. And with a manhunt that intensive..."

She left the rest unsaid, because the outcome was only too obvious. If the manhunt did heat up like that, there was every likelihood of their being found. In the process, far too many people would hear of their whereabouts, presenting a situation much more dangerous than his silence.

"Look," Gloria pressed him, "it will be all right. I got him to agree, as long as you tell me, that for now no one else needs to know, including him. And you know I'll keep it strictly to myself, Mitch."

Damn. He was squeezed into a corner. She had left him with no other option.

"Are you there?"

"Yeah." He hesitated. "Okay, I don't like this, but we're in Utah. A little bump on the road called Silver Dollar, and that goes no further than you."

"You can count on me, though this whole thing frustrates the hell out of me."

"While we're on the subject of frustrations, what about mine over this police search for me? I thought you were going to pull some strings to get that called off."

"Nobody has that kind of influence, not with the kind of evidence the Milwaukee police department has collected. Unless you turn yourself in and submit to a full investigation, they refuse to listen. And how do you know there is a search?''

He briefly explained about his close call in Wyoming with the sheriff.

"You see, that's all the more reason for you not being this—this loose cannon in the wilderness."

"Gloria?"

"What?"

"Merry Christmas, and stop worrying. I'll talk to you later."

Mitch rang off before she had the chance to lay into him again. Then, hands thrust into his pants pockets, he went and stood by the window where he persuaded himself that he had done the right thing in trusting Gloria. In any case, he'd been left with no choice.

The view from the window was a bleak one. He could see Silver Dollar's ghost town up on the snow-covered mountainside, a collection of crumbling gray structures from a lost era. The sky above the mountain peaks was the color of dull pewter, now that the sun had vanished under a mass of clouds. He hoped the change didn't mean bad weather.

Mitch sensed he was no longer alone. Turning away from the window, he discovered Madeline in the open doorway that connected their two rooms.

The sight of her standing there, with tumbled red hair and a bath sheet snugged around her slim figure, made him catch his breath. Now, this was a view he could appreciate. She was fresh and glowing from her bath, and he swore he could smell the fragrant scent of the soap she had used, although at this distance that was impossible.

She had that kind of effect on his imagination, which was already busy savoring what was beneath that towel. The lush vision of warm, naked flesh had the blood rushing to his groin. He was in danger of a sweet, aching arousal.

That was before he realized that Madeline had appeared

without a sound to indicate her arrival. That she continued to stand there in absolute silence. Her eyes were fastened on him, and even from this far away he could see the accusation in them.

The tightness that threatened one area of his body transferred itself to another, this time settling deep in his gut in the form of a gnawing guilt. He had waited too long to tell her. She *knew*.

Hoping to salvage the situation, Mitch started toward her. But she held up one hand, warning him to keep his distance. He stayed where he was, allowing her to move a few safe steps into the room. There was more now than accusation in her gaze as she confronted him. He could see it plainly in her face, a stricken expression of betrayal.

"It's true, isn't it," she said, her voice low and controlled. "You're Julie's 'Mickey.'"

"Madeline—"

Not listening to him, she went on in that quiet tone that was somehow worse than if she had stormed into his room, raging with anger. "I knew there was someone in Julie's life, even though she never talked about him much. I guess he was just too special for her to discuss him casually with someone she didn't know all that well. I was too new a friend, and maybe Julie didn't easily trust people. But you'd know more about that than I do."

"Madeline," he tried again, "let me explain."

"And whenever Julie did refer to him," she continued as if he hadn't spoken, "it was always as Mickey. Little things she'd mention in passing, like, 'Mickey is out of town this week,' or, 'Wonder if Mickey will like these earrings.' Never any other name, just Mickey. I thought it was his real name. I didn't know it was Julie's pet name for—"

Madeline broke off, her gaze slowly searching him. Mitch knew she was looking at his ears, really seeing them for the first time, verifying what she must have finally understood while she was bathing.

"For *you*," she finished softly. "Julie must have teased you about them. Who was she comparing you to, Mitch? But I don't have to ask, do I? Because there's only one Mickey famous for his ears. So that's what she called you, Mickey for Mickey Mouse. That's how it would have started, and then the name stuck. That's right, isn't it, Mitch?"

"Yes."

"I thought that had to be the answer. Nothing else explained all of it—the way you whipped around in the office when the man from the garage called out for Mickey and how sensitive you seemed about your ears when you caught me staring at them back at the farm. Not because you minded their size but because you were afraid I'd figure it out." Her finely shaped eyebrows drew together in a frown. "But why did you feel you had to hide it from me?"

"Neil," Mitch said. "Neil was convinced you wouldn't stay with me if you knew of my connection to Julie, that you'd run."

"And you couldn't risk that." Her frown deepened in further understanding. "You were buried out there at the farm. I see now why that was. You were grieving for Julie. And that's why you resented my being there. I was an intrusion."

Mitch made a mistake then. He offered no word of acknowledgment. He was silent, and his silence was all the explanation Madeline needed.

"Oh, no," she murmured. "It's worse than that, isn't it."

"Look, there's something you need to hear."

She shook her head vigorously. "I don't have to hear it. I can see it in your face. I've seen it all along, only I never understood it. You blame me for Julie. You think I'm in some part responsible for Julie's death."

Mitch didn't answer her. He turned away and went back to the window. He stood there for a moment, looking out again on the mountainside without seeing it, seeing himself instead as he'd been in those long weeks after Julie died, suffering over her loss, haunted by his failure to be there for her. All of it came back in a fresh rush of hurt and anger.

An anger that he directed at Madeline when he swung away from the window and strode to the center of the room where she stood. Now that he no longer had to conceal anything from her, now that it was all out in the open, he could release the bitterness that he had struggled to contain ever since her arrival at the farm.

"Suppose you tell me exactly how innocent you are," he said, hearing the sharpness in his voice, knowing he wasn't being in any way gentle about it, and yet not caring. "Just what did happen that night?"

"But you must know. Neil must have shared it all with you."

"Come on, Madeline, I want your version."

She shut her eyes briefly, looking pained, as though silently telling him that she had already described the events of that night over and over and couldn't bear to relate them again. But Mitch refused to free her from his demand.

When her eyes opened again, meeting his gaze, there was decisiveness in them. And a note of defiance in her voice. "All right, here it is, everything I told Neil and his partner when they questioned me the next morning. Julie and I were working late at the Phoenix that night. It was a chance for us to make some extra money serving a private party upstairs."

"Consisting of who?"

"Griff and some of his business associates who'd come in from the East."

"What happened at that party?"

"Nothing. They talked politics and sports, and we served them supper. It was all very ordinary."

"And afterward?"

"Julie and I were in the bar area downstairs, stacking all the clutter on trays so that it would be ready for the kitchen staff to take care of the next day. Everyone had gone by then."

"You telling me the club was empty?"

"The Phoenix is a big place. I don't know who was still around. A few cleaning people, anyway. All I'm saying is we were alone when Julie remembered about the earrings."

"Earrings?"

"She'd asked me to make a pair for her in an ankh shape. I had brought them that night and given them to her while we were upstairs. She put them aside when we got busy, and forgot about them until we were in the bar."

"So she went back upstairs to get the earrings?"

"Yes."

"A cleaning woman says she overheard you sending Julie upstairs."

"Well, she's wrong," Madeline insisted. "All I did was remind Julie that she'd laid the earrings next to the microwave in the serving pantry up there."

"Go on."

"I finished stacking the trays. Julie didn't come back."

"And you didn't wonder about that?"

"Of course I wondered. I started to go looking for her, but on the way I stopped at my locker for my things, thinking we'd leave together. Her locker was next to mine. It was open—her stuff was gone, and so was her car when I checked the lot out back."

"So you figured she was already on her way home."

"Yes."

"And it never occurred to you that maybe she hadn't left the club, that maybe something had happened to her upstairs? Something involving Matisse or one of his men."

Madeline hesitated, and Mitch thought, *She hasn't told me everything. There's something she's holding back.*

"Come on, Madeline," he challenged her, "you must

have known by then that Matisse and his friends had a bad reputation."

"I—I was beginning to realize it, yes."

"But you didn't quit. Even after Julie died like that, even though you must have wondered just how and why she was killed, you stayed on with Matisse and his club."

She gazed at him, a deep sadness in those wide amber eyes. "And that's what you can't forget or forgive, isn't it, Mitch. That's what makes you convinced that I betrayed Julie, even though there was never any evidence that her death was connected with anyone at the Phoenix."

Mitch didn't say anything, although he knew Madeline was waiting for him to soften his anger, to tell her that maybe he had been wrong about her.

"I'm sorry, Mitch," she said gently. "I'm sorry you lost Julie. But you should know that I lost her, too. That, even though I knew her for only a few weeks, she was someone I cared about."

Mitch still couldn't bring himself to tell her what she wanted to hear.

Madeline's voice sank to a whisper. "You must have loved her very deeply. And hated me for her loss. Probably still do, resenting me for keeping certain things to myself I prefer not to discuss."

Mitch realized that he could no longer remain silent, that this time he had to speak. "We have to talk about this," he said earnestly.

"We're talking now."

"Not like this. Not with all this hurt getting in the way. Why don't you get dressed, and we'll go down to that store and buy what we need? Then we can bring it back here, sit down to eat and calmly talk it all out."

She didn't answer him. Her gaze left him and traveled slowly around the room. "I don't like motel rooms," she said absently. "They have no identity, no real color or feeling. But then, I guess they can't be something intimate."

"Groceries," he reminded her impatiently. He promised himself that while they were eating he would make an effort to learn what she was hiding.

Her gaze returned to him. "You'll want to clean up, too, won't you?"

Mitch knew he was overdue for a bath. Cleaning up in rest-stop washrooms had been adequate under the circumstances, but it was no substitute for a shower. "Give me twenty minutes," he said. "Okay?"

"Okay," she said.

MADELINE SHUT the connecting door behind her and went and sat on the edge of the bed in her room. She was too shaken to get into her clothes.

She must have been huddled there in her misery for a full five minutes before she understood what was wrong with her. It wasn't learning about him and Julie that shocked her, made her desperately unhappy. It was something far worse.

Madeline didn't know how it had happened, or just when, but somewhere on this taut journey she had fallen in love with Mitchell Hawke.

With the fists of both hands pressed tightly against her mouth, she tried to deny that love. But her effort was useless. It was there, and it was impossible. Frightening.

Her thoughts, trapped by panic, flew in every direction, like the beating wings of a bird seeking escape. In the end, mind quiet but filled with despair, she wondered how she could bear to go on staying with him, loving him as she did. Knowing what he felt about her, knowing how much Julie had mattered to him. And she didn't think that would change, *could* change, even though there were things about herself she hadn't told him and feared she might never be able to tell him.

He wanted to talk, but all that really mattered had already been said. Anyway, she didn't trust another conversation.

Didn't trust that she could mask her feelings for him, now that she knew exactly what those intense emotions were.

She could hear the sound of the shower in his bathroom next door. Rising from the bed, she began to dress. She wondered what to do, what she could do that made any sense in this impossible situation.

There were no answers. It certainly made no sense that she felt herself smiling as she put on her clothes. Evidence, she supposed, that she suddenly found herself appreciating the wry humor of her mistake. Leave it to her to fall in love with a man who had no use for her. She supposed that qualified her as the classic victim of heartbreak. The tears, she knew, would come later.

The water was still running next door when the phone on her bedside table rang.

THERE WAS NO ANSWER when Mitch tapped on the connecting door. Had she stretched out on the bed in there, fallen asleep? She had looked tired enough for a nap.

"Hey, Madeline," he called, "time to go."

Silence. Beginning to feel uneasy, he tried the door. It was unlocked. He opened it and poked his head inside. She wasn't there.

Cursing under his breath, fearing the worst—that she had run out on him—he damned himself for being too harsh with her. Why hadn't he been more understanding, more willing to listen?

He had to find her, had to get her back! It was dangerous for her to be out there on her own. Where could she have gone in this isolated place, anyway?

Grabbing his coat from his room and taking his gun with him, Mitch tore out the door and down the long hallway toward the motel's front entrance. It was possible that she hadn't run away, that she had somehow been snatched—and that scared the hell out of him. He couldn't lose Madeline. She was his responsibility.

That she might mean much more than that to him was something he refused to consider, because that, too, scared him.

Bursting into the office, he came to a stop. He stood there, breathing deeply in vast relief. A bench was situated on the other side of the office, just inside the front door. Madeline, looking a bit forlorn, was parked there with her suitcase and jewelry satchel at her feet. Mitch's things had also been dumped beside the bench.

Her head was bent over something. She was either too occupied to be aware of his arrival or else chose not to notice him. As Mitch started toward her, he realized she was not alone on the bench. She had found a companion.

Chapter Eight

The kitten was probably the homeliest Mitch had ever seen, all patchy gray and tan and with a face that was somehow wrong. As he approached the bench, he could also see that it had a pronounced kink in its tail.

Neither Madeline nor the kitten seemed to care what it looked like. He could hear it purring contentedly in her lap. Head lowered, she stroked the animal with a slow, patient tenderness. Mitch couldn't help smiling at the sight of them. She was like a little girl with her first pet.

"I see they managed to haul the car down," he said, nodding toward their things on the floor.

Madeline didn't look up. She went on fondling the kitten. "Mickey Schultz called the room to let me know one of the brothers had brought our luggage to the office."

"The guy couldn't even bother delivering it to our door? He's as sour as his wife is sweet."

Madeline smiled, indicating the closed door behind the desk. "I think they're back there now somewhere having a few words on that subject."

"You might have told me you were going out."

"I knocked on the bathroom door. You didn't hear."

"You should have waited."

Her head lifted this time. "I couldn't. I had to make sure

the satchel was okay.'' She looked at him as if he should have known that.

The precious jewelry tools. They were a priority with her.

''I'm sorry if you were worried,'' she said. ''I thought I'd get back before you were dressed.''

Instead of which, he thought, she'd been distracted by the creature curled in her lap. ''Looks like your friend has gone to sleep,'' he said.

She looked down at the kitten and smiled serenely. Mitch realized that he, too, was in a decidedly calmer state of mind. Their seething emotions had been spent.

For a moment Madeline didn't say anything. Then, with a wistful expression on her face, she confided, ''I've always loved cats. Dogs, too. But I was never able to have one. Adam was so terribly allergic to them.''

Adam. Mitch didn't miss the way she sounded the name, caressing it with the same tenderness she stroked the kitten. Did he want to know who Adam was? Maybe not. Maybe he wasn't going to like hearing just how important this Adam was to her. Maybe he would hate the guy, hate her because of him.

On the other hand, he'd better learn about Adam, whoever he was. Something told Mitch that Adam was the missing piece, the secret Madeline had been withholding from him.

Not waiting for an invitation, Mitch settled on the bench beside her. She didn't object, though she was silent for another moment. He waited patiently, sensing this was difficult for her.

''It's not easy for me to talk about Adam,'' she said. ''There's so much hurt there.''

''That why you haven't mentioned him before?''

''I'm always afraid people won't understand, won't see how sensitive and gentle he was.''

Was. Mitch didn't miss her use of the past tense. But he didn't interrupt.

"I suppose very often people who are frail on the outside are sensitive and gentle inside. I suppose not being strong can make you...I don't know, forgiving about the flaws in others. Adam was like that. He never minded that sometimes he was mistaken for being soft or weak. 'Don't resent them, Maddie,' he'd say. 'They don't understand.' Well, I did mind, but that's all right. I was strong enough for both of us."

"Because you had to be," Mitch guessed, beginning to see where she was taking him.

She glanced at him with an expression of gratitude. "We were all each other had after our parents were gone. My mother walked out on us when I was too young to remember much of anything about her. To this day, I have no idea where she is or even if she's still living. Dad tried to raise us, but I'm afraid he didn't have a lot going for him. He was forever losing jobs. He was headed for another job interview when his car was run off the highway in the fog near Big Sur."

"Leaving you with Adam." He was her brother, Mitch realized. Adam was Madeline's brother. He experienced a relief that he didn't permit himself to question. "How old were you?"

"Old enough to leave school and go to work to support Adam and me. I wasn't going to have them stick us in a foster home somewhere."

She said this last with a fierceness worthy of a proud warrior. For the first time since she had walked into his life, Mitch viewed her with genuine respect, admiring her courage and independence.

"And your brother?"

"Adam was fourteen. But we were fine on our own. Dad had left some insurance—not much, but it helped. I won't say it wasn't a struggle for a few years, because it was.

Eventually, though, I paid off all of his debts. We were in the clear. Things were looking up, until—''

She broke off, a catch in her voice. Mitch waited for her to compose herself. He offered no word of sympathy, sensing she wouldn't appreciate it, that she was determined not to lose her self-control.

Clearing her throat, she said simply, ''Until Adam got sick.''

''How sick?''

''Very sick. Leukemia.''

Mitch's heart went out to her. He had a sudden urge to take her in his arms, soothe her with comforting words, but again he knew that would be a mistake. For both of them. He was silent.

Madeline slowly scratched the kitten behind its ears. It went on sleeping in her lap. ''Adam was in and out of the hospital,'' she said. ''The medical expenses were awful. That's why I went to work at the Phoenix.''

''Where you ignored the rumors about Griff Matisse.''

''I couldn't afford to listen to them. The salary was so good, better than anything I'd been earning and with benefits I needed. And when Griff learned about Adam, he insisted on helping. He couldn't have been more generous.''

She paused, and Mitch knew she was struggling with guilt.

''All right,'' she admitted, ''maybe I shouldn't have ignored those warnings about Griff being connected to a crime syndicate. But I convinced myself that a man that kind about Adam couldn't be what people said he was, that it was just spite because they envied him his success.''

''But you did deceive yourself,'' Mitch pointed out.

''Yes, for a long time. But all that came to an end when Julie died.''

''Are you telling me that you do know what happened to Julie that night?''

Madeline shook her head emphatically. "No, everything I told you before was the truth. I don't know what Julie might have seen or heard when she went upstairs to get those earrings, or if anything at all happened to her while she was in the club. But early the next morning, when I learned she'd been found in the bay after a fisherman caught his line on her body…"

"What?"

"I knew that Griff could have been responsible in some way. Or, if not him, one of his crowd. That's when I decided I could no longer lie to myself and that I had to get out. I went to Griff first thing and told him I was quitting, that I had a better job offer."

"And?"

"He listened, and then he smiled. It wasn't the smile of a friend. He must have seen right through me, because he informed me that I wasn't going anywhere, that I was staying and that I was going to do just what he told me to do, including keeping any suspicions I might have to myself, or—"

"What?"

"He made certain threats about Adam. I believed them."

Which, Mitch thought, explained why Madeline had been evasive when Neil questioned her afterward. Madeline had been scared, not for herself but for her ailing brother. She had been protecting Adam.

Mitch could understand all of it now—why she had remained silent, why she had continued on at the Phoenix after Julie's death, why she had even permitted herself to be known as Matisse's girl, accompanying him wherever and whenever he ordered.

"All those weeks after Julie died I held my tongue," Madeline said. "I hated every day of it, but I held my tongue."

She fell silent, and her hand that had been scratching the

kitten went still. But Mitch knew she wasn't finished with her story, that she was steeling herself for the toughest part.

"And then this fall..." she said, pausing to draw a steadying breath. "This fall Adam's condition changed. He'd been in remission, but the leukemia became active again. This time the doctors weren't able to save him. He— He just seemed to slip away. You know?"

Mitch didn't think there were any words he could use to express his understanding. Instead, he reached for her hand, squeezing it gently to tell her that he knew just what grief over the loss of a loved one was all about. Madeline didn't respond to the pressure. Her hand was lifeless in his, but he went on holding it.

"Adam bought my freedom with his life," she said, her voice hollow now. "Griff had nothing to threaten me with anymore. I didn't have to stay with him. I could go far away and try to make a new life for myself. After I buried Adam, I took what money I had left out of the bank and went to the club. Smart or not, I needed to do that. I needed to find the guts to tell him I was finished and that I was leaving."

"Instead," Mitch realized, "you witnessed Matisse putting a bullet in that undercover cop."

She nodded. "And whatever courage I had flew out the window. All I could think about was how ruthless Griff was and what happened to people who saw or heard what they weren't meant to see. People like Julie and that undercover cop. That's why I didn't trust the police to protect me, not when they couldn't even protect their own officers. That's why I ran and kept on running."

"Why didn't you tell me all this before?" Mitch asked. "Why didn't you let me know about Adam?"

She turned her head and gazed at him in faint surprise, as if he should have known the answer to his question. "You weren't ready to hear it," she said simply. "I tried several times to make you understand, but you didn't want to listen to anything that might make you realize I wasn't as bad as you were convinced I was. Besides, I didn't want to use Adam to make you see just who I am. I wanted you to find that out for yourself.''

She was right. He hadn't deserved to have her share with him a subject so private and precious as Adam. But he knew now the brave and decent woman Madeline Raeburn was. He just wasn't certain how he was going to apply that knowledge to his own churning emotions.

''I don't want to run anymore, Mitch,'' she confided softly. ''I'm just so tired of running.''

He could see how drained she was, that she needed to rest. ''Let's get you back to the room, although we should visit that grocery store before it's too late.''

She shook her head. ''Why don't you go down and buy what we need? Right now, all I want is a long nap.''

''I'll see you settled in the room first.'' Mitch released her hand and got to his feet. ''Uh, you have a little problem,'' he said, reminding her of the kitten in her lap.

''Betty Schultz said this was the last kitten in her cat's litter. She was able to find homes for the others, but no one wants this poor mite, including her husband.''

The expression of longing on Madeline's face told Mitch exactly what she was feeling. ''I know what you're thinking,'' he said, ''but we can't take it. You know we can't.''

''I know, but I hate the idea of what might become of it.'' She rose reluctantly from the bench, gently depositing the kitten on the floor.

''Come on,'' he urged, collecting her suitcase and his own things, leaving the satchel for her. ''You can worry about it later.''

Madeline was silent when they reached their rooms. Mitch feared she was still thinking about the kitten. He couldn't forget the look of yearning on her face when he'd insisted the cat was not their problem. He was beginning to feel like a prize heel.

He watched her kick off her boots and stretch out on the bed. "You okay?"

"Yes."

"I'll let you sleep, then." He started toward the connecting door to his own room, wanting to drop off his gear before he left for the store.

"Spare me a few minutes before you go," she requested, drawing herself up against the headboard and indicating the easy chair by way of invitation.

He didn't think it was a matter of her wanting his company. There was something on her mind. He settled in the easy chair, waiting for her to tell him what that something was.

She was silent for a moment, and then she asked him quietly, "Tell me about Julie and you."

Why did she want to know? What did it matter?

At his hesitation, she added a quick, "Please, I'd like to understand. I mean, we are friends now. Or aren't we?"

Were they? Mitch wondered. He supposed that her confession in the office *had* changed their relationship. He just wasn't sure how to define that change. But he didn't tell Madeline that. Instead, he answered her with a careless, "Yeah, I guess we are."

Where did he begin? Even after all these months since her death, it wasn't easy for him to talk about Julie. He realized, however, it was time that he did.

Madeline tried to help him. "How did the two of you meet?"

"I was on a case, trying to locate a runaway teen for this couple in Carmel. I did a lot of that kind of work. Most PI's do. It usually involves questioning all the young drifters hanging out on the streets of big cities like San Francisco, because that's where these kids head for."

"Was Julie one of them?"

"Well, she wasn't a kid by then, but, yeah, she was

living a pretty rough existence when I stopped to talk to her on that street corner.''

"And you helped her," Madeline said. "She told me if Mickey hadn't gotten tough with her, she never would have turned her life around. That's true, isn't it?"

Mitch shook his head. "I don't know why I picked on her in particular. She was no more deserving than a lot of the other young people panhandling on the streets, or worse, just because somewhere along the way they'd had a rotten time of it. Except, there was something that drew me, made me want to rescue her.''

"Bet she didn't want to be rescued, huh?"

Mitch grinned over the memory. "We battled all the way. She had a smart mouth and was as hard as concrete. The only way to survive on the streets. Underneath was something else, though. Underneath, she was vulnerable and needy as hell. I suppose that's why I was attracted to her.''

"And fell in love with her," Madeline said softly.

"Eventually, yeah."

"Then when you lost her…"

"Bad," he admitted. "The worst. I blamed myself for not being there for her. I was in Los Angeles when Julie died, hunting for another runaway.''

"But it wouldn't have made any difference if you had been in San Francisco. You couldn't have prevented her death.''

Mitch shook his head. "Guilt doesn't work that way. Even when things happen that you know you wouldn't have been able to change, the guilt is still there.''

"Yes," she said, and he knew that she understood.

"I wasn't much good to myself or my clients after that. Remember the character in that old Alfred Hitchcock movie *Vertigo*? The guy who was haunted by all the places in San Francisco he'd shared with the woman he'd loved and lost, and how he kept looking for her in every face? That was me. Only, unlike in the movie, the woman I longed for really was dead and would never come back.''

Mitch paused, fingering the zipper on his coat. This was hard, harder than he'd thought it would be. Madeline silently waited for him to go on.

''I must have looked like hell,'' he continued, hearing the gruffness in his voice. ''Neil said he was shocked by the change in me when he came back to San Francisco to finalize the sale of his house. 'You can't go on like this,' he told me. 'You've got to get away from this town.' My family had already asked me to do just that, only I hadn't listened to them.''

''But you did listen to Neil,'' Madeline pointed out.

''Yeah, I did. I think it was because Neil had been through the same kind of thing when he lost his wife last spring, so I figured he knew what he was talking about. He told me about this farm for rent, just far enough outside Milwaukee that no one would bother me but still close enough that he could be there for me if I needed him. All I had to do was shut down my office until I was ready to come back to San Francisco and join him in Wisconsin. It sounded right—a place where I wouldn't be reminded of Julie every time I turned around. Somewhere where I could try to forget.''

''Until I came along,'' Madeline said.

There was a note of apology in her voice, and Mitch knew it didn't belong there. Not anymore. ''Sure, I resented you,'' he admitted, ''but if you hadn't come along, I'd still be at the farm wallowing in misery. You took me out of that, Madeline Raeburn.''

Why hadn't he understood this before? he wondered. Why hadn't he realized that her arrival and her subsequent need for his protection had saved him, forced him out of his isolation and brought him back to life?

''I can live with myself again because of you,'' he said.

He watched a faint blush of pleasure tint her cheeks, and it tugged at something deep inside him.

"And Julie?" she asked softly.

"I still miss her. I guess I always will, but the grief is no longer so overwhelming."

She nodded in acceptance, but there was a questioning look in her eyes, as though she might be wondering if he was still hurting. A moment later, unable to resist her exhaustion any longer, those eyes turned drowsy and drifted shut.

Mitch left his chair and went to the wardrobe. Inside, he found an extra blanket tucked on a shelf. He unfolded it, took it to the bed and covered Madeline's sleeping figure. She stirred only long enough to ease herself full length on the bed.

For several moments he stood there, watching over her. She had turned on her side, her full, sultry mouth slightly parted, thick lashes resting delicately against the side of the tiny crescent-shaped scar at the corner of her eye. Strands of red hair brushed one cheek. He fought a longing to reach out and smooth them back, and a more powerful longing to crawl in there beside her and hold her in his arms.

She was damn seductive like this, and he was a fool in danger of losing his self-control again. There was another desire he experienced as he stood there, a much safer, less complicated one. He wanted to do something that would make her happy, and never mind why he felt this sudden need. Maybe just because it seemed as though she hadn't known much happiness in her life, and she deserved to do so.

Glancing at his watch, he put that thought on hold. If he didn't get down to the store, he risked finding it closed. Besides, if he went on standing here savoring the alluring sight of Madeline on that bed... Yeah, she was definitely an invitation to a region of his anatomy he didn't trust. It would probably be much wiser if he cooled down, out in the winter air.

Making sure her door was locked and the security chain in place, he went out through the connecting door, which he also locked behind him along with his own room door. He didn't like leaving her alone, even though he knew it was necessary and that she would be safe.

He'd make his errand a fast one, Mitch promised himself as he exited the motel and headed down the hill. And maybe he could find something in the little store that would serve as a Christmas gift for Madeline.

THE EARLY DUSK OF WINTER had wrapped itself around Silver Dollar when Mitch returned to the motel, armed with two plastic bags of groceries of the variety that required neither a stove nor a refrigerator. None of it was exciting fare, but it would feed them adequately through the morning after Christmas.

His presence in the store had aroused no particular interest, for which Mitch was thankful. Silver Dollar was obviously used to visitors, even though this was the wrong season for them. Even so, he would be happy when they could leave this place. And until then, he planned for them to keep to themselves as much as possible.

Nowhere in either of the two bags was his intended gift for Madeline. The store had offered nothing that would qualify. But the motel had. It was waiting for him when he entered the office, where it wound itself around his ankles, mewing a plea for attention.

Mitch looked down at the scruffy kitten, recognizing an inspiration when he saw one and at the same time calling himself an absolute fool for even considering it. Less than an hour ago he had been damning Madeline Raeburn as a trouble he didn't deserve. Now, as much of a sentimental idiot as she was, he was prepared to take on this insane responsibility just because he knew how much it would please her.

He smiled wryly and spoke to the kitten. "It's not a done deal yet, so stop looking at me like it is. Wait right here, huh?"

The kitten was either smart enough to know this was an opportunity, or else it was in a mood to park itself under the bench, where it sank on its haunches. Mitch went on to his room, where he relieved himself of the groceries, unlocked the connecting door and checked on Madeline. She was still asleep on the bed.

The kitten was waiting patiently under the bench when he returned to the office. Stepping over to the desk, Mitch started to ding the bell that would summon one of the Schultzes from their apartment. He paused, hand hovering over the bell. There was a small Christmas tree on one end of the counter. It was one of those artificial tabletop varieties that came already decorated. All you had to do was plug it in, and you were in business. Actually, it wasn't much of a tree. Its plastic ornaments were pretty awful. But what the hell—if the Schultzes were willing, why not?

He smacked the bell, and Betty Schultz came bustling in from her apartment, smiling at Mitch enquiringly.

"Betty, how would you like to get rid of a kitten and rent a Christmas tree?"

She was delighted when he explained what he wanted, insisting that he take her spare litter box, enough litter and cat food to last until they could buy more when they were on the road again, and two plastic bowls for water and food. Mitch asked her to charge all the extras, including the use of the tree, to his bill, but he doubted she would. She was too thankful that the kitten was being adopted to think about profiting from the deal.

It took him three trips to haul everything down to their rooms. On the last one he fetched the kitten, cradling her in his arms as he carried her along the corridor. She seemed pleased about the arrangement, looking up at him with what he was convinced was a smug expression.

"You're gonna be trouble, aren't you."

She yawned with an attitude of feline superiority.

"Yeah, I can see you're gonna be trouble."

Traveling with a cat. That was a piece of insanity right there, never mind the potential problems with it once they got to where they were going. But, hey, if it made Madeline happy...

He found her still asleep when he slipped back through the connecting door into her room. Nor did she stir as he moved about quietly, making his preparations. The kitten, which had followed him, prowled around the room, investigating every corner. He filled one of the bowls with water and placed it on the floor for her before setting up the litter box in the bathroom. Food wasn't necessary at the moment, since Betty had indicated the kitten had already been fed.

Remembering the Christmas tree, he brought it from his own room, placed it on the table by the window and plugged it in. Not bad. The tiny glowing lights forgave the tree its worst features. His last task involved a red satin bow, which he plucked off the top of the tree.

Scooping up the kitten, he settled in the easy chair facing the bed. "Be cooperative now," he whispered to the animal, "or you're out of here."

She was a docile creature, and she permitted him to fasten the scarlet ribbon with its attached bow around her neck. When he was finished, the kitten licked his thumb with her small, sandpapery tongue.

"You're work," Mitch said gruffly. "Do you know that? And watch those claws." But she had already stolen a piece of his heart, and when he stroked her fur, she settled down peacefully in his lap.

Gazing at Madeline as he waited for her to waken, he was aware of how defenseless she looked, curled there on her side. He'd felt lonely, seeing the lights in several windows down the road on his way back from the store, missing Christmas with his family. Mitch no longer felt that way, knowing that the woman on the bed needed him. Or was it the other way around? Did he suddenly need her? It was a disturbing question, one he preferred not to answer.

The kitten, growing restless, jumped down from his lap. Before he could recover her, she sprang onto the bed, lowered herself onto her haunches inches from Madeline's nose and began to wash herself.

The kitten's purring must have penetrated Madeline's sleep. Her eyes opened, focusing slowly on the furry bundle close beside her. Mitch, who had started to rise from the chair, sat back and enjoyed the emotions that drifted across her face. Bewilderment was followed by disbelief, then a long, silent wonder.

Finally accepting the reality of the kitten, she sat up abruptly on the bed. She looked at Mitch and then at the tree on the table. Eyes wide and shining, she was like a little girl enchanted by the delights of Christmas morning. Anyway, that was what Mitch, grinning with pleasure as he watched her, chose to believe.

His joy lasted until her gaze cut back to him. This time he saw accusation in those dark eyes. Heard it when she blasted him with a fierce, "Oh, you fool! You silly, sentimental fool!" And then she burst into tears.

It was a very noisy, wild sort of weeping that had Mitch instantly on his feet. In two quick strides he was at the bed. Perching on its edge, he reached for her. She went into his arms without an argument, sobbing loudly against his shoulder.

"Hey, this isn't exactly the reaction I was counting on." She choked out something muffled that he was unable to understand. "What are you saying?"

Managing to gain control of herself, she pushed away from him with an angry, "Damn it, I never cry, and here

I am blubbering like some idiot! What have you gone and done to me?''

"Yes, that's what I thought you said. Merry Christmas to you, too."

Dabbing at her eyes with a corner of the blanket, she gazed at him in an awkward embarrassment.

"Sentimental slob, huh?" he said.

She smiled at him and shook her head. "Fool. That's what I said. A sweet, wonderful fool."

"That's better."

They sat there looking at each other. It was a tender, innocent moment. Or would have been, if she weren't so incredibly sexy with that lush mouth and sleep-tousled hair.

The kitten prevented him from taking Madeline into his arms again. She had stood there the whole time, blinking at them patiently. Now, demanding attention, she inserted herself between them. Madeline gathered her up and hugged her to her breasts, rocking her gently.

"What are you going to call her?" Mitch asked. "Betty assured me it is a female, by the way."

Madeline didn't hesitate. "Hannah. Her name is Hannah. Aren't you, sweetheart?" she crooned to the kitten.

"Where did that come from all out of nowhere?"

"It didn't. I've been saving it. Ever since I was a little girl I promised myself that if I ever had a dog or a cat, she would be Hannah."

"Why not? She looks like a Hannah. But now that you've opened your present, you'd better get rid of the ribbon before Hannah there strangles herself with it."

Madeline wanted the details—how he'd secured the kitten, the supplies for her and the tree. While he told her, she removed the ribbon and bow from around Hannah's neck. Her excitement this time was pure and effusive. Scrambling off the bed with Hannah in her arms, she went over to the table to admire the tree.

"It's a poor excuse for a Christmas tree," Mitch pologized.

"Don't say that. It's perfect." She swung away from the able in sudden realization. "But, oh, Mitch, I don't have thing for you."

"You can remedy that by fixing dinner. Or what has to ass for it, anyway," he said, indicating the sacks of roceries.

"Done. Just let me repair myself." She put the kitten own on the floor and headed for the bathroom. At the oor, she turned to him. "And, Mitch?"

"Yes?"

There was a sober expression on her face. "Over dinner ere's something I'd like to say. Something I haven't told ou yet."

Did he like the sound of that?

Chapter Nine

Madeline was suddenly shy with Mitch as they faced eac
other across the table with its offering of sandwiches, potat
chips and fruit. She couldn't imagine why. It wasn't be
cause she was nervous about what she intended to say t
him.

On the other hand, maybe there was a good explanatio
for this attack of timidity. Madeline could deal wit
brusqueness and male insolence—attitudes Mitchell Hawk
had exhibited frequently since she had walked uninvite
into his life. But to learn, as she had earlier, that this ma
was all mush under his tough exterior…well, that wa
something against which she had no defense. The troubl
was, it made him so impossibly, irresistibly sexy.

It didn't help that she was in love with him, which wa
a serious enough problem in itself. And to find that lov
deepened by her discovery that there was an essential co
of sensitivity carefully hidden inside him was a knowledg
that unsettled her.

Yes, she was shy with him. She had a right to be, whe
he sat there across from her with that lazy smile on his bol
mouth and those distinctive ears she longed to touch.

Needing to avoid the pair of potent blue eyes watchir
her, afraid she was about to blush under his scrutiny, Made
line looked away. She pretended to examine the litt

Christmas tree, which they had slid to one side. The red bow had been restored to its top.

Mitch had managed to secure a bottle of red wine from the grocery store. Lifting his plastic cup, he saluted Madeline. "Merry Christmas, Ms. Raeburn."

Madeline toasted him back with her own cup. "Merry Christmas, Mr. Hawke." She sipped from the cup, hoping the wine would relieve her infuriating shyness with him.

"So," Mitch said, lowering his cup, "what about it?"

He was asking her to tell him what she had so mysteriously referred to earlier. Except, there wasn't anything mysterious about it. She did regard it, however, as the last barrier between them that she intended to remove, for whatever it was worth. Finding her courage, Madeline leaned toward him earnestly.

"The relationship between Griff and me," she said. "The intimate side, I mean. I'd like you to hear the truth about that."

"No," he said quietly, "you don't have to tell me. I don't need to know."

"But *I* need you to know," she insisted. "It didn't matter all those months I was with Griff what others thought about us. As long as Adam wasn't affected, it wasn't important enough for me to care. But now…"

"Maddie—"

"No, let me finish. About intimacy between Griff and me…well, there wasn't any. None at all. I know what everyone assumed, and there was every reason for them to think it, but I never slept with him. Nor did he ever suggest that I go to bed with him."

Mitch looked at her as if he found this impossible to believe. "You telling me he was never interested in you in that way?"

"It's true. And although I was relieved, I used to wonder about it, until one of the other girls at the club told me she was pretty sure Griff was incapable of sex."

"Impotent?"

"I think so."

"So Matisse had you go everywhere with him becaus[e] he needed a great-looking woman on his arm to protect hi[s] image." Mitch nodded in understanding. "Yeah, the mas[-] culine ego had to be satisfied."

"I think it was even more than that. Griff has this passio[n] for rare and exotic things. He has all sorts of valuable co[l-] lections. And I guess on some level I'll never understan[d] I qualified." She shuddered. "But I was the one item i[n] his collection that got away, and he wouldn't forgive that."

"You were his trophy girlfriend?"

"Something like that."

"Well, why not. Hell, Maddie, don't you realize what [a] beautiful woman you are?"

She felt herself go warm, and knew by his grin that sh[e] was blushing, after all. The curse of a redhead. Mitch p[ut] his hand across the table and squeezed her fingers.

"Matisse is not going to get you back," he said, his lo[w] tone taking on a savage edge, "either for his collection [or] to eliminate you."

His touch made her breathless. There was more in it tha[n] just the promise of her safety. But before she could lear[n] what, he removed his hand and helped himself to one [of] the peanut butter and jelly sandwiches she'd arranged on [a] paper plate.

Mitch tucked into the sandwich with the enthusiasm [of] a man tackling a steak and a baked potato. Removing [a] baby carrot from a bag, she asked him what Christmas ha[d] been like with his family. He told her about holida[y] traditions he had known growing up in Chicago. How eac[h] Christmas Eve the angel, a little shabbier every year an[d] with this goofy smile painted on its face, had been place[d] faithfully by his father at the top of the tree. How h[is] brothers and sisters had squabbled over their presen[ts] Christmas morning. How aunts, uncles and grandparent[s] alking over one another, had joined them at a groaning dinner table.

There was nothing extraordinary about the Hawke celebrations, but Madeline relished hearing about them. The Hawkes were a big, loving family that gathered annually or the kind of holiday she had always yearned for.

And all the while, as Mitch talked and she listened, there was this thing humming between them. An awareness of each other that grew more intense with each passing moment. She felt it, and she knew by the way Mitch looked at her that he felt it, as well. It was both wonderful and frightening.

The spell was broken by the time they finished the meal with doughnuts and instant coffee from the small coffeemaker that the motel provided for each room. Both of them were silent. Madeline struggled with her uncertainty. She had been foolish enough to fall in love with a man who, until today, barely tolerated her. And now? Well, he desired her. That had been evident for some time. But could desire be enough for her, when he didn't return her love? When he was perhaps still in love with the woman he had lost?

Julie. That was why she had asked him about his Julie this afternoon. She had needed to know. But she didn't want to think of Julie now. She wanted to think only of Mitch and her and this humming thing between them. It was with them still, stronger than ever.

She couldn't be imagining it. Mitch wanted her as much as she wanted him—

"Dinner was great, better than turkey," he said cheerfully, shoving back from the table and getting to his feet. "See you in the morning."

She came to her own feet and stood there, bewildered, trying to hide her vast disappointment as he moved toward the connecting door to his room. Unable to bear his desertion, she was ready to turn away, when he hesitated by the door and looked back.

"Uh, maybe," he said, "I ought to look around your room before I say good-night. Check it out just to make sure everything is secure. After all, that is supposed to be my job. What do you think?"

She met his gaze. There was an unmistakable gleam in his eyes. They both knew there was nothing that needed to be checked. She could have smacked him for teasing her, except the sight of his lean, solid figure leaning casually against the side of the door was too mouthwatering to resist.

"I suppose," she said carelessly, "that would be a good idea."

"Right." Pushing away from the wall, he sauntered toward the window. The heat of his body deliberately brushing against hers, as he passed her on his way to ascertain that the window was locked and the drapes tightly closed, made Madeline light-headed.

Satisfied with the window, he moved to the hall door. "Let's make sure the chain is still in place," he said. "Yep, it's good." He looked around. "Everything seem okay to you in here?"

"I think so."

She played his game, pretending to survey the room. Hannah had been busy while Madeline had fixed the sandwiches earlier. The kitten had managed to snag one of the plastic Christmas balls off the tree, entertaining herself during dinner by batting it around the floor. The ball rested now in a corner. Exhausted by her activity, the kitten had appropriated the easy chair for herself and was stretched out on its cushion. She didn't bother opening her eyes as Mitch continued to move around the place, investigating the bathroom and the interior of the wardrobe. Madeline was waiting for him when he circled back to her.

"All clear?" she asked.

"Nothing could be more clear."

She knew he wasn't talking about the room.

"You know," he said, his voice so husky it made her

shiver with anticipation, "it wasn't necessary for you to tell me you weren't involved with Matisse. It wouldn't have made any difference to me, Madeline. Not anymore."

The uncertainties she had experienced moments ago suddenly didn't matter. Not when he looked at her like that, his eyes caressing her. Because whatever happened when they reached California, they had the magic of tonight. It belonged to them, and for now she was prepared to forget all the rest.

GRIFF MATISSE WAS ENTERTAINING. The Christmas Eve party for friends and business associates was taking place in his high-rise apartment on Russian Hill. The setting, with its finely appointed rooms, was even more sumptuous than his office suite at the Phoenix.

None of his elegantly attired guests was connected with his crime operations, at least not directly, which was why Griff was annoyed when a member of his house staff murmured into his ear that Angel was waiting for him in the library. He wasn't happy about Angel paying him a visit in his home—not when his present company preferred not to be reminded that certain profitable investments he had arranged on their behalf were less than savory.

Excusing himself, Griff left the party and went to the library. "This had better be important," he said, shutting the door behind him.

It was a thick door. He could no longer hear the music or the conversation of his guests. He and Angel were alone in the silence. Matisse knew when the skeletal Angel rose from the sofa and faced him, his eyes glowing his triumph, that it was important.

"We got her, Griff!" he reported in that deep, whispery voice.

"Where?" Matisse demanded.

"Utah. A little burg called Silver Dollar. She and this private-eye character are holed up there in some motel."

"You're sure that's where she is?"

"Came through from our usual reliable source less than an hour ago."

"What's to keep her from slipping away from us again?"

"They ain't going anywhere. Their car broke down, and it won't get fixed until the day after Christmas. They're sitting ducks, Griff."

Matisse crossed the room and stood by the tall windows. The view, overlooking the lights of the city and the darker mass of San Francisco Bay, was magnificent. He could see reflected in the glass the image of one of the three Christmas trees in the apartment. From its boughs was suspended a valuable collection of crystal and silver filigree ornaments. It made an impressive display against the glossy dark paneling of the library.

Griff was fiercely determined to preserve all that the tree behind him represented, the high-rent view, the apartment and all it contained. But because of one woman, Madeline Raeburn, he could lose everything. That must not happen. He knew there was a grim smile on his face when he swung away from the window.

"How soon can you get to her?"

"I looked into it," Angel said. "There's a flight out after midnight. Only, the closest airport is Salt Lake City, so that means a long drive from there in a rental car to this Silver Dollar. Probably sometime tomorrow morning."

Griff nodded. "I don't want you tackling this alone, not with this PI on the scene. Take one of the boys with you. And, Angel?"

"Yeah?"

"Don't lose her."

THE VITAL THING BETWEEN THEM was no longer humming beneath the surface. It was out in the open, pulsing so strongly it made Madeline tremble with longing.

Mitch's dark eyes locked onto hers. For a moment they stood there in absolute silence, their gazes communicating a raw desire. His eyes continued to hold hers as he peeled off his gun holster, slung it over a chair and moved toward her with a maddening slowness.

When he reached her, his gaze still unwavering, he stood so close she could feel the rush of his warm breath, smell his distinctive masculine aroma mingling with the shower soap he had used.

The pulsing had escalated into a wild throbbing. He had to be hearing it as she did, feel it raging through his blood. Then, why did he go on standing there like that, tormenting her with his restraint? Why didn't he reach out for her?

"It's always better if you wait for it," he said, his voice deep and raspy.

Had she voiced her frustration without even realizing it? Or could he already read her that well?

"How long?" she whispered.

Those midnight-blue eyes teased her. "We have all night."

"What if I decide, instead, to wait for Santa Claus?"

"He couldn't fill your stocking the way I can."

"You think?"

"I think."

He offered her proof in the shape of his mouth descending on hers. His big hands framing her face, he kissed her so deeply, so thoroughly that Madeline became drunk with all the sensations he lavished on her: the slight stubble of beard on his square jaw rubbing pleasantly against her chin, the clean taste of him in her mouth, his probing tongue tantalizing hers. There was a roaring inside her head when his mouth finally lifted.

"See?"

Her breathing was ragged, but she managed a response. "Are all the Hawke men as conceited as you are, or do you have a monopoly on it?"

"I prefer to think of it as a skill we offer. We instinctively know all the right spots to please. This, for instance." He placed the forefinger of one hand against the scar at the corner of her eye.

"I don't think that qualifies as an erogenous zone."

"Are you sure?"

He angled his head down toward hers again, the tip of his tongue demonstrating his boast by slowly tracing the shape of the scar. Madeline would have sworn the area was in no way sensitive. She was wrong.

"Bet there's a story connected with this scar."

She fought for self-control. "Uh, there is. I slugged a boy when I was nine for making fun of Adam."

"Looks like he slugged back."

"Wearing his father's ring. It was a heavy ring."

"That when you got interested in jewelry?"

"That's when I got interested in boys. Particularly their ears."

Madeline's hands came up on either side of his head and began to investigate his ears, satisfying a yearning she had had since the farm.

"What is it about my damn oversize ears that fascinates women?"

"Can you blame us? We have this irresistible urge to tug on them." She wasn't tugging the lobes, however. She was fondling them. *Definitely* fondling them. How could something so ordinary as a pair of ears feel so good to the touch? She didn't know, but his did.

"There're other places I'd be much happier for you to tug."

"Being?"

"Let me show you."

Swinging her up into his arms, he carried her to the bed, placed her across its width and stretched out beside her.

"Shouldn't we take off our shoes?"

"We'll get around to it. But right now…"

Reaching for her in a manner that was clearly proprietary, he drew her up tightly against his hard length. His lips were equally possessive when they trailed fire down her cheeks and across her throat, before settling on her mouth in another long, breath-robbing kiss.

Madeline didn't object to his aggressive tactics. In fact, she welcomed them. And when it came to permitting him access to her breasts, she even assisted. Willingly. Because, although he had no trouble lifting her sweater, dragging it over her head and throwing it away, his eager, impatient fingers were defeated by the clasp of her bra.

Taking pity on him after he muttered a curse of frustration, she insisted, "Here, let me."

She released the hooks, allowing the bra to fall away.

He groaned, his hot gaze exploring the swollen flesh that lay beneath the silky fabric. His hands seared it. And his mouth positively devoured it.

Madeline happily withstood the exquisite torture of his tongue branding the tender fullness of her breasts. But when his lips closed in turn around the hard buds of her nipples, drawing them deeply into his mouth, she spoke up.

"I am," she managed to gasp, "just a little confused here."

He lifted his head and grinned at her. "Are you complaining?"

"No," she assured him quickly. "No, absolutely not. But, um, wasn't it supposed to be the other way around? The tugging, I mean."

"Oh, right."

He hastily removed his shoes, her shoes and any other article of clothing that might come between them. Which, by Mitch's definition, meant stripping them until they were both naked.

Riveting. It was the only word Madeline could think of to describe his powerful body fully exposed now to her view.

Her admiration must have been evident, because he told her slowly and with a voice thick with emotion, "I like what I see in your eyes. And I like what mine are seeing. Oh, yes, I do."

She felt the heat rise in her as his gaze stroked the length of her. "About that tugging," she reminded him.

"Let's start here."

He took her hand and guided it to his rigid arousal. Madeline's fingers closed around his hardness. Within seconds, she brought him close to climaxing.

"Easy, sweetheart," he warned her hoarsely. "There's only so much tugging a man can take. And, anyway, there are other areas waiting to be satisfied."

"Where are they?"

"Happy to oblige."

And he did. His mouth and hands were all over her, plundering her lips, breasts, belly, thighs. And by the time his roving tongue reached that most vulnerable place of all, Madeline was on fire and aching for him. Mitch accommodated her.

They joined with an urgency that had no lingering trace of resistance. A wild, luscious business of whispered endearments, blinding rhythms, deep, intense joy. Madeline's love for him consumed her in an ultimate flare of pleasure that was followed by his own blazing release.

The aftermath, as he lay tightly beside her, the fingers of one hand stirring over her contented flesh, was mellow, peaceful. Or it was, anyway, until he suddenly stiffened and bellowed a loud "Damn!"

Madeline's eyes flew open. She lifted her head and discovered they were no longer alone on the bed. The kitten had awakened and joined them, landing squarely on Mitch's chest. Having been ignored long enough, Hannah demanded his exclusive attention by bumping her head against his chin.

"You little nuisance," he grumbled. "I knew you were going to be trouble."

Madeline smiled. "I think someone has decided to attach herself to you."

"Hey, stop that!"

The kitten, disappointed in the results of her first method, had switched to another. Her dainty pink tongue was licking the chin against which she'd been rubbing.

"Cut it out. That tickles."

But Madeline noticed that Mitch made no effort to remove Hannah from his chest. Nor did the kitten's applications with her tongue prevent the laughter that rumbled from deep inside his chest. That wonderful, rich laughter that made Madeline go all soft and weak was as endearing as the gentle way he stroked the cat.

These qualities had once surprised her, and she still had trouble associating them with the man, even though Madeline knew now the infinite tenderness of which Mitchell Hawke was capable. Oh, yes, after what had happened between them tonight, she knew very well.

"Whoa, not my whole face!"

"Don't scold her," Madeline said. "She can't help being in love."

No, Hannah couldn't help loving him. Nor could Madeline. It was a love that hurt, though, because, as he went on playing with the cat, there was something else Madeline understood. She and Mitch weren't going to talk about the magic they had shared just minutes ago. Nor was she going to hear any commitment from him.

She had told herself going in, that it would be this way, had even prepared herself for it. So she had no right to feel all hollow inside. But she did. Silly of her. Because how could you lose something you'd never had to begin with?

Chapter Ten

Mitch answered the tentative knock, drawing the door back cautiously on its chain. Betty Schultz stood there in the hallway. She was dressed to go out and bearing a plate of Christmas cookies.

"Good morning," she said brightly, "and merry Christmas."

Mitch returned the greeting and waited for her to explain her errand.

"I brought you these," she said, indicating the cookies. "It's kind of early, so I hope I didn't—"

"No, we're both up and have had breakfast." He had, in fact, already showered and shaved and had been dragging on a clean shirt when she knocked. "Hold on a second."

Closing the door long enough to remove the chain, he opened it again, thanking Betty for her thoughtfulness as she handed him the plastic-wrapped plate.

"Mickey and I are spending Christmas at our son's farm over in the next valley. I'm afraid you'll be alone here in the motel for most of the day."

"We'll manage," Mitch assured her.

She hesitated. He figured she maybe wanted to ask about the kitten, and he was prepared to tell her Hannah was doing fine. But she had something else on her mind.

"I just hate the thought of the two of you all on your own for Christmas, and it occurred to me…"

"Yes?" He hoped she wasn't about to invite them to her son's farm.

"Well, it's just possible that you could join your friends in Salt Lake City."

Mitch was immediately interested. "How is that?"

"Ben Crowder. He's always looking for a way to earn money, and if he's still on the outs with his daughter, he won't care how he spends Christmas. You might be able to hire him to drive you down to Salt Lake City and back. It would give you a few hours with your friends, enough to share Christmas dinner with them, anyway."

"How do I find this Ben Crowder?"

"He has a little place up in the ghost town. You can't miss it. It's the only building that isn't a shell. I'd offer to call him for you, but he doesn't have a phone. He does have a dependable car, though."

Mitch was at the window, gazing up the side of the mountain, several minutes later when Madeline emerged from the bathroom. He still had the plate of cookies in his hand.

"Did we have company?" she asked.

He set the plate on the table and earnestly explained Betty Schultz's visit.

Madeline nodded solemnly when he was finished. "Since these friends of ours are a fiction, I'm assuming that if we can get to Salt Lake City, your intention is to— what? Buy another car, rent one?"

"Whatever it takes to get us back on the road again. I don't like us sitting here in this motel, even if it's only for another day."

"What about the Schultzes? Do we just run out on them?"

"I'll leave an envelope behind the front desk with a note and enough money to cover our bill."

"And the station wagon?"

"It's expendable. Come on, Madeline, this is the smart thing to do."

He could see she wasn't happy with his plan. He watched her cast her gaze slowly around the room. He sensed she was thinking about last night's intimacy between them, her mind seeing this ordinary setting as something special, bearing a magic. Well, it was true. The lovemaking they had shared here had been fantastic, making him long to be inside her right now. But that memory also confused and worried him. In another day or so they would reach their destination, and soon after that, if everything worked out as he hoped, he would turn Madeline over to Gloria Rodriguez as promised. What then?

Mitch hadn't thought that far in advance, hadn't permitted himself to think about it. And he couldn't do so now, couldn't afford to do anything but concentrate on delivering Madeline safely to the people who were counting on him.

But he wasn't kidding himself. After last night, she was in his blood. Love? No, it wasn't anything like that. He couldn't allow it to be love. Not after Julie. Because, whatever the outcome of this journey, he wouldn't risk another loss like that. Not ever again, he promised himself. Love like that just had too much potential anguish attached to it.

"All right," Madeline said reluctantly.

"You'll be all right here on your own, won't you? I won't be long—just whatever time it takes to find this Ben Crowder."

"I'm going with you," she insisted. "Please, I can't take another hour of being cooped up here."

Mitch had wanted both of them to remain behind locked doors, to have as little contact as possible with other people. But he also didn't want to waste time on a long argument. Besides, it was probably better that he keep her with him.

THE AIR WAS PURE and bracing, with a few flakes drifting down from an overcast sky, as they set out for the ghost town. To Mitch's satisfaction, they were alone in the land-scape as they trudged up the snowy lane leading to their destination.

Silver Dollar seemed deserted, its few inhabitants either celebrating Christmas behind closed doors or, like the Schultzes, visiting families elsewhere. The only sign of life came from a small, white-framed church down along the highway. Recorded carols poured from a loudspeaker mounted in the belfry, the music floating out over the valley.

The ghost town, its sagging structures ranged along a natural terrace on the breast of the mountain, was not as distant as it had seemed. Probably a climb of less than two hundred yards from the motel below.

The weathered buildings might have appealed to Mitch on some other occasion. At the moment he was interested only in Ben Crowder's place, which he identified as being the only intact structure in the collection. It was the last house on the right, though it was more of a shanty than a house. They mounted the crumbling porch, and Mitch rapped on the door.

While they waited, hoping for an answer, an exuberant version of ''White Christmas'' issued from the loudspeaker below. Flurries came in little bursts from the higher elevations of the mountains, stopping, then starting again. The house was silent. Mitch knocked again, but no one came to the door.

''He can't be home,'' Madeline said. ''There's no car in sight.''

''Could be both Crowder and his car are out back. Wait here while I check.''

Mitch left Madeline on the porch and made his way around the corner of the house. He was disappointed when he reached the parking area off the rear of the building. There was no sign of a vehicle. The tire tracks, just visible in the snow, weren't fresh ones, indicating that Crowder must have left the scene some time ago.

They would not be hiring Ben Crowder to take them out of here. They were stranded in Silver Dollar.

Nothing to do but accept the situation, Mitch thought. He was turning away, when Madeline raced around the side of the house, joining him at the back. There was a sense of urgency in her haste. Realizing at once that something was wrong, his hand moved automatically to the pistol at his belt.

"What is it?" he demanded. He could see now that she was badly shaken.

"They're here!" she cried. "Two of Griff's men!"

He swore savagely before asking quickly, "Where?"

"Down on the highway! They were on foot, headed toward the motel!"

"You're sure? From this distance?"

"Mitch, even that far away I'd know them. One of them is a former wrestler called Lucky. A big hulking brute with a shaved head and a reputation for meanness. And the other one is Angel. I'd recognize *him* anywhere." She shivered at the mere mention of the deadly Angel.

"Did they spot you?"

"I tried to get out of sight as fast as I could, but, yes, I'm afraid they did."

"And with your red hair," he said grimly, "they'll be pretty certain you're the woman they want."

"Mitch, what are we going to do? They must be on their way up here."

On their way, and bound to be armed, he thought. A shootout? Forget it. With two of them out there, any confrontation like that would be suicide. And if he and Madeline tried to make a break for it down the open mountainside, they would be cut off.

Retreat, he decided. It was their only choice. But where? Farther up the mountain? Not possible. From this point it rose too precipitously for any easy climb. They would be picked off its face if they tried.

In the end, there was just one possible avenue of escape, and Mitch didn't hesitate. Yards away to their right was a low cyclone fence, and almost directly behind it was an elevated bed. There were parallel tracks on that bed. They rounded a bend before vanishing into a yawning cavity cut into a sheer spur of the mountain. Mitch knew he had to be looking at a corner of the railroad museum and that the major portion of its park must lie somewhere on the other side of that tunnel.

It had taken him less than a minute to make his decision, but these were precious seconds they couldn't afford. They had to move. But what about Madeline? She had sounded close to hysteria when she'd rushed to his side. Could she handle it? He faced her squarely. She was staring at him anxiously, waiting for his instructions, but her panic had ebbed.

"We're going over that fence. You ready?"

"Yes," she said, and he silently blessed her for not wasting time asking for an explanation, and for the courage she had summoned and was struggling to maintain.

Luck was on their side when they left the covering of the house and ran toward the fence. Another snow shower had descended from the peaks, concealing them in its curtain of white but also making it impossible for Mitch to know how close their enemies were.

"How could they have found us in Silver Dollar?" Madeline asked him breathlessly, as he boosted her over the barrier and scrambled after her.

He knew there was only one possible answer to that question, but it would have to wait. Right now, he had time for nothing but saving her, though he did feel relief that he hadn't left her behind in the motel, where she almost certainly would have been ambushed.

And by now, dead.

The realization left a tight feeling in his gut and renewed a fierce determination not to lose her.

HER NERVES STEADY NOW, her composure recovered, Madeline concentrated on their survival. That was all on the surface, of course. Underneath, she was sick with terror as Mitch helped her up the embankment, as they sprinted between the rails toward the hole in the mountain. She understood his destination now.

Flakes settled on their footprints behind them, but she didn't delude herself that it was enough to entirely cover their tracks. Sooner or later Griff's henchmen would discover and follow their trail.

Where were they now? she wondered. Searching the area around Ben Crowder's house or already at the cyclone fence? Already close behind them. She could almost hear the bark of a gun, feel a bullet stinging her flesh. And all the while the loudspeaker in the hollow below mocked them with a rousing rendition of "Jingle Bells."

"This is it," Mitch said.

Madeline had been so busy tormenting herself that she'd failed to realize they had reached the mouth of the tunnel. Giving her no chance to look back through the swirling snow, he caught her hand and fled with her inside.

They were less vulnerable in here. But the place was eerily silent. The only sound bouncing off the raw stone walls was the slap of their boots on the hard gravel bed.

She wondered if the railroad museum had constructed the tunnel. Or was the museum merely using what was Silver Dollar's long-abandoned silver mine? And what did it matter as long as this thing didn't dead-end somewhere inside the mountain, leaving them cornered?

An unwanted thought, and one that seemed horrifyingly possible when it was darker than twilight in the tunnel. So dim, in fact, after the glaring whiteness outside, that Madeline could scarcely see where they were going.

Her near blindness cost her, because when, to her relief,

they did finally approach the end of the tunnel, she stubbed her toe against one of the ties. The jolt was so unexpected that she stumbled, twisting her ankle under her as she went down. When Mitch, whose hand still grasped hers, started to pull her to her feet, she gasped in pain.

"You're hurt!"

"I turned my ankle. It's nothing. Help me up."

But when she was standing again, with the ankle bearing her weight, the throbbing became intense.

"You sure you can walk?"

"I'm fine," she lied. "Let's go on."

The ankle was of far less concern to her than their enemies. She turned her head and looked back through the tunnel. Still no sign of them.

They left the tunnel and the tracks themselves where they turned off to the left. Directly in front of them, and resembling a hangar, was an enormous metal shed wide-open on both ends. Madeline could see that the structure housed the museum's collection of historic trains.

"Through here," Mitch said, leading her into the lofty shed.

"Where are we going?"

"If I've got my bearings right, there should be an old depot somewhere straight down on the other side of this place."

"How do you know that?"

"There was a brochure in our rooms promoting the museum. It had a map indicating the location of the attractions. One of them was a restored depot housing the park's office."

"Which must be closed at this time of the year—so what good will the depot do us?"

"It won't, but the snowmobile parked at the side will. I hope."

She understood then what Mitch intended, as she recalled what he obviously had already remembered. When they'd checked into the motel yesterday, they had overheard the young man from the garage telling Mickey Schultz that he'd repaired the caretaker's snowmobile and left it at the side of the depot at the museum. If they could get their hands on that snowmobile, it would mean a swift escape.

But there was something else. "The key," she said. "He mentioned he left the key where Mickey asked, but he didn't say just where that was."

"Yeah, it's a problem, but if we can't find the key, maybe I can hot-wire the snowmobile. Let's go."

At this point distance was everything to Madeline. She could feel the ankle swelling inside her boot, and by the time they reached the other end of the shed she was limping noticeably. She could see the depot down below with the covered snowmobile under its eaves. It was still a long way off, however, and the pain of carrying her own weight had become unbearable.

Mitch was aware by now of her condition. "It's bad, isn't it."

"I'm sorry," she said, coming to a halt, "but I don't think I can make it."

There were steps that mounted to a raised wooden platform for viewing one of the trains. She leaned against its railing in an effort to ease the tender ankle. Mitch gazed at her, and she knew by the look on his face what he was thinking.

"Don't say it. You can't carry me. We could never move fast enough. We'd be targets out there in the open. Look, there must be someplace in here where I can hide while you get to that snowmobile."

The vast shed offered scores of possibilities, crammed as it was with passenger trains ranging from steam to diesel, ornate to streamlined.

"No good," he said. "Every coach is sure to be locked up tight."

"That one isn't."

She watched the surprise register on his face as he cast his gaze in the direction of the train she indicated on the next track. A sign identified the three cars as the private coaches of a wealthy nineteenth-century industrialist. A stool had been wedged in the back entrance of the rear car, to prop the door open.

"Hang on," Mitch said.

She continued to lean against the railing as he went to investigate the mystery of the gaping door. He was back at her side in a moment.

"Looks like they were doing some restoration work in there. You can still smell a slight odor of varnish."

Madeline understood. "And one of the workmen must have propped open the door to help the varnish dry."

"And neglected to come back afterward to close and lock it."

"Leaving me a place to hide."

Mitch shook his head. "I don't like it. The thought of leaving you on your own—"

"We don't have a choice. You know we don't. And we're wasting time."

Madeline waited tensely as he considered her plan. She wasn't so naive as to believe they had managed to lose Angel and Lucky. The two gunmen were somewhere out there, still hunting for them, and if they didn't hurry—

"All right," Mitch reluctantly agreed. "At this point it's probably safer for you here than out in the open. If nothing else, it's an opportunity for me to lure them away from you."

Offering his support, he helped her to the other train and up the steps to the platform. Shoving the stool out of the way, he held the door open for her.

"Lock it behind you if you can," he instructed her, as she slipped inside and turned to face him. "I guess I don't need to tell you what to do after that. Just promise me you'll stay safe until I come back for you.''

His gaze held hers for a moment that was taut with an emotion she was afraid to question, and then before she could tell him to be careful, he was gone. The door swung shut, closing her inside the car.

From one of the windows at the side, she was able to catch a glimpse of Mitch leaving the shed. He was bent over in a defensive crouch, his pistol in his hand as he sprinted in the direction of the depot. The snow had stopped again. There was nothing to conceal him.

When he disappeared over the brow of the slope, Madeline said a silent prayer for his safety and turned away from the glass to deal with the door. But its old mechanism wouldn't permit her to secure it from the inside. It would have to remain unlocked.

The ankle was worse. Easing around, she hopped carefully along the length of the shadowy coach, searching for a place to hide. It was a grand Victorian affair with plush seating, bronze chandeliers and thick carpeting. As Mitch had indicated, the faint odor of varnish that had been used on the dark paneling still lingered in the air, even though the work must have been done days ago when the weather was still mild enough.

Not satisfied with anything the parlor section of the car offered in the way of concealment, Madeline moved on to the next area, which contained an elaborate dining facility. In a corner, behind a stained-glass divider, was a reed organ. There was just enough space between the organ and the wall. Madeline squeezed in and lowered herself to the floor. It was a relief to rest the ankle at last.

Huddled there in the gloom, she tried not to mind the raw, bone-chilling cold in the car. Instead, she thought about Mitch and his single-minded determination to safeguard her. Either he was that conscientious about his promise to Neil, or else his desperation was more personal.

Could she be that important to him? She wanted to think so, longed for it in her love for him, but she would be foolish to convince herself it was true. Their intimacy last night might not have been as meaningful to him as it had been to her.

A depressing thought. She tried to distract herself.

Would it be necessary for Mitch to hot-wire the snow-mobile? Did he have enough skills to even attempt it? But if he couldn't locate that key, and with time a vital factor... Yes, that was the awful part. He was out there on his own, risking himself against the viciousness of a pair of gunmen who wouldn't hesitate to kill him.

Another unwanted thought. Better to keep her mind occupied with something more positive.

Like the music from the loudspeaker in the church. It was far away now, muted by both distance and the walls of the coach, but she swore she could still faintly hear it, even recognize the melody: "I'll Be Home for Christmas." Ironic under the circumstances, but the poignant song made her want to cry.

She listened for a minute, and then suddenly the music was overwhelmed by another sound. Not far away this time but out there in the shed. The loud, jarring noise of one metal door after another being rattled. Madeline stiffened in alarm. They were here! Trying the doors of the trains to learn whether any of them were unlocked, searching for Mitch and her.

Unnerved, Madeline listened to the racket that echoed hollowly in the immensity of the shed. At any moment she expected the enemy to reach her train, learn the door in the last car was unlocked. Then, just as suddenly as it had erupted, the clamor stopped. The long silence that followed was more unsettling than the banging had been.

Had they given up, gone away?

Madeline strained her ears, listening for any further treacherous sound. Was she imagining it, or had she caught the faint *click* of a latch? There. The unmistakable, cautious tread of footsteps. Someone was inside the coach, stalking whoever might be hidden here.

She curled herself into a tight ball and was absolutely still, praying she wouldn't be discovered down here in the thick shadows. That they wouldn't look behind the organ.

And then, to her horror, as she risked carefully peering around the edge of the instrument, she saw it. Out on the floor were traces of snow that her boots must have deposited along the length of the coach, leaving a trail that was certain to betray her.

Chapter Eleven

Before Madeline had a chance to act, either to try to brush the snow out of the aisle or to slip away to another place of concealment, he was there. The white deposits led him straight to the corner where she was huddled.

"Just like the bread crumbs in that fairy story, Maddie. Left a perfect trail. I can't figure out whether you were real careless or maybe just anxious to see me again. Guess it doesn't matter."

She had forgotten how chilling that low, breathless voice was. How gloating the smile on his thin, hollow face.

"Get up," he commanded. "We're going for a walk."

The wicked gun in his hand left her no choice. Using the organ as a support, she pulled herself to her feet. Angel backed away, leaving her space to move out into the aisle. He gestured with the gun, indicating she was to walk ahead of him in the direction of the rear entrance to the coach.

Pain stabbed through Madeline's ankle under the weight of her body. Her injury must have been apparent to Angel. He made a sound of sympathy behind her. There was nothing genuine in it.

"Hurt yourself, huh? Now, that's a real shame."

She remained silent, refusing to give him the satisfaction of complaining, though the long, slow walk to the door, down the steps and along the hard platform between the trains was difficult for her.

Where was Mitch? Madeline frantically wondered as Angel drove her ahead of him toward the front of the shed. What was happening with him? And where was Angel's brutal companion?

"Where are you taking me?" Madeline demanded hoarsely as she limped out into the open. She hoped they weren't going far. The ankle was agony.

"Someplace where you won't have to worry about that ankle anymore. That way," he snarled, directing her off to the left.

A joyful "Winter Wonderland" came very faintly from the distant loudspeaker as they crunched through the snow. Then there was another startling noise that sounded like the popping of a gun. They reached the brow of the hill. Below them, several hundred yards away, was the depot and a sight that made Madeline cry out in anguish.

Sprawled in the snow in front of the gaping door of the depot was the lifeless figure of Mitch. Lucky stood over him, gun in hand.

Angel chuckled softly. "Guess your friend already has nothing more to worry about."

Madeline was facing her own end, but it didn't matter now because her heart had already died inside her. Then, suddenly, the snow came down again in another furious flurry, obscuring the cruel scene below as though a curtain had dropped.

Angel, growing impatient, forced her to move on ahead of him. Madeline shuddered at the sound of another shot. That would be Lucky putting a last bullet into Mitch to make sure he was finished. The ankle was no longer excruciating. Like the rest of her, it had gone numb with grief.

She and Angel continued to bear left, and after a moment something huge and black loomed out of the snow. As they approached, she could see it was another ancient locomotive parked on a siding with its tender coupled behind it.

"Got something special here, all picked out for you, Maddie."

When they rounded the locomotive, a pair of structures appeared through the snowfall. Both structures were mounted on stiltlike frameworks above the tracks. The first of them supported a huge barrel-shaped vessel fashioned out of wooden staves. Madeline thought it must be an old-time water tank for filling the boilers of the early steam locomotives.

The second and lower structure, only a few feet from the first, had to be a coal hopper. Situated over the siding, its chute would have dropped coal directly into the tenders as they passed underneath.

Why had Angel brought her to this place? Why hadn't he killed her back in the train shed?

"Interesting thing about that water tower," he said, stopping her on the tracks. "There's a trapdoor on the roof of the tank. I spotted it from the top of the hill before I went looking for you in the shed. They must use it to get down in the tank for repairs and to make sure it's good and dry inside, come freezing weather. Door can probably be bolted from the outside, too."

He was clearly taunting her. Madeline refused to answer him.

"Turn around," he instructed.

When she hesitated, he pressed the muzzle of the gun against her ribs. She swung slowly until she was facing him.

"That's much better," he said. "I want you looking at me when I tell you what's going to happen to you. Remember the last time we met, Maddie? You ran out on me, left me trapped in that elevator. Maybe you forgot, but I didn't."

He thrust his bony face down into hers, his eyes burning,

his voice a fierce whisper. "That tank, see, is like an elevator stuck forever between floors. Just hanging up there in midair, all cramped and dark down inside. It's waiting for you, Maddie. You're going into that tank, and you're never leaving it. Go on, climb."

When she didn't move, he nudged her with the gun. What did it matter? she thought. Now that Mitch was gone, nothing mattered. But as she turned and hobbled toward the ladder fixed permanently to the side of the tower, she remembered Hannah. Who would be there to love Hannah when they didn't return to the motel? Would Betty Schultz find the kitten another home? And she remembered with an infinite sorrow the man who had given her the kitten. The man who had been so tough on the outside and so wonderfully sentimental inside.

"Keep moving," Angel urged her, waiting at the foot of the ladder as she drew herself slowly, rung by rung, toward the tank above her. "When you get up there, I'll follow. Make sure you're tucked inside, all snug and cozy."

The falling snow had thinned again. Only a few light flakes now. In her despair, she scarcely noticed them.

It wasn't until Madeline reached the level of the neighboring elevated hopper with its massive load of coal, so close to the water tower that she brushed against the long chain suspended from a lever on its side, that the reality of her situation struck her.

What was she doing? She was climbing into her own coffin without a fight. All right, she had to die, but she didn't have to go willingly.

"Why have you stopped?" he demanded when she halted on the ladder and looked down at him. "Get moving."

"No," she said, "I'm not going to help you. If you want me inside that tank, you're going to have to shoot me first and carry me up there yourself."

Ignoring his violent curses, she started to come down.

And that's when she saw it. The most marvelous sight in the world. Stealing around the side of the locomotive, pistol in hand, was the figure of Mitch!

She didn't cry out this time, but perhaps Angel caught the joy that must have registered on her face or sensed trouble. Gun raised, he whipped around. Both men fired simultaneously.

Mitch's bullet tore into Angel's shoulder while Angel's bullet struck the weapon in Mitch's hand with such force that the pistol seemed to leap out of his grip. It landed in the snow several yards away. Mitch was defenseless.

Ignoring his wounded shoulder and with a menacing smile on his face, Angel advanced slowly on his helpless target. He stopped a safe distance away from Mitch, but close enough this time not to miss him. Standing directly under the coal hopper, he pointed his gun at his victim's chest.

Mitch would not survive a second time.

No!

The word screamed in Madeline's head. She would not permit Angel to destroy him. Acting from instinct spawned from desperation, she launched herself from the ladder. Her whole body wrapped itself around the long chain attached to the lever. That lever, dragged at with sufficient force, would activate the mechanism that opened the hopper. That was what she hoped, anyway.

And she wasn't wrong. Her full weight on the chain was enough to release the door of the chute. Tons of coal exploded from the hopper, roaring down on the tracks. A cloud of black, choking dust billowed into the air, and when it cleared revealed a mountain of coal on the spot where Angel had stood. The gunman was no longer visible. The avalanche of coal had buried him.

For a stunned, giddy moment Madeline went on hanging there, clinging to the slowly swaying chain. Then hands, strong, welcome hands, were suddenly there and reaching for her, helping her to slither down, catching her as she descended.

On solid earth again, she collapsed weakly against Mitch's solid body. His arms went around her, holding her close. Nothing had ever felt so secure, so warm and comforting.

"It's all right now," he murmured. "It's finished, and thanks to you we're both safe. *That,* Madeline Raeburn, was one cool performance."

She shook her head. "It wasn't logic. It was pure rage."

"You okay?"

"Yes. How about your hand?"

"Bullet didn't hit me. But it struck the gun so hard I couldn't hang on to it."

She removed herself from his embrace and turned her head. The dust had settled on the silent mound of coal. "Mitch, we have to try to dig him out! We can't let him die under there like that!"

She would have rushed to the mound, started to claw at the coal, but he stopped her.

"Maddie, it's too late. Even if the bastard deserved to survive, it's too late. We could never get to him in time. If all that weight on top of him didn't kill him outright, he'll have suffocated by now."

Madeline accepted his explanation, though she shivered from both horror and remorse. "Whatever he was, I killed him. And to be responsible for a man's death—"

"Sweetheart, it wasn't murder. It was self-defense, the same as it was for me outside the depot."

"Lucky—"

"Wasn't so lucky in the end. Look, you need to sit down."

Gazing around, he spotted one of the park's benches nearby. He led her there, brushed the snow from the bench's surface and saw her settled before seating himself beside her.

"How's the ankle holding up?"

"Maybe it's not so bad now," she lied. "Just what did happen down there, Mitch? I thought you were dead."

"I nearly was. He sneaked up on me just after I broke into the place. There was a mail slot on the door, and I figured the key for the snowmobile might have been slipped into it and be lying on the floor inside. Turns out it wasn't, so I still don't know where the key is."

"Go on."

"There's this elaborate model train that takes up most of what used to be the old depot's waiting room. Lucky and I played hide-and-seek around the damn thing until I realized he was alone. That meant he was keeping me busy while Angel hunted for you. I was bolting for the open door to get back to you, when he fired at me."

Which explained the first shot she'd heard, Madeline thought.

"The bullet grazed me," Mitch went on, touching an area on the side of his head that thankfully showed no sign of injury. "It was enough to stun me. When my head cleared, I was lying out in the snow and Lucky was standing over me. He figured he'd hit me, that I was down and helpless. He was ready to put another bullet into me. Only, I still had my gun in my hand, and I used it before he could use his."

The second shot, Madeline thought. The one she'd heard after the sudden snow flurry had eclipsed the scene, making her assume the worst. Dear God, how mistaken she'd been and how thankful she was for being so wrong!

Mitch finished his story with a brief, "I was racing back to the train shed when I came across your tracks. Even with the new snow, they were still clear enough to lead me here."

"What happens now?" she asked.

"We get out of here and back to the motel."

"We'll need to phone the police, won't we?"

"Maddie, we can't go to the police about this. Not now. Not until after you're safe in California."

"But we can't just walk away from two bodies."

"We have to. All right, maybe we could explain what happened here this morning, manage to clear ourselves. But they'd send me back to Wisconsin, and that would leave you vulnerable again. Because taking out Angel and Lucky isn't going to stop Matisse. Once he realizes he's lost his two boys, he'll be more determined than ever to destroy you, and if Angel and Lucky knew where to find you…"

"That means someone is still passing information to Griff."

"Exactly, which is why we have to keep Angel and Lucky to ourselves and count the minutes until we can leave Silver Dollar—before Matisse sends someone else to hunt you down."

"But we can't keep two bodies a secret."

"Why not, when the park is shut down and Schultz won't be checking the place again until sometime tomorrow, if then? And by that time, I intend, one way or another, for us to be far away from Silver Dollar. Look, with one of them under a pile of coal and the other hidden in a snowbank—which is where I've got to bury Lucky," he said grimly, "they aren't going to be found."

"But when Mickey Schultz does check and discovers the break-in and that pile of coal, he's sure to call the police."

"Yeah, but until he gets around to removing the coal, he and the law are going to think what happened here was a case of vandalism, and they have no reason to connect that with the nice couple who stayed in his motel."

Madeline wasn't happy about his plan, but she recognized Mitch's tough wisdom and offered no argument.

"You going to be all right here for a few minutes?"

She had to be. "Yes."

"I won't be long."

He slipped away. While she waited on the bench, Madeline avoided looking in the direction of the mound of coal, tried not to think about what lay beneath it.

Mitch was back in short order to tell her he had dealt with Lucky and fastened the door to the depot. "I didn't have any luck with the snowmobile, but I've got this," he said, indicating the toboggan he had with him. "Found it leaning against the side of the depot," he explained. "Schultz probably uses it to move supplies around the park, and now I'm going to use it to get you back to the motel."

Madeline was grateful for his intention. The ankle would never have permitted her to reach the motel on foot. They returned to Silver Dollar by way of the back road that led to the front entrance of the museum. The route was longer but easier to manage.

They were silent as Mitch drew the toboggan behind him. She didn't press him into conversation, knowing he wanted to remain alert for any possible trouble. But they encountered no one who might challenge them.

They were in sight of the motel when Mitch dragged the toboggan into a grove of evergreens. "We'll leave the toboggan here," he said. "I don't want anyone catching us with it and mentioning to Schultz that they know what happened to his missing sled. Think you can limp the rest of the way?"

"I'll manage."

But the ankle continued to be a problem, aching with every step as they headed toward the motel. When she could no longer hide from him what she was suffering, he brought them to a halt.

"The hell with this," he said.

Before she could object, he scooped her up into his arms and carried her toward the entrance. She should have insisted she could make it on her own, that she was too heavy a burden.

But the truth was, Madeline was much too comfortable snuggled against his solid warmth to offer any resistance.

The situation they were dealing with did not warrant any sighs of contentment, nor a feeling that as long as Mitch's strong arms were around her she was secure. But that's exactly what she did experience, and relished every second.

The magic deepened with a renewed snowfall. Not a furious flurry this time, but a steady, gentle snowfall accompanied by the soft, sweet strains of "Silver Bells" from the church down the highway.

"This snow is good," Mitch said. "It'll cover all sign of our tracks."

He didn't speak again after that. They met no one either approaching the motel or in the office. The Schultzes would still be at their son's farm. Not until Mitch had her back inside her room and the door locked behind them did he release her. She regretted the loss of his closeness when he placed her on the bed. And the need to be practical.

"Maybe you should see a doctor," he said, gazing down at the ankle with a concerned frown after helping her remove her boot and sock.

"I don't think it's serious. All I need to do is keep it elevated and apply ice."

"Maybe, but if that swelling isn't down by tomorrow, we've got to find somebody to look at it."

Hannah was unhappy with them. The kitten, bored with her long solitude, wanted attention and sprang onto the bed. But Madeline was too distracted to play with her. The time had come to address a subject they had postponed out of necessity but which she knew had to be worrying both of them.

"Mitch."

"Yeah?"

"How did Angel and Lucky know we were in Silver Dollar?"

Mitch had known it would come to this. He could no longer avoid telling her. "Because I told Gloria Rodriguez where we are when I phoned her yesterday."

She stared at him. "Are you saying— What are you saying?"

He explained to Madeline just what he had shared with Gloria and why. He knew it was no use damning himself when, at the time, his decision had seemed a wise one. The best thing he could do now was to try to make up for his error in judgment.

Madeline was still staring at him, disbelief in her eyes. "It's hard to imagine. That the assistant district attorney would actually—"

"Don't say it," Mitch interrupted, "because there's no way Gloria is an informer for Matisse. She's as honest as Neil was. I would never have trusted her, otherwise."

Madeline looked bewildered. "Then, how did Griff learn where we are, if Gloria never revealed that knowledge to anyone and her phone is as absolutely safe as she swore to you it is?"

Mitch shook his head. "Our conversation must have been taped somehow, and that would require access to Gloria's office. I've seen those offices. They're secure. They have to be, with the sensitive material that's handled there. Which means it's someone inside, someone on the DA's staff who's connected with Matisse."

"What are you going to do?"

"Get you some ice for that ankle."

It wasn't all he was planning to do, but he would tell Madeline the rest when he got back with the ice. Taking the plastic bucket from the tray, he went down to the little room, off the office, containing the ice machine and several vending machines. There were extra plastic liners there for the buckets. Filling the bucket, he returned to the room with the ice and a supply of liners.

"I'm going out for a little while," he told her, handing her one of the liners he'd stuffed with chunks of ice.

She looked surprised that he would leave her after all that had happened.

"I have to," he explained, withdrawing a set of keys from the pocket of his coat. "I took these off Lucky before I put him under the snow."

"Car keys?"

"Probably from a rental. They must have left it somewhere close by. If I can find it, we'll have transportation out of here. We won't have to wait until tomorrow and hope for the best with the station wagon."

He didn't like the thought of leaving her on her own, even though the immediate danger was behind them. Didn't like exposing himself again to recognition, remote though that possibility was. But it was imperative that they get away from Silver Dollar as soon as possible.

Insisting she keep his pistol with her and making sure both of their doors were locked behind him, Mitch left her occupied with her ankle. The snow was falling gently in fat white flakes as he left the motel.

He remembered that Madeline had seen Angel and Lucky on foot when she'd first spotted them from the ghost town. So, where was their car? Somewhere within easy walking distance but tucked out of sight. They wouldn't have wanted to risk being observed arriving in a vehicle, choosing instead to sneak up silently on the motel.

That seemed the obvious explanation, but Mitch couldn't find the car. He trudged up and down the highway in both directions, looking for some sign of it without result. In the end, wet and discouraged, he abandoned the search, fearing someone would notice his presence and decide his behavior was suspicious.

"No luck," he reported to Madeline when he returned to their rooms.

This had to be the worst Christmas Day any two people could experience, Mitch thought. And the longest. He spent a portion of it prowling around the room, until Madeline, exasperated, told him that if he was going to pace endlessly like that, would he please do it in his own room.

He couldn't help it. He was restless with worry. Worried about Madeline's raw and tender ankle, though her repeated applications of ice did seem to be easing the swelling. Worried that the station wagon wouldn't be repaired tomorrow—and what would they do, then? Worried, too, about the mole supplying Griff Matisse with information.

It was this last concern that frustrated him the most. Taking up a vigilant post at the window, where he absently ate one of the sandwiches he had fixed for them, Mitch concentrated. He was still missing something here, something that continued to escape him. He couldn't shake his earlier feeling that it was connected somehow with one of those three cops who had been Neil's friends: Morrie Swanson, Dave Ennis, Hank Rosinski. Whatever was missing, his mind refused to grasp it.

It was after dark when Mitch went down to the office again for more ice. The Schultzes were back. He could hear a TV behind the door to their apartment. He had filled the bucket in the little room off the office and was eyeing the soda machine, wondering if Madeline would appreciate a fresh drink, when Betty came out to the desk to greet someone who had come through the front door.

"Saw your lights when you drove up. What can I do for you, Deputy?"

Immediately alert, Mitch hugged the wall at the side of the ice machine. His position afforded him no view of Betty or the cop, which meant they didn't know he was in here. He planned to keep it that way.

"Got a little problem, Betty," the deputy explained. "There's this car Earl Stokey reported parked behind his shed. He doesn't know who it belongs to or how it got there."

Mitch, listening to the exchange, knew he had to be referring to the car that had brought Angel and Lucky to Silver Dollar.

"Checked the registration," the deputy continued. "It

turns out to be a rental from an agency down in Salt Lake City. You got any guests who might be responsible for this vehicle?''

"We're empty except for one couple," Betty told him, "and their car is down at the garage waiting for repairs, so it can't be theirs."

Mitch tensed. Would the deputy question her about that couple? If the sheriff in Wyoming *had* ended up identifying Mitch and issuing an APB… To his relief, the deputy didn't pursue it.

"Well, we'll follow up with the rental agency. Chances are, it's not abandoned and someone is just visiting in the neighborhood and with this snow didn't realize where he was leaving it."

"Is it still coming down?"

"No, it's stopped and the plows are out, so the highway is clear."

"It made a pretty Christmas Day, though."

"Not for me. I've been on duty for most of it."

Betty made sympathetic noises. "I bet your girlfriend didn't appreciate that. Is she still working at the courthouse over in Fraser?"

"Still there."

Seconds later the deputy departed, and Mitch heard the apartment door closing behind Betty as she went back to her TV. Mitch was alone again in the office area. And his brain was on fire with what Betty Schultz's casual question had triggered in his memory. He knew now what had been eluding him.

MITCH, CIRCLING RESTLESSLY AGAIN, explained it to Madeline back in her room. "Carol," he said, his excitement mounting. "Her name is Carol. I don't think I ever heard a last name. It doesn't matter. Gloria will know."

"Slow down and tell me again. This Carol is *who?*"

"Hank Rosinski's girlfriend. One of Neil's friends on the

force in San Francisco. I heard Neil asking him about her once when we were all together. Something about Hank's going over to see her in the Bryant Building where she worked, and one of the other guys joking about how hot she was for him. The Bryant Building houses the DA's office."

"And that's all? On just that little, you're saying Hank Rosinski is the traitor in the ranks and that his girlfriend is feeding him information he passes on to Griff?"

"My instincts have been telling me ever since Neil's death that he would never have let anyone get that close to him but a friend he knew and trusted. Like one of his three buddies from the San Francisco force. Both Morrie Swanson and Dave Ennis seem to be unlikely candidates, especially Ennis. Dave once took a bullet for Neil when he was shielding him on the job, and he was like a brother to Neil when he lost his wife. All right, so I can't entirely rule him out, Swanson, either, though the last I heard he was on sick leave and in no state to hurt anyone. That leaves Hank Rosinski, and maybe the evidence isn't enough, but it fits. It's strong enough, anyway, to get Gloria onto it."

"Mitch, this is Christmas night."

"Christmas or not, I've got to try reaching her at home. I can't call her at her office anymore, that's for sure."

Gloria's home phone would be safe, he thought. He remembered her once having mentioned that her husband was there all the time, working out of his home office. That meant Matisse's informer would have had no access to her house, or any reason to record calls there, anyway. The problem was, Mitch didn't know Gloria's home number. He could only hope it wasn't unlisted.

Settling in a chair beside Madeline's bedside table, he reached for the phone. Berkeley, he thought as he dialed Directory Assistance. Yeah, he was sure Gloria lived in Berkeley. But Directory Assistance had no number for a Gloria Rodriguez in Berkeley.

Her husband? Mitch wondered. Was the number listed under her husband's name? What was his name? Julio. Yeah, Julio sounded right.

This time Directory Assistance was able to provide him with a number. He dialed and waited through three rings. A man answered. Mitch gave him his name. He could hear the laughter of kids in the background. Seconds later a door closed, shutting out their sounds, and the phone was picked up.

"Mitch, what is it?"

Good. For a change, Gloria wasn't chewing him out. She had realized he wouldn't call her at home on Christmas night unless it was urgent.

"Something you're not going to like," he said. "You alone?"

"Yes, in the study with the door closed. Go on."

She listened, obviously horrified, as he described all that had happened at the railroad museum.

"Mother of God, how did they find you? How *could* they find you?"

"We told them, Gloria, you and I, that's how. You got a Carol Somebody working in your offices?"

"Carol Donatti. Yes, she's one of my two assistants."

"Well, I think your Ms. Donatti is recording calls off your private line, my call in particular, and that if you get a team in there to search, they're going to find a concealed device she managed to plant."

"I don't believe it! Carol is one of our most trusted people!"

"You'd better start believing it, because if I'm right, she's the pipeline to Matisse through her boyfriend, Hank Rosinski. Whoever killed Neil was someone he knew and trusted and I think that someone was Rosinski and that an investigation will prove it. He's working for Matisse, Gloria. It has to be the explanation."

Gloria was silent for a few seconds, digesting his information. "All right," she promised him, "I'll handle it. But you have to understand, Mitch, that this is a sensitive matter needing a cautious investigation. The DA's office can hardly accuse one of its own people of collaboration with a murder suspect without evidence."

"Get it!"

"And what will you be doing?"

"Getting your witness away from here, one way or another, the first thing tomorrow—before Matisse learns his two gunmen failed him."

"I don't have any argument with that one, but I want you to call me again when you're back on the road. Maybe I'll have news for you by then. In any case, I need to be kept informed."

"Oh, I like that. Me calling you again on that *secure* phone of yours."

"Yes, I get your point. My personal cell phone, then. I'll keep it with me at all times, and whenever you call I'll make sure we don't talk until I move to a safe area." She gave him the number, and Mitch jotted it down. "There's one more thing," she said.

"Being?"

"You walked away from a pair of dead bodies."

"Not good, huh?"

"I would say not."

"Well, hell, I'm a wanted man, anyway. What's two more? Look, I'll deal with it when all this is over with."

"Mitch—"

"Later, Gloria."

He rang off before she could remind him that, as the assistant district attorney, she had no business condoning the actions of a fugitive, much less aiding them.

Madeline was waiting to hear about Gloria's end of the conversation. He told her, and she nodded in silence, accepting their decisions. He went on gazing at her, propped against the headboard of the bed, her hair all tumbled, her face without makeup, her pant leg hiked up and revealing her red, swollen ankle.

She had never looked more tempting to him. He wanted her, wanted her just as much as he'd wanted her last night.

And he did nothing about it.

To MITCH'S RELIEF, the station wagon was delivered to them late the next morning. He paid the bill on both it and the motel, loaded their gear in the back, saw Madeline settled in the passenger seat with the kitten in her lap and headed down the highway.

Things were looking up again, he thought with satisfaction. They were putting distance between them and a place that had proved to be dangerous for them. The car was performing smoothly, and even Maddie's ankle was on the mend, the swelling almost gone. Yeah, they were going to be all right.

And then he glanced at Madeline beside him and wondered who he was kidding. She sat there quietly entertaining Hannah, slowly tickling the ecstatic kitten beneath its furry chin. It had cost him a massive dose of self-control, but he had kept his distance from her all of yesterday afternoon and last night. She had said nothing to him about it either then or this morning, but Mitch knew she had to be puzzled and hurt that he had avoided any intimacy with her, had elected to sleep in his own room.

He'd told himself that after what happened at the railroad museum, he couldn't afford to be involved with her like that again, that he'd almost lost her because his eternal longing for her had weakened his alertness. That only by concentrating exclusively on getting them out of this mess, with no more distractions, could he keep her safe.

It was all true, but Mitch knew there was another reason for his resistance. One that was far more complicated. He feared that if he touched her again, he would never be able to let her go. And in the end he knew he would have to do just that. They hadn't discussed the future, and he wondered if she even realized there was every likelihood that once Madeline testified, she would be urged to enter the witness protection program.

He wouldn't see her again. They would part, their lives taking separate directions. He would have to accept that, but his emotions were in a turmoil over the prospect. The truth was, he wasn't sure what he really felt about Madeline. He just knew he was confused, unhappy and struggling with a self-denial that was a constant ache.

MITCH WAITED until they were far away from Silver Dollar and approaching the border into Nevada before he called Gloria Rodriguez from a rest-stop pay phone. She answered immediately.

He identified himself with a cautious, "Can we talk?"

"Hold on a few seconds—"

There was a pause, and he imagined her moving off to an area where there was no risk of their being overheard.

"Okay, I'm back, and you were right. Your calls to me were being taped. Carol has been removed from the scene, but she isn't talking yet. Her lawyer refuses to let her answer our questions, but with enough pressure..."

"What about her boyfriend, Hank Rosinski?"

"We have two witnesses who report that over the past several weeks he was seen at night entering and leaving the back door of the Phoenix."

"What does he have to say for himself?"

"Nothing, because he isn't here. He's on vacation in L.A."

A working vacation for Matisse, Mitch thought. One that had taken the bastard to Neil in Milwaukee. And now he was using L.A. as a cover.

"Two officers are on the way to take him into custody," Gloria continued. "He's being returned for questioning."

"Good, but not good enough."

"I don't like the sound of that. What is it now?"

"I'm not bringing Madeline to San Francisco."

"What!"

"There's someplace else I'm taking her, and we're going to hide out there until you can assure me Hank Rosinski has been apprehended, that Matisse and his people no longer stand a chance of getting anywhere near her, and that the situation is absolutely secure from all angles."

"Mitch, I don't like this."

"What's new. You haven't liked anything I've been doing since Milwaukee, but if I hadn't done it, Madeline Raeburn would be dead by now. It's not negotiable, Gloria."

He promised he would contact her again when they got to where they were going, and rang off. There was another call he needed to make. He had to phone the rental agency in that little mountain town in northern California to reserve the cabin, which in this season shouldn't be a problem. But before he did that…

Leaving the phone, he walked toward the parked station wagon where Madeline was waiting for him. It was time he let her know about that cabin. He was afraid she wasn't going to be very happy with him.

Joining her in the car, he filled her in on his conversation with Gloria. Then he told her about the isolated cabin and his intention for them to wait there. The explosion he feared didn't occur. She was silent for a moment before she responded with a quiet, perceptive, "This isn't something you just now thought of, is it."

"No," he admitted.

"You've been planning it since—when? From the start?"

"Something like that."

"Why didn't you tell me? Why didn't you trust me to know?"

"Maybe because I thought you'd be angry, reject the whole idea."

"What makes you think I'm not angry now?"

"Are you?"

"No, but is it really necessary for us to go there?"

"Maddie, you know it is. Until Matisse is no longer a danger, we've got to put you somewhere where neither he nor his people can find you."

"Yes, I understand." She was thoughtful again. "How do you know about this cabin?"

"I stayed in it once before."

She gazed at him in another silence that made him uncomfortable, made him wish he had never suggested the cabin.

"You went there with Julie, didn't you. That's why you didn't want to tell me."

"Look," he assured her, "it's going to be all right."

"Is it, Mitch?" she said sadly. "Or are the memories going to be too much for you? Are you going to hate me again because it will be me in that cabin with you and not Julie?"

Chapter Twelve

Something had gone wrong.

Angel had promised he would phone from Utah when the job was done. That call should have come to Griff no later than Christmas night. This was late afternoon on the day after Christmas, and there had been nothing but silence from that direction.

Sitting at his desk in his office at the Phoenix, Griff considered acceptable explanations for Angel's failure to contact him. But there was no satisfying explanation. He was convinced something had gone wrong, *seriously* wrong. He had an uneasy feeling he knew what that something was, but he needed to be certain.

There was only one way to find out, Griff thought, eyeing the phone in front of him. He and his informant were careful about their association, limiting their contacts to essential matters. It would have been dangerous to do otherwise. But this was essential. He had waited long enough.

Reaching decisively for the phone, Griff dialed a private number, which was answered immediately. After he explained what he wanted, there was reluctance in the voice on the other end. Griff was prepared for that.

"Do I have to remind you all over again," he said coldly, "exactly what you owe me?" There was a murmured answer. "All right, that's better. It shouldn't be too difficult for you to find out what happened to them, not with your connections.''

Ending the call, Griff rose from his desk and moved restlessly around the room. He stopped by the fish tank, but this time the exotic tropical collection, with all its brilliant flashes of color, didn't soothe him. His handsome face was tight with rage and a ruthless self-promise.

It would make no difference if Angel and Lucky were dead. One way or another Griff was going to destroy Madeline Raeburn, even if it meant ending her life with his own two hands. It would, in fact, give him considerable pleasure to do just that.

IT WAS THE AFTERNOON of the next day when Mitch and Madeline arrived in the old logging town of Ardmore, tucked between the mountains in northern California. The small, quiet community was near enough to the coast that its climate, even in winter, was a mild one. Snow was rare, but the rain and mist that made the lush evergreen forests possible were frequent.

This was exactly the kind of dismal weather they met, with a thin drizzle falling, when they stopped at the rental agency to collect the keys to the cabin. There was no telephone up at the cabin, so after they came away from the agency they found another public phone outside a service station.

Reaching Gloria on her cell phone, and making sure she was in a safe area, Mitch asked a blunt, ''Results?''

''Carol still isn't talking,'' the assistant DA reported, ''but Hank Rosinski was apprehended in L.A. and is on his way back here for questioning. Somehow we'll prove that Matisse was getting fed everything he needed to know, probably from the start when Madeline turned herself over to Neil Stanek in Milwaukee.''

Mitch was satisfied with her information, but he was not

going to take any chances. "Okay, but I'm still not bringing Madeline to you until—"

"Mitch, listen to me. There's been a new development. The FBI has come in on the case."

"The feds? What's their angle?"

"I'm not sure. You know how reluctant they are to share their intentions."

"Come on, Gloria, you can do better than that. This is about the witness protection program, isn't it?"

"I think so."

Mitch wasn't surprised. Hadn't he expected this? Though not so soon. The realization that it must already be in the planning stage left him with an anxious feeling in his gut. A sense of loss.

Gloria went on. "Two of their agents are asking to meet with Madeline right away. Mitch, she needs to see them. What they have to say is vital to her welfare."

He could appreciate that. A meeting that would offer Madeline a guarantee of her future safety was not only important but essential. And with Gloria's assistant removed from the scene and her boyfriend in custody, there was no reason not to agree to such a meeting. Except he wasn't forgetting what had happened in Utah. He was not going to risk walking into any more traps.

Gloria read his reluctance. "Mitch, you don't have a choice. The DA is demanding that you cooperate with them. And if you don't comply and let these two agents speak to her, the FBI is going to treat your refusal as a kidnapping, and if that happens…"

"Yeah, I get it. There'll be no place we can hide." He would have to agree to this meeting, but he intended it to be on his own turf and on his own terms.

"Ardmore," he instructed Gloria. "It's a little town north of San Francisco. Make sure they understand that's not even close to where we'll be holed up, just where we'll meet them.'' The cabin itself was several safe miles away from Ardmore, a location he wasn't going to reveal.

''Where in Ardmore?''

Across the street from where he stood was a small restaurant. The sign out front identified it as the Redwood Café. ''There's a café called the Redwood,'' he said. ''It's on the main street. Tell them to be there tomorrow morning. Ten o'clock.''

''Good.''

''Not good. How will I know these guys are the genuine article?''

''Mitch, they will have identification.''

''Anyone can get their hands on identification, including Matisse and his crowd.''

Gloria thought about it for a moment. ''Suppose we get Dave Ennis to accompany them,'' she suggested. ''He's an officer you're familiar with, and he can vouch for the two agents.''

Ennis was an officer with the best of records, and now that Mitch knew Hank Rosinski was the traitor in the ranks... Yes, Ennis would be all right. ''Tomorrow, then. And, Gloria?''

''Yes?''

''You tell them Madeline is not going anywhere near that café until I go in first and check them out.''

''Understood.''

Ending the call, he joined Madeline in the car where he told her about the two FBI agents. ''What do you suppose they want?'' she asked him.

To put her in the witness protection program, Mitch knew, but he didn't want to worry her over this until it was a certainty. ''Maybe just to question you.''

She didn't pursue the matter, though he wondered if she had already guessed what the two agents intended to propose. They filled the wagon with gas, found a supermarket where they bought groceries and headed out of town on a deserted back road that took them up into the Coast Range.

The route had once been a logging trail and was still narrow and unpaved, but it wound through majestic forests of Douglas fir and tall redwoods, offering spectacular glimpses of the mountains on its sharp turns. They met no other car.

Ardmore was several miles behind them when they left the road, taking a private lane that led them at last to the cabin. Nothing could have been more secluded, or more inviting. The small log structure was nestled in a grove of fragrant pines and boasted a stone fireplace and modern conveniences.

After climbing the porch, unlocking the door and releasing Hannah inside, Madeline helped Mitch to carry their things in from the car. When they returned, they found the kitten investigating the interior of the cabin. It was a simple arrangement, a long room across the front with a kitchen at one end and a sitting area at the other. Behind this were two tiny bedrooms with a bathroom between them.

From the moment of their arrival, Mitch had felt Madeline watching him in silent concern. It wasn't until he got to his feet after lighting a fire on the stone hearth that he offered her the reassurance he knew she'd been waiting and hoping to hear.

"It's okay, Maddie," he said softly. "Julie's ghost isn't here with us. Turns out that whatever memories I've got of this place are peaceful ones."

She nodded without comment, but he wasn't sure she believed him.

The gray light at the windows faded into dusk. While the early night of December wrapped itself around the cabin, they made dinner in the tiny kitchen. Mitch, preparing the steaks they had bought in town, eyed Madeline chopping vegetables for their salad. Her mouth was as silently busy as her hands as she concentrated on her task. That habit was as endearing to him now as it was familiar.

He continued to enjoy the sight of her across the table from him as they ate their dinner, the rain pattering softly on the roof. And afterward, seated beside her on the sofa in front of the snapping log fire, his eyes, with a will of their own, refused to look away from her.

Madeline was playing with Hannah, tossing balls of paper for the kitten to pounce on, and she had never looked more alluring than with her red hair gleaming in the firelight, her amber eyes smiling down at the kitten. Mitch knew he could no longer deny his desire for her. He wanted her, hadn't stopped wanting her since Silver Dollar, and all of his wise arguments weren't enough to matter. Not now, not tonight.

"You know, don't you," he said hoarsely, "that this could be our last night alone together? I may have no choice tomorrow. Turning you over to them, I mean."

She stopped playing with the cat and gazed at him. Her eyes were solemn now. There was a moment of silence, no other sound in the snug cabin but the crackling of the fire.

"Yes," she finally murmured, "I've been thinking that, too. How we don't know what tomorrow is going to bring, how we have just tonight."

It was the invitation Mitch had been praying for all evening. He reached for her, and suddenly she was in his arms. His mouth devoured hers in a long kiss that was sometimes slow and sweet, sometimes hot and fierce.

When his mouth finally lifted from hers, he whispered, "Do you have any idea how beautiful you are, Madeline Raeburn? Not just here." His hand touched her face, then trailed down to touch the area of her heart. "But here, too, inside."

"You didn't always think so," she reminded him.

"Because I was a fool."

"And now?"

"I'm no longer blind."

He began to kiss her again. The fire went on burning while they made their own glow there on the sofa. Strained against each other, clothes shed, their bodies joined in a feverish lovemaking that abandoned all caution.

IT WAS IN A DIFFERENT MOOD, a decidedly sober one, that they readied themselves for their return to Ardmore the next morning. Their conversation was meager. They didn't discuss the joyous rapture they had shared last night. Madeline was conscious of a certain constraint between them as they finished a quick breakfast, made sure Hannah was supplied with food and water, and left the cabin.

It had stopped raining, but the sky remained overcast, the trees wet and dripping. The weather reflected Madeline's own state of cheerlessness. They were silent on the drive down the mountain, each occupied with private thoughts.

As they neared town, Madeline was no longer able to restrain herself from asking the question that had been nagging at her since Utah and which, until now, she hadn't found the courage to frame. Probably because she feared the answer.

"It's coming to an end, isn't it, Mitch. If these FBI agents tell us what I think they will, we could be on our way to San Francisco this afternoon. What are you going to do when it's all over and done with? Do you know?"

He hesitated only briefly before telling her, which meant he had already made his plans.

"I'll have to go back to Wisconsin, settle everything around Neil's death and see about the farm. Clear up things in Utah, too, before I can get on with my life."

No mention of any *we*, she noticed. She was not included in his plans. "Do you intend to reopen your agency?"

"Probably."

He kept his gaze on the road. He didn't look at her.

Madeline didn't pursue the subject. When they reached the edge of Ardmore moments later, Mitch armed her with instructions.

"As unlikely as the possibility is, we're going to be careful not to walk into any trap. I'll leave you in a safe spot while I check out these agents. When I'm sure they're who they're supposed to be, I'll come back for you."

Madeline was too depressed by then to argue with him. They approached the rendezvous from a back route. Mitch pulled behind the service station across the street from the Redwood Café. There were rest rooms here with outside entrances not visible from the café.

"Lock yourself in the ladies' and don't come out until I tell you it's okay."

His perpetual caution was beginning to seem excessive to her, Madeline thought with annoyance. It wasn't until she was inside the rest room, with the door locked behind her and gazing at herself in a badly spotted mirror above the sink, that she realized what her irritation was all about.

She wasn't angry over Mitch's caution. She was angry with his intention to return alone to Wisconsin. He hadn't discussed it with her, hadn't considered her feelings in the matter. Once she was safe, he meant to turn his back on her and walk away. Just like that. Out of her life, with no emotional attachment to restrain him, no regrets. Finished.

And then, as suddenly as it had flamed, her anger died with the realization that, of course, he must leave her. What else could he do? Because whatever had been between them, however potent it had been, it wasn't enough. Not when he was still in love with Julie. She understood that now. Julie was gone, but Mitch was still in love with her.

Placing her hands on the edges of the sink, needing its support, Madeline stared at her reflection in the clouded mirror. She was still looking at the image of that unhappy woman when Mitch rapped on the door.

"You can come out," he called.

Squaring her shoulders, resolving not to let him see her misery, she turned away from the mirror, unlocked the door and joined him outside.

"They're legitimate," he reported.

They crossed the street, entered the almost deserted café and walked to the back of the room where the three men waited for them at a corner table. The trio got to their feet when Mitch and Madeline arrived. Brief introductions were performed.

Madeline had already met Dave Ennis when he and Neil Stanek had questioned her after Julie's death. She remembered she had liked him. Sandy-haired and affable, and with a boyish face, he greeted her courteously.

The two FBI agents were of a more serious nature, what Madeline would have termed Washington types. Unlike Dave, who was casually dressed, they wore dark business suits that were so alike they could have been uniforms. They even had similar faces. Only the fact that one of them had liberal amounts of gray sprinkled through his hair allowed her to tell them apart.

When the five of them had seated themselves around the table and the waitress had retreated after bringing fresh coffee, the senior agent, Goldman, leaned toward Madeline. He spoke to her in a low, earnest tone.

"I'll get straight to the point, Ms. Raeburn. The FBI is involved in this case because the man you saw murdered at the Phoenix was working for us. We had reason to believe that Griff Matisse and his crowd were involved in an illegal arms activity, and that's a federal matter."

"Then, why did you wait until now to come forward?" Mitch asked him.

"We were waiting for Ms. Raeburn to surface. And in the meantime it seemed wiser to let Matisse think that no one but the San Francisco district attorney and police department were working on the murder."

"I've already agreed to testify," Madeline said, "so why are you here?"

"To offer you immunity, Ms. Raeburn. Your testimony means everything in this case. In fact, it *is* the case. Without it, it won't be possible to convict Matisse, nor even arrest and charge him."

"Which means she's damn important to you," Mitch said. "So important I want to hear that you and San Francisco are going to do everything in your power to see that she's safeguarded until Matisse stands trial and is sentenced."

Johnson, the younger agent, who had been silent until now and looked like he was having trouble hiding his resentment that Mitch was here at all, joined the conversation. "That will happen. It's afterward that worries us. That's the immunity we're talking about."

Madeline stared at him, understanding what they were telling her because it had already occurred to her. "The federal witness protection program. That's what you mean, isn't it? But is it really necessary?"

Goldman nodded solemnly. "I'm afraid it's the only way to guarantee your safety, Ms. Raeburn. Because even if Matisse doesn't manage somehow to get off, if he ends up behind bars for life or receives California's death penalty, you're still at risk from his mob friends. They have long, unforgiving memories."

"It's your choice," his partner said, "but we are urging you to accept."

Agent Goldman seemed anxious for her to understand. "You know how the programs works, don't you, Ms. Raeburn? We give you a new identity and relocate you to another part of the country."

"And," she murmured numbly, "I would have no further contact with my former life or friends. Yes, I know how it works."

"Well, of course, any family member or loved one can elect to go with you into the program."

"I have no family," Madeline said.

Mitch spoke up. "Look, I realize you need to know her decision as soon as possible in order to undertake the arrangements, but the lady needs time to think."

"Yes, I'd like to go back to the cabin for that. Anyway, all my things are still there."

Agent Johnson consulted his watch. "My partner and I are going to have to leave. We have a plane waiting for us at the local airfield. Dave here will escort you by car back to San Francisco. You can give us your decision through him."

"Want me to follow you to the cabin?" Dave asked them.

Madeline shook her head. She needed time alone with Mitch. There were things that had to be said. Private things. "Give us an hour before you meet us up there."

"I'll need directions to the place," Dave said.

Madeline waited for Mitch to provide Dave Ennis with the directions, but he was hesitant to do so. The officer was not only quick to realize that but seemed to understand Mitch's reluctance.

"Look, Mitch," Dave solemnly reassured him, "if you don't want to tell me, okay, but you should know by now that you can trust me. San Francisco wouldn't have sent me otherwise."

Mitch considered, then nodded slowly. "All right," he said, and proceeded to give Dave the directions.

They were quiet on the drive back to the cabin. Madeline knew that Mitch was allowing her to think about what the two agents had proposed. But she didn't need to ponder their offer. She had already made up her mind. It was the only solution to a situation she could no longer bear.

Mitch held his silence, even when they reached the cabin, but he kept sliding anxious looks in her direction. She knew he was impatient to hear her decision. But she couldn't seem to find the courage to tell him what he needed to hear, as she moved around the cabin, collecting her belongings and placing them beside the front door.

They both understood that, whatever her choice about her future after the trial, an immediate return to San Francisco was necessary, as well as possible now that Matisse's pipeline had been disconnected. But Mitch seemed in no hurry to gather his own things. He followed her from room to room as she straightened up the cabin and washed their breakfast dishes. Their stay here had turned out to be a brief one, after all, and she was sorry about that.

"What are you doing?" he challenged her, a note of irritation in his voice. "The agency has a cleaning service that comes in afterward. They'll take care of all that."

But she needed to keep busy. Hannah, looking forlorn, had stationed herself by the front door. Did the kitten fear she was about to be abandoned? Madeline picked her up and held her in her arms, stroking her fur and murmuring reassurances to her.

Mitch could no longer stand the suspense. "Maddie, the hour is almost up. Dave is going to be here in a few minutes. What have you decided?"

She could no longer delay telling him. "I'm going to do what they want me to do," she said softly. "I'm going to enter the witness protection program."

He gazed at her, his face unreadable, and then he nodded slowly, accepting her decision. "Yeah, I guess that's the only way to make sure you stay safe."

That was part of it, yes, but there was another, equally important explanation for her decision. She knew that Mitch would eventually return to his work in San Francisco. And she didn't trust herself to be anywhere near him—not loving him as she did, not when she knew he didn't return that love. But the witness protection program would take her far away from the temptation of Mitchell

Hawke, prevent her from ever returning to San Francisco. A clean, swift break. It was the only way she could survive their parting.

"All right," Mitch said. He took a slow, deep breath and then released it before declaring recklessly, "And I'm coming with you into the program."

Madeline couldn't stand it. *Don't,* she pleaded to him silently. *Don't do this to me.*

"You're a rash fool!" she told him angrily, and she could feel her mouth twist in anguish. "Do you think I'd ever allow you to do such a crazy thing? Give up your PI work, your friends and family. Your *family,* Mitch. If you've forgotten how much they mean to you, I haven't."

"I can live with it," he said stubbornly.

"But I can't." Here it is, she thought. The moment she'd been dreading. They both had to face the truth. "Why, Mitch? Why would you even suggest joining me in the program?"

"Do you have to ask? You must know how I feel about you."

"No, I don't know. Just what do you feel?"

"Madeline—"

"Is it more than desire? Are you in love with me? Can you honestly say you love me?"

His silence was all the answer she needed. It meant what she had feared all along. He couldn't let Julie go. He was still in love with her.

She heard the sound of a car pulling up in front of the cabin. Dave Ennis had arrived. Thank God, this painful moment needn't be prolonged.

Mitch had heard the car, too. "Look," he said quickly, "we don't have to settle this here and now. We can sort out everything on the way to San Francisco."

Madeline's response was emphatic. "I'm not riding with you to San Francisco. I'm going with Dave in his car. I want us to say our goodbyes here and now." *Because if we don't,* she thought, *I might never again find the strength to part from you.* As it was, knowing she had to walk away from him was tearing her up inside. "Please, Mitch, it's better this way."

"Maddie, listen to me—"

Hastily kissing Hannah on top of her head, she thrust the kitten into Mitch's arms. "There's too much involved in trying to take her with me. I'll miss her, but she'll be happier with you. You were always her favorite, anyway." She picked up her things and opened the door. "I won't try to thank you for everything you've done for me, Mitch. There aren't words enough."

He didn't try to stop her. He let her walk out the door and close it behind her.

Dave was waiting for her by the car. He stepped forward and took her suitcase as she came down the steps. "Where's Mitch?"

"He isn't coming with us. He'll drive himself to San Francisco, maybe this afternoon."

"Oh?" The detective was obviously surprised, but he didn't press her. However, the stricken expression that must have been evident on her face did concern him. "You all right?"

"Fine. Can we go now, please?"

Madeline looked out the window from her side of the car as they drove away from the cabin, keeping her head turned so that Dave Ennis wouldn't see the tears swimming in her eyes and try to question her again.

The tears blurred her vision, and the awful ache that caused them made her inattentive. That was why, when they reached the point where the lane joined the road, she didn't notice that Dave turned right and not left in the direction of Ardmore. Several seconds passed before she became aware of his error.

"We're going the wrong way."

"It's all right," he assured her. "I took the time to study

the map while I was waiting to pick you up. This is a much quicker route back to the main highway. It'll save us a lot of miles.''

Madeline didn't argue with him. He seemed so sure. But when the winding road climbed higher into the mountains, growing narrower with each turn, and the forest grew thicker on both sides, a sense of uneasiness surfaced. Something was wrong.

Turning her anxious gaze away from the wilderness outside the passenger window, she started to tell Dave to go back. And her eyes met a far more troubling sight.

The detective had a smile on his mouth and one hand on the wheel. The other hand held a gun close to his side and pointed at her.

''Just keep still, Maddie,'' he instructed her softly, ''and we won't have any accidents.''

Chapter Thirteen

Mitch stood there in a rigid silence, staring at the closed door and feeling as though he had just been kicked in the gut. She was gone. Just like that, and without looking back, Madeline had walked out of his life.

At first he felt nothing but anger and bewilderment. A sense of abandonment churning inside him. Then, gradually, the bitter emotions receded, leaving him with something else. Something far more painful. A vacuum, an emptiness so deep and lonely that it seized him with a wild panic, had him desperate to understand.

What had just happened. And *why* had it happened?

Hannah squirmed in his arms, making him aware of her presence. He looked down, and he could swear that in the kitten's wise eyes gazing up at him there was an expression of accusation.

"Don't look at me like that," he said, his voice harsh. "What have I done to deserve *your* judgment?"

But Mitch knew what he had done. He had let Madeline go without making any real effort to stop her.

"All right, so it is my fault. I didn't fight to keep her, because I was scared. Satisfied?"

Scared? Of what?

The answer came to him at once. Or maybe it had always

been there and he hadn't allowed himself to recognize it until now.

Of telling her that you're in love with her.

My God, it was true! Somewhere on the long road from Wisconsin to California, he had fallen in love with Madeline Raeburn!

"Hannah, did you hear that? I'm in love with Maddie!"

Speaking the words aloud, with wonder and sweet relief, not only made them real but gave him the explanation for what had just happened and why. He had let Madeline go because he had been afraid to tell her how he felt, afraid to admit the truth even to himself.

Julie. It was because of Julie. She had been so much a part of him that he'd refused to let her go, had feared betraying her memory by falling in love again, had feared even deserving to love like that again. But Julie would have been the first to tell him that he *did* deserve to love again, that finding and needing Madeline in no way diminished what he and Julie had once shared.

Need. That was what the hollowness inside him was all about. He needed Madeline to fill it. She was as necessary to him as air and water. He couldn't give her up, couldn't live without her, even if it meant losing both his identity and his cherished family by going into the witness protection program with her. He'd suffer any sacrifice, just as long as he and Madeline were together.

"Yeah, I hear you," he said to the kitten. "She's on her way to San Francisco. Listen, don't worry. I'm going to get her back. Whatever it takes, I'm going to get Maddie back."

Satisfied with his promise, Hannah leaped down from his arms and began to groom herself. Mitch grabbed up his coat and the keys to the station wagon. Banging out of the cabin, he flung himself behind the wheel of the wagon, started the engine with a roar and tore along the lane. Dave's car had a head start on him, but he was confident

e could overtake them before Ardmore. Providing he
idn't kill himself speeding down a mountain road.

He was about to swing out onto that road where the lane
oined it, when he caught a movement out of the corner of
is eye. His head swiveled for a better look. There, through
gap in the forest high above him, where the road doubled
ack on itself as it climbed the mountainside, was a slowly
noving car.

Mitch knew that dark sedan. He had stood beside it out-
ide the Redwood Café in Ardmore, while giving the owner
irections to the cabin. It was Dave Ennis's car.

What were Dave and Maddie doing up there? Mitch
new the road didn't go anywhere in that direction. After
everal twisting miles it dead-ended at a wilderness trail
ading back into the forest to a waterfall he and Julie had
nce visited.

The dark sedan was swallowed again by the ranks of tall,
piky evergreens. Mitch didn't hesitate. Throwing the
vheel of the wagon over to the right, he went after the
ther car. He tried to quell his alarm as he sped recklessly
long the twisting road, but he had a bad feeling about this.
'hat feeling escalated with each sharp bend in the road.

"BEING A COP tests your skills," Dave informed her ear-
estly. "Sometimes you find it necessary to do risky things,
ke driving one-handed in city traffic while keeping a gun
ained on your passenger with the other. Of course, this
n't the city. It's a back road with no traffic at all. Still,
vith all these turns it's a real challenge. We'll take it slow,
nough, and as long as you behave yourself, Maddie, we'll
e all right. Sure would hate to go over the edge. It's a
ng way down, huh?"

A smile continued to hover at the corners of his mouth,
ut Madeline could see there was nothing friendly now
bout that boyish face. Dave Ennis was her enemy.

"You two have a lover's spat?" he asked her.

Madeline didn't answer him. Squeezed against the passenger door, not daring to move, all she could do was stare in terror at the muzzle of the gun that was directed at her.

"You and Mitch, I mean," Dave explained. "I could see in that café how it was with the both of you, how protective he was about you and how you must have fallen for each other. So I figured that since the café, you maybe had a spat. Otherwise, he wouldn't have stayed behind at the cabin. It was a break for me. It would have been a lot harder if he'd come along. Harder, but not impossible."

Madeline found her voice then. "It was *you* that Gloria's assistant fed the information to, not Hank Rosinski."

"I started seeing Carol after she broke up with Hank. I gave her what Hank couldn't. I satisfied her. You know?"

"*Why?* Why did you let Griff Matisse use you?"

He glanced at her, then gave his attention back to the road. "Addiction, Maddie."

He must have felt her shock and revulsion, because he laughed. "No, not that kind of addiction. Gambling. Gets in a man's blood. Sometimes so bad that you end up owing the wrong people, owing them a lot and doing things for them that you just can't help doing. No choice about it."

Griff, Madeline thought, understanding. Griff owned Dave Ennis. That was the explanation for what was happening to her.

"Poor Carol," he said, bobbing his head in regret. "She hated my habit, was always after me to give it up. But I was in too deep. Don't ever get involved with a gambler, Maddie. But that's right, you never will, will you?"

She wouldn't get the chance. She would be dead. That's what he meant. But why hadn't he killed her already? What was he planning?

"Where are we going?" she whispered. "Where are you taking me?"

"Like I told you before, Maddie, I studied a map of the area. Had a chance during that hour down in Ardmore to

rrange things. Now, no more talk. I've got to concentrate
n the road. I swear it's got more zigzags than Lombard
treet.''

There was silence in the car, a fearful, strained silence
s they continued to crawl along the tortuous road. On the
vooded mountainside above them were bands of mist like
ong, trailing scarves. And when they climbed higher, those
eils licked the sides of the car, depositing tiny beads of
noisture on the windows.

The raw winter air seemed to penetrate the car, making
Madeline shiver where she huddled against the door. Or
erhaps it was pure fear that had her hugging herself
rotectively.

Mitch. She needed Mitch. But Mitch couldn't help her.
He didn't know what was happening to her. He was back
t the cabin. She had only herself to rely on, and she could
hink of no way to save herself. Not with that gun gripped
ghtly in Dave Ennis's hand.

The road leveled, rounded a last bend and ended in a
mall clearing. Dave pulled to the side of the road and
irned off the engine.

''Get out,'' he instructed her, unbuckling his belt. ''We
valk from here. And don't try running away from me. You
vouldn't get five yards.''

Madeline released her own seat belt and fumbled for the
andle on the door. Once outside, she was aware of the
oreboding silence. The only sound was the faint drip of
ollected moisture dropping from the hemlocks and red
edars.

And then, her heart lifting with hope, she saw it. There
vas another car parked deep under the trees, long and sleek
nd black. They weren't the only arrivals in this isolated
lace. Someone else was already here. Someone who rep-
esented the possibility of rescue.

''Forget it, Maddie,'' Dave said in a voice of mocking
orrow as he rounded the hood of the sedan, his gun still

trained on her. "It isn't someone up here for a nature hike. He came on business. You."

Her heart sank again.

"Come on," Dave said, waving the gun toward the mouth of a footpath that plunged into the forest. "He's eager to see you again."

It was then, with a terrible certainty, that Madeline understood who was waiting for her at the end of that trail.

"COME ON, SWEETHEART," Mitch pleaded aloud with the old station wagon as it labored valiantly up the mountain, "don't fail me now. I'm counting on you."

There was another, equally urgent plea that he expressed in silence. *Don't let anything happen to you, Maddie. Hang on until I get to you. Do you hear me, Maddie? Stay safe, just stay safe....*

Every warning system in Mitch's body had convinced him by now that Madeline was in danger. That it was Dave Ennis, not Hank Rosinski, who had betrayed them. It was the only explanation for Ennis's pursuit of a road that ended in remote wilderness.

Mitch had had no further glimpse of the dark sedan, but he knew that it was somewhere ahead of him. He searched after each bend around which he heedlessly swung, but the vehicle continued to elude him. And with every passing mile his frustration mounted.

Madeline. He couldn't lose Madeline as he'd lost Julie. Madeline, who had become everything to him. The thought of anything happening to her had him wild with fear.

His silent plea became a silent prayer. *Dear God, protect her until I can.*

A moment later he blessed the faithful station wagon which delivered him to the end of the road. Ennis's car was there, but there was no one inside.

His gun. Mitch needed his gun. He'd placed it in the glove compartment for safekeeping after coming away from

he café. Madeline, no longer able to bear all that was associated with it, had wanted the weapon out of sight now
that it was no longer necessary. But it *was* necessary. Leaning over, he popped open the glove compartment.

Gone! That bastard, Ennis, must have lifted it while waiting for them at the cabin. He'd have to rescue Maddie
without a gun.

Not until Mitch sprang from the wagon did he notice the
other car parked under the trees. They weren't alone, then.
Ennis must have arranged for someone to meet them up
here. Mitch's insides tightened at the thought of just who
that someone might be.

But where were they? There was no one in sight. The
footpath. It was the only choice. They had to be on their
way to the falls.

The dim forest swallowed him as he raced along the trail
among the dense ferns and lofty redwoods. His swift feet
were silent on the thick bed of damp needles. The only
sound was his hard breathing. But gradually another sound
reached his ears—the muffled roar of the waterfall somewhere ahead of him.

Mitch paused when he arrived at a narrow gap in the
thick vegetation on the lip of a sheer, rocky ledge. The path
turned here to the right. He remembered that a bit farther
on it descended in easy stages through a loop that formed
a switchback at a lower level. From the sharp edge of the
gap he could see that section of the trail about seven or
eight feet directly beneath him, snaking along the rim of
the deep gorge where the waters tumbled below the falls.

And then he saw them. Dave Ennis, gun in hand, driving
Madeline ahead of him. They were down there on the
switchback, approaching from the right. There was no sign
of anyone else.

Mitch, peering through the vegetation that screened him,
was frantic by now. They would be under him in another
few seconds. If he didn't act, it would be too late.

He needed a distraction, something to divert Ennis's attention long enough to permit him to jump him before he could put a bullet in Madeline. A pebble would do.

Crouching, he snatched up a small stone from the score of them strewn over the top of the shelf. Then he stood, missile in hand, his body tensed and ready for action. His timing had to be just right.

And it was.

As Ennis started to pass below him, with Madeline still out in front, he pitched the stone. It landed with a *crack* on the rocky path several feet behind Ennis. Coming to a startled halt, the detective whipped around, prepared to fire.

That was when Mitch hurled himself from the ledge overhead, landing on top of Ennis. Forceful though his impact was, it wasn't enough to knock the gun out of Ennis' hand. The detective hung on grimly. A fiercely determined Mitch dragged him to the ground, where the two men, slugging and cursing, fought for control of the weapon.

The pistol discharged, sending a bullet pinging into the hard face of the ledge. Mitch feared that the next shot might not be a wild one, that it would strike Madeline before he could wrest the gun from Ennis's iron grip. He was conscious of her hovering nearby, her eyes wide with shock.

"Maddie, get the hell out of here!" he yelled. "Out of the range of his gun! Go!"

Madeline went, but not because Mitch ordered it and not to run away. The joy and surprise of his sudden arrival was replaced by an urgent desire to help him overcome Dave Ennis. She needed a weapon, a heavy rock or a stout limb. Her frantic gaze revealed nothing in the immediate area.

A few paces away, in the direction of the falls, the path curved around a thicket of rhododendrons. Praying there would be something she could use on the other side of that dense growth, slipping and sliding on the mossy path in her haste, Madeline rounded the rhododendrons. And found herself staring down the barrel of a revolver.

He had either been lurking there the whole time or, impatient over the delay, had come to meet them. Madeline, gaze lifted to that coldly handsome face with its pitted jaw tight with rage, realized she had made a fatal mistake. In a desperate moment, she'd failed to remember that Dave Ennis had been delivering her to the man who held that revolver.

Griff Matisse, who must have arrived separately in Ardmore and waited there in hiding until Ennis had been able to direct him to this lonely rendezvous. Griff, who wanted her dead and this time would make sure she did die by accomplishing the business himself. She could see by the hot, eager glow in his eyes that he expected to relish every second of her destruction.

He couldn't have heard over the thunder of the falls, which was only steps away now, the scene in progress on the other side of the thicket. Madeline couldn't hear the struggle, either, didn't know what was happening. But Griff must have had his suspicions and intended to confirm them.

"Turn around!" he commanded her sharply.

When she hesitated, he grabbed her by the wrist and forced her around. She felt him pressed against her back and the gun held to her head. Using her as a shield, he made her walk back around the thicket.

Madeline felt the slick leaves of the wild rhododendrons brush wetly against her cheeks, heard a roaring in her ears and wasn't sure whether it was the falls or her own fear.

Suddenly, there on the other side of the rhododendrons, she saw Mitch rising from the unconscious figure of Dave Ennis, the detective's pistol in his hand. But her hope was defeated before it could take root.

"Drop it," Griff ordered Mitch, "or I shoot her here and now!"

Mitch froze in a half crouch. Madeline could see that he was considering Matisse's command. She knew what he must be thinking—that if he released the pistol, they would both die, anyway. Once it was on the ground, Griff wouldn't hesitate to kill them.

Mitch's action, when he dove behind a shoulder of rock that protruded from the face of the ledge, was so swift and unexpected it confounded Matisse. His surprise resulted in a few vital seconds of delay, because although he fired at Mitch, his shot came too late to matter. Mitch was already out of sight.

That's when Madeline understood Mitch's intention. He wasn't saving himself. He was buying time for her. As long as he was on the loose and armed, Griff wouldn't kill her. He still needed Madeline to protect him.

There was something else Griff Matisse suddenly realized. She could see it in his worried gaze when she looked over her shoulder and caught him searching the top of the ledge. Madeline realized it, too. If Mitch swarmed up that wall of rock and positioned himself above them, Griff would be vulnerable. That could already be happening behind the shoulder of rock.

"Back!" he shouted at her.

His arm coiled around her waist like a steel band, continuing to use her as a shield, he dragged her back around the clump of rhododendrons. Nor did he pause there. He went on retreating, drawing her with him in the direction of the falls.

Madeline scanned the top of the ledge. There was no sign of movement in that thick undergrowth up there. Where was Mitch?

They were nearing the waterfall now, an impressive cataract that plunged over a lofty precipice into the bed of the gorge, a hundred feet or more below the trail.

But the trail didn't end at the side of the falls. It crossed in front of them, spanning the gorge in the form of a footbridge. A structure that had Madeline gasping when, gun to her head, Griff forced her to mount it with him.

Step by perilous step, he backed them across the narrow

bridge. The falls were so close she could feel the spray on her face.

He stopped them midway along the span. "Look down!" he yelled into her ear above the rage of the torrent.

Madeline made the mistake of obeying him. It was a sickening drop to the bottom of the chasm where the waterfall met the rocks in a chaos of white spume.

"That's where I promised myself the pleasure of sending you!" he said viciously. "That's where you belong, where you'll never be found and where you'll never bother me again!"

But he couldn't kill her yet. He continued to need her as his hostage, now more than ever. When Madeline lifted her gaze and discovered Mitch at the approach to the bridge, hope swelled again inside.

There was an awful moment then, in which the two men faced each other in a tense stalemate. Mitch couldn't fire, not with Madeline squeezed against Matisse. But Mitch had no such cover. He was a clear target, and his enemy realized that.

Madeline felt the revolver draw away from her head as it turned in a new direction, felt Matisse's grip on her relax as he concentrated on his aim. It was an opportunity, and she seized it. Before his arm could tighten on her again, she slipped through his grasp and threw herself facedown on the floor of the bridge, allowing Mitch an unobstructed target of his own.

There was a sharp barking sound. Over the din of the falls, she couldn't be sure whether she heard one gun or both of them. Flipping around and looking up, she saw an expression of utter surprise on Griff's handsome face. The revolver left his hand and clattered on the planks at his feet. Then, clutching himself, he sagged and began to slowly crumple.

Heels digging into the wood, Madeline scooted back to avoid his crushing weight. But his body toppled sideways, crashing into the railing with such force that a section broke away. To her horror, Griff went with it, plummeting to the rocks below.

Madeline started to scramble to her feet, but the floor was wet and slick and, without a railing to grab, she began to slither off the edge of the bridge. Then, suddenly, a pair of strong arms were around her and hauling her safely to her feet.

Mitch! Mitch was here! Collapsed against his solid length, her hands began to feel every part of him she could reach. "You're all right!" she blubbered. "He didn't touch you! *You're all right!*"

"He's a lousy shot," Mitch shouted over the roar. "Or was," he added grimly, glancing down at the broken body sprawled on the rocks far beneath them.

Madeline shuddered in Mitch's arms.

"Come on," he said, "let's get you off this thing."

With one arm protectively around her waist to guide her, Mitch led her back along the bridge. "No," she said when he wanted her to rest after they reached the side of the gorge, "let's go on." She needed to get away from the scene, away from the sight of that body in the chasm below.

Mitch led her up the trail and around the thicket of rhododendrons. It seemed almost quiet here after the boom of the falls. And empty.

"He's gone," Madeline said, realizing that Dave Ennis's body was no longer stretched out on the path.

Mitch nodded without concern. "As hard as I hit him, he should have stayed unconscious, but I guess that head of his survived my fist. Hey," he said, realizing she was trembling, "you need a chair."

He made her sit down on the flat surface of a boulder before settling himself close beside her.

"Listen!" she said, lifting her head and straining to hear. Faintly through the woods came the sound of a car door slamming, followed by the urgent gunning of an engine. "He's getting away!"

"He can't hurt us anymore. Let him go. The cops can deal with him. It's over, Maddie. For us, it's all over."

She turned her head and looked at him soberly. "Just how final is it, Mitch?"

He caught her face between his hands. "Not that kind of *final,* so don't get any ideas about walking out on me again. I've got a few things here to straighten out with you."

"Like?"

"For starters, there's this love I should have been expressing a lifetime ago."

"What are you saying?"

"That I'm thankful to be sitting here on this boulder next to the woman I want beside me for the rest of my life. I'm in love with you, Madeline Raeburn, just in case you have any doubts about it."

"When did you realize that?"

"About three seconds after that cabin door closed behind you."

"How much in love?"

"What?"

"Just how much in love with me are you?"

"*This* much."

And that's when he began to kiss her. She knew then that his love was genuine. And considerable. It was, after all, a very long kiss—sometimes tender, sometimes ferocious and always possessive. *Entirely* possessive. He demonstrated that when his mouth finally lifted from hers.

"Look, just don't get away from me again. Okay?"

"Is that a threat?"

"Damn right it is. Here's the plan. You either love me like I love you, and you marry me, or—"

"Or what?"

"There will be serious consequences."

"Oh." She thought about it. "Then, in that case I do and I will."

Chapter Fourteen

Mitch was worried.

All right, so the setting was pure magic. From the open door of the small chapel where he had been restlessly pacing, he could look out through the massive arches into the cobbled courtyard. It was all out there—a luxuriant bougainvillea vine that flamed against the wall of the bell tower, swallows that swooped from the roof tiles, masses of flowers on the rim of the pool where the ceremony would take place to the accompaniment of the dripping fountain.

And the weather couldn't be better, a balmy afternoon with sunlight spilling into the courtyard. And all this in January! But then, this place, an historic mission several hours south of San Francisco, with restored facilities available for private functions, had always been blessed with a sweet climate, whatever the season.

Even the music was great. There was a harpist, and she played softly while the guests milled around the scented courtyard, nibbling refreshments from the trays offered by a trio of strolling servers. Everyone who mattered was here—friends, his entire family.

Mitch's wedding day was everything it was supposed to be. And he was worried. Something was wrong. He didn't know what, but he had been feeling it all week.

"What are you doing hiding out in here?"

The lanky figure of his brother appeared in the doorway. Roark, who operated his own branch of the Hawke Detective Agency in San Antonio, was to be Mitch's best man, which was why he wasn't sporting his usual Western garb.

Roark advanced into the room, wearing his perpetual grin. "Are we maybe a nervous groom?"

"Where's Madeline?"

Roark shrugged. "In that room on the other side of the church, making herself into your glowing bride, I imagine."

"Did you see her?"

"No, and what are you so anxious about?" he teased. "Afraid she won't show?"

Mitch was beginning to think that could happen. The possibility made him sick. "Have you got the rings?"

"Right here." Roark patted the pocket of his suit coat.

"Show me." He needed to see them. Needed to reassure himself with some form of physical evidence that his marriage to the woman he loved *would* be a reality.

"What's the matter? Don't trust me? All right, all right, here they are." Roark withdrew the two simple gold wedding bands from his pocket and displayed them in his palm for Mitch's approval. "See, all safe and sound. Satisfied?"

"Ah, the happy bridegroom!"

The small, ample figure of Gloria Rodriguez joined them. She was carrying a champagne glass from which she'd been sipping.

Roark returned the rings to his pocket. "The uptight bridegroom is more like it. You see what you can do to distract him," he instructed the assistant district attorney. "I've got to help Ma keep Pop from trying to tell that poor assemblywoman exactly what's wrong with California politics."

Roark retreated, leaving Mitch with the beaming Gloria. "Well, maybe I do have something to distract you, if that's what you need. My office called me on the way down regarding Dave Ennis.''

''What about him?''

''They finally caught up with him trying to cross into Mexico. He's being returned to San Francisco. As for Hank Rosinski...well, it turns out there's a very innocent reason why he was seen going in and out of the back door of the Phoenix at night. Seems that after Carol Donatti dumped him, he'd begun keeping company with the pastry chef at the Phoenix.''

Mitch was glad to hear all of this and told Gloria so, but he wasn't much interested when she went on to talk about the case they'd already begun preparing against Ennis. He was still concerned about Madeline, and the more he thought about it, the more he was convinced that something was definitely not right.

He even knew when it had all started. Last week he and Madeline had flown back to Utah. They had been accompanied by an FBI agent, who had helped to clear them in the deaths of Angel and Lucky. While dealing with the police there, the agent had received a phone call from San Francisco.

The contents of that call, which he'd communicated to them afterward, had a sobering effect on both Mitch and Madeline. Gloria's former assistant, terrified now that her lover was exposed, had cut a deal with the DA's office. The charges against her would be mitigated in exchange for her full cooperation. Carol had talked.

They'd learned it was Dave Ennis who had informed Matisse that his barman was an undercover cop. Dave who had made a quick trip to Milwaukee to persuade his former partner to reveal to him where he had hidden Madeline Raeburn and who had knocked Neil unconscious when he'd tried to reach his gun and afterward shot Neil with Mitch's pistol. And, hardest of all to hear, Dave who had killed Julie after she'd caught him accepting a payoff from Matisse. Knowing who he was because of his connection with Mitch's friend Neil, Julie had realized he was a cop gone bad.

Mitch had been shaken by the explanation of Julie's death. And angry all over again. Madeline had been troubled by that, had asked him about it that night in Utah.

"Do you still miss her, Mitch? Will the hurt ever go away?"

He'd taken Madeline in his arms, his love for her swelling inside him. "Sweetheart, I want you to promise me something. That you'll never again have any doubts about this. Here it is. I loved Julie, yes, and I guess there will always be a tiny corner of my heart that belongs to her. Or, at least, to her memory. But I think I'd already begun to let Julie go before you came into my life. I just had a tough time accepting that."

"And now?"

"Now it's time to say goodbye. I can do that, and without regrets, because of you. Do you realize how thankful I am for you, Maddie, and just how much I love you?"

He had been so fiercely earnest about it, so intense in their lovemaking that had followed, that he could have sworn she was completely satisfied by his pledge to her. But he'd been uneasy about the change in her the next morning. She was suddenly quiet and thoughtful. Something that, if he hadn't known better, could be defined as secretive. Had she failed, after all, to believe him last night? Then, over breakfast, to his considerable disappointment, she'd announced her intention not to go on to Wisconsin with him and the FBI agent.

"You don't need me there, Mitch. And with the wedding coming up…well, I should be back in California handling all the arrangements for that."

When he pressed her, she had insisted there was nothing else on her mind. He had let her go. And been feverishly impatient to get back to her the whole time he'd spent in

Wisconsin sorting out Neil's death with the police, packing his belongings at the farm and arranging to have his pickup recovered from the Milwaukee garage and delivered to him in San Francisco.

Madeline had greeted him with such warmth when he finally, eagerly landed back in Frisco that Mitch had convinced himself he'd been imagining her remoteness. But in the days that followed her passionate welcome, she was preoccupied again and seemed to have almost no time for him. When he sought an answer, she pleaded the wedding.

"I'm sorry if I've been neglecting you, Mitch, but there's just so much to take care of. I never realized that planning even a simple wedding could be such a frantic thing. And look at how busy you've been yourself getting your agency rolling again."

Her explanation had been a reasonable one. Only, it hadn't satisfied him. She spent far too many hours mysteriously absent from the apartment they'd taken. Even Hannah missed her....

Gloria was still talking about the case. Realizing how inattentive he'd been, Mitch made an effort to listen.

"We still don't know who fired on Madeline in the Milwaukee safe house. It couldn't have been Ennis on that occasion, since he was on duty in San Francisco. Probably a mob hit man from somewhere back in the Midwest that Matisse arranged for when Carol passed him the word through Ennis that this was where Madeline was hiding. Anyway, I guess the important thing is, with Matisse dead now and Madeline no longer needing to testify, she doesn't have to go into witness protection. You must both be happy about that."

"Yes," Mitch agreed.

"It means you can concentrate on reopening your agency, and Madeline can get back to earning that degree. I hear she's planning a career in jewelry design."

"That's right."

"Tell her I'll be at the head of the line when she opens her first shop." Gloria paused. She must have realized that his mind was elsewhere. "Listen to me running on. This is your wedding day. You don't want to hear all this. All you want to do is stand next to your bride at that fountain out there."

Yes, Mitch thought, that's exactly what he wanted to do. But when Gloria kissed him on the cheek and wandered back into the courtyard, panic seized him again. What if it didn't happen? What if Madeline didn't appear at his side to exchange their vows? What if, all this time, she'd been uncertain about their marriage, and decided at the last minute to call it off? He was suddenly terrified. The idea of not having her as his wife was unbearable. He couldn't wait. He had to know.

Striding out of the chapel to find her, he started along the arcade. And that's when he saw her. From the room on the other side of the church, Madeline darted out onto the arcade. He stopped to gaze at her. Even at this distance, she took his breath away. She was a vision in flowing, champagne-colored silk with a wreath of pale blossoms crowning her radiant red hair.

She hadn't seen him. Framed in one of the arches, she was much too busy scanning the crowd in the courtyard. Not in any idle manner, either. There was a tenseness in the way she held herself, something that expressed urgency.

As Mitch watched, her searching gaze settled on the figure of Roark, who was standing in the shade of a peppertree talking to their sister, Eden, their eldest brother, Devlin, his wife, Karen, and Dallas McFarland, the husband of the youngest Hawke sibling, Christy.

Madeline waited anxiously until Roark looked up and she was able to catch his attention. When she beckoned to him, he excused himself from the group and crossed the courtyard to join her on the arcade. The two of them disappeared into the building.

Roark? What could Madeline possibly want from his brother and best man? Mitch intended to find out. Moving swiftly down the long colonnade, he turned into the open doorway. He found the two of them on the far side of a room that had once been a monastic office.

They stood close together, talking in hushed tones. It struck Mitch that their conversation had an intimate quality. Reasonable or not, he experienced a rush of jealousy. Those pangs intensified when they glanced around at his entrance and immediately drew away from each other, as if they had been discovered in some conspiracy.

"Would someone mind telling me what's going on?" Mitch demanded.

"Uh-oh," Roark said, his mouth widening in a grin.

"Do I get answers or not?"

Roark and Madeline exchanged glances. "You'd better give them back to me, Roark," she instructed him quietly.

"You sure that's smart?" She nodded. "Okay." He dug into his pocket and handed her whatever she must have passed to him before Mitch's arrival.

Mitch couldn't see what it was. Madeline's fingers closed tightly the instant she received it from Roark. Still wanting that explanation, Mitch started toward her. Before he could reach her, Christy floated into the room. Actually, *waddled* would have been a more accurate term, since she and Dallas were expecting their first child, and from the size of her, Mitch wouldn't have been surprised if she went into labor then and there.

"What are *you* doing here?" she challenged him. "Hasn't anyone told you it's bad luck to see your bride before the ceremony?"

Mitch dearly loved his blond, feisty sister, but at the moment he wanted her elsewhere. Roark understood that, which is why he drew Christy toward the door.

"Come on, little mama, they need some privacy."

"They'll have a lifetime of that after the ceremony. All

right, okay, I'm coming. Madeline," she called back over her shoulder, "I've got your bouquet. Holler for it when you're ready."

There was silence in the room when they were gone. Madeline gazed at him, her face without expression. Mitch, suddenly contrite, went to her. "I'm sorry if I'm behaving like a jerk," he apologized, "but it's been a bad couple of weeks for me." Looking down into her amber eyes, which had widened in surprise, he went on to describe what he'd been suffering since they'd parted in Utah. "I don't know what's going on, but frankly, Maddie, you're scaring the hell out of me."

Her face now expressed sympathy and wonder. "You poor darling, I had no idea that all this while— I mean, I knew you had concerns, but I thought they were around getting the agency up and running again. And, of course, I wasn't really paying attention, because I had to keep inventing fresh excuses in order to sneak off to— Well, after all, claiming wedding preparations was wearing pretty thin, so—"

"Maddie," he pleaded, "what are you talking about?"

She held up her fist and opened it slowly. "Look," she said softly, showing him what Roark had returned to her.

A pair of matched wedding bands lay in the hollow of her palm. Not the plain gold ones Mitch had purchased and given to Roark to keep for the ceremony. Even at a glance, he could see these were something very special, something that had been crafted with loving attention to every minute detail. They were exquisite.

"I don't understand," he said. "You picked out the others yourself when we went to the store. I thought you liked them."

"I lied. Mitch, I create custom-made jewelry, remember? You didn't think I'd settle for something ordinary when I married the only man I'll ever love." She smiled at him hopefully. "Do you mind? Say you don't mind."

Mind? How could he possibly mind what in every way was an expression of her love for him? She must have devoted countless hours to the making of these rings. No wonder she had been so preoccupied and so frequently absent from his side.

"It's a fantastic surprise," he assured her. "But where? How?"

"Kim," she explained, referring to the super at her old apartment building. "That dear man rescued all the larger equipment I had to leave behind and kept it for me in a storeroom in the basement. One of the girls I worked with at the Phoenix let me set up in a spare room in her apartment. Not that I wasn't also as busy as a squirrel seeing to the wedding preparations. But here, Mitch, look at your ring."

Madeline handed him the larger, wider band, urging him to examine it. Her pride evident, she began to point out the details.

"The white gold symbolizes the purity of our union," she explained. "The knot designs stand for family and the continuity of life, and the interlocking circles represent the constancy of our love. There's engraving inside."

He turned the ring to see the inscription. *Forever yours,* it read, followed by the date and their initials.

She was anxious for his approval. "Is it all right, Mitch? Do you like it?"

Well, damn, he was suddenly not only having trouble swallowing, but also actually felt the prick of tears behind his lids. If he wasn't careful, he'd end up bawling, he was that emotional. Not just with joy but with a grateful humility that this woman, whom he'd come close to losing in his failure to appreciate all that she was, would soon become his wife.

"Oh, yeah," he said, his voice gruff in his effort to control himself. "I like it. Enough to wear it, sweetheart, for the rest of my life."

Squeezing his fingers tightly around the ring so as not to drop it while he attended to a vital matter, he took her in his arms and kissed her slowly and deeply. And when he finally, reluctantly released her, his happiness was so vast that, much to his relief, instead of shedding tears he gave a rumble of rich, robust laughter.

Madeline smiled up at him, a gleam in her eyes.

"What?" he asked.

"Do you have any idea," she said, "how absolutely sexy that laugh of yours is?"

"It is, huh? Well, you're going to be hearing it a lot," he promised. "Starting when I get you behind the door of that honeymoon hideaway waiting for us in Carmel."

"And since that can't happen until after the ceremony…"

"It means we're wasting time," he growled impatiently. "Come on, let's you and me get married."

Arm around her waist, he hurried her out into the sunlit courtyard, where the harp played, the fountain bubbled and the company waited eagerly to celebrate their nuptials.

Forever yours, Mitch thought, remembering the inscription inside the ring. No words could be truer.

HARLEQUIN®
INTRIGUE®

**Elevates breathtaking romantic suspense
to a whole new level!**

When all else fails, the most highly trained, covert
agents are called in to "recover" the mission.
This elite group is known as

THE SPECIALISTS

Nothing is too dangerous for them...
except falling in love.

DEBRA WEBB

does it again with an explosive new trilogy for Harlequin
Intrigue. You'll recognize some of the names from her
popular COLBY AGENCY series, but hang on to your
hats this time out. Because THE SPECIALISTS are more
dangerous, more daring...and more deadly than any agents
you've ever seen!

UNDERCOVER WIFE
January

HER HIDDEN TRUTH
February

GUARDIAN OF THE NIGHT
March

Look for them wherever Harlequin books are sold!

HARLEQUIN®
Makes any time special ®

Favorite Harlequin Intrigue® author

REBECCA YORK

brings you a special 3-in-1 volume featuring her
famous 43 Light Street miniseries.

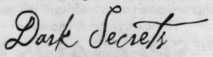

"Rebecca York's 43 Light Street series just keeps
getting better and better!"
—*Romantic Times*

Available in December 2002 wherever paperbacks are sold.

Visit us at www.eHarlequin.com

BR3DS

eHARLEQUIN.com

community | membership

buy books | authors | online reads | magazine | learn to write

buy books

Your one-stop shop for great reads at great prices.
We have all your favorite Harlequin, Silhouette,
MIRA and Steeple Hill books, as well as a host of
other bestsellers in Other Romances. Discover a
wide array of new releases, bargains and hard-to-
find books today!

learn to write

Become the writer you always knew you could be:
get tips and tools on how to craft the perfect
romance novel and have your work critiqued by
professional experts in romance fiction. Follow
your dream now!

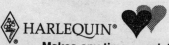

HARLEQUIN®

Makes any time special®—online...

Visit us at
www.eHarlequin.com

HINTLTW

The Gallagher family
is back in a gritty
new novel of
romantic suspense

Amanda Stevens

GALLAGHER JUSTICE

Justice was in her blood

While investigating police
corruption, Fiona Gallagher
finds herself pitted against
the entire Chicago Police
Department, including her
three lawmen brothers. The
only one who can help her
is Detective Ray Doggett,
a man with dark secrets
of his own.

*Coming to stores
in January 2003.*

HARLEQUIN®
Makes any time special ®

Visit us at www.eHarlequin.com

PHGJ

Steeple Hill Books is proud to present
a beautiful and contemporary new look
for Love Inspired!

As always, Love Inspired delivers
endearing romances full of hope, faith and love.

Beginning January 2003
look for these titles
and three more each month
at your favorite retail outlet.

Steeple
Hill®

Visit us at www.steeplehill.com

LINEW03

C O O P E R ' S  C O R N E R

Welcome to Twin Oaks—
the new B and B in Cooper's Corner.
Some come for pleasure, others for
passion—and one to set things straight...

Coming in January 2003...
ACCIDENTAL FAMILY
by Kristin Gabriel

Check-in: When former TV soap star Rowena Dahl's biological clock started ticking, she opted to get pregnant at a fertility clinic. Unfortunately, she got the wrong sperm!

Checkout: Publisher Alan Rand was outraged that a daytime diva was having *his* baby. But he soon realized that he wanted Rowena as much as he wanted their child.

HARLEQUIN®
Makes any time special ®

Visit us at www.cooperscorner.com

CC-CNM6